DANGEROUS DESIRES

OF GOLD & BLOOD
BOOK TEN

Jenny Wheeler

Published by Happy Families Ltd

ISBN 978-1-99-117259-4 (Large print)
ISBN 978-1-99-116202-1 (Paperback)
ISBN 978-1-99-116201-4 (EPub)
ISBN 978-1-99-116200-7 (Kindle)

OF GOLD & BLOOD SERIES

Poisoned Legacy #1

Brother Betrayed #2

Double Jeopardy #3

Tangled Destiny–A Christmas Novella and Prequel #4

Unbridled Vengeance #5

Hope Redeemed–A Spanish Novella #6

Book Bundle Of Gold & Blood Series One, Books 1–3.

Book Bundle Of Gold & Blood, Series Two Books 1 & 4–Elanora's Story.

Tainted Fortune #7

Captive Heart–A Hawaiian Christmas Novella #8

Ancient Deception #9

Book Bundle Of Gold & Blood, Three Holiday Novellas
(Books 4, 6 & 8)

Dangerous Desires #10

In Memory of Alinvesh Kant, 1978 - 2021

\#

Show me a prison, show me a jail,
Show me a prisoner whose face has gone pale
And I'll show you a young man with so
many reasons why
And there but for fortune, may go you or I
Phil Ochs–"There But For Fortune"–
Published 1964

Remembering Stephen Stratford, 1953 - 2021
A 'scholar and a gentleman'– and one of
New Zealand's finest editors.

One

Hector de Vile, California senator to Washington, sank his bare shoulders beneath the swirling rose-scented water and exhaled. The Imperial Spa on Montgomery Street was the most recent evidence that San Francisco matched London and Paris as one of the most metropolitan cities in the world, with its faux Greco-Roman baths open to any gentleman who was a paid-up member of the Imperial Club next door.

Hector closed his eyes and allowed himself to float off on a cloud of happy imaginings. His newly discovered son, Kaleo, installed at De Vile Holdings, married to de Vile's young business partner Sarah, producing a brood of brilliant grandchildren. His old friend, the Countess Elizabeth, in an elegant yet simple wedding gown, eagerly awaiting his arrival at the altar.

He lay back, let the hot water caress his neck and shoulders, and exalted in the moment. The only sound in the secluded, dim space was the mesmerizing bubbling of the moving water, pumped through jets into the mosaic-tiled private pool.

His eyes flickered open briefly, taking in the sense of luxurious enclosure the intimate bathing cubicle afforded. Like a Roman catacomb, lit by fluttering candles set in alcoves in rough brick walls.

He allowed himself a breathy chuckle. A catacomb, maybe, but one for the living. At fifty-one, he might near the end of his earthly years, but he had much he still wanted to accomplish.

He sank deeper, and when the heat grew intolerable, he rose like a breaching whale, the water streaming off his shoulders, and he again laughed silently to himself. He'd been a whaler in Hawaii. And he'd moved on to know the celebrated and the notorious identities of the young state of California.

John Sutter, the adventurer who started the whirlwind that became California when a worker found gold on his ranch. Jack Porter, the notorious bandit who'd hung out on Sundays at the Mission Dolores roadhouse, with his black beard, flowing hair, and glittering restless eyes, prompting fascinated terror as he drank with prominent Californios and soldiers before his crazed misdeeds caught up with him.

Hector had ridden the Pacific Coast north from the collection of huts that had been Yerba Buena to view the masses of seals on the rocks below Cliff House, before there even was a Cliff House.

And now he was a national figure, one of the richest men in the state, and about to propose to a woman for only the second time in his life.

Belatedly, he was hoping to enjoy a family life he'd not known in adulthood. He'd accumulated children. Yes, by some miracle he didn't deserve, he'd raised a treasured adopted son, and he'd found the children who'd been withheld from him for over twenty years. Now he'd add a wife to the story and his life would be complete.

The candles audibly guttered. A subtle change in the surrounding airflow made him look toward the arched doorway. His eyes widened. A woman, a barely mature blonde child draped in a towel which slipped to her waist, revealing pert breasts, approached him across the stone floor. Before he had time to draw breath, she'd perched on the bath edge close to him.

She dangled slim white legs into the roiling hot water and paddled them, smiling from under long black lashes, as if it were the most natural act in the world for her to be keeping him company in the nude.

Alarm rose in his throat. What was this? Some plot? Entrapment? There were men, he knew, who fancied young girls, but he was not one of them.

He'd settled his haunch on one of the top steps leading down into the pool and now he reflexively sank to a lower level, distancing himself from the mirage.

"There's some mistake," he said. His normally deep voice sounded breathy and cracked. "You've got the wrong place."

She smiled again and shook her head. Still, she remained silent.

Her hand went to her throat, and it was then he noticed something hung from a leather cord between her breasts, making a light rattle as she pulled the cord free.

"Oh nooo," she cooed like a dove. "No mistake."

She pulled the emblems out for him to get a closer look.

He peered through the steamy bath vapor.

What looked like two bone amulets—like the whalebone teething rings mothers gave their children in Hawaii—hung threaded through the leather string.

"Madame Moonlight says you'll be most interested in these…"

She leaned into him and rattled them under his nose.

"*Nera Come La Notte* is certain. You're to meet her in her private box at the opera on Thursday."

She stared into his eyes, seductive, flirtatious, offering the token.

"Moonlight? What the devil does Moonlight have to do with me? Or any of this?"

He pushed himself up the steps again, the water sloshing and slapping the bath's sides as he moved, releasing a cloud of rose-scented air.

"That's for her to know, and you to find out." The outer corners of her lips turned up in a coquettish question mark. For a child—what was she—twelve, thirteen? She had a precocious knowingness.

He stilled inside, his sixth sense overcoming the rush of anxiety.

Here be dragons.

He'd seen it on the old maps when he'd sailed the China route.

The territory of ancient cartographers, marked as unknown and dangerous. By the time he'd been a captain, they included it more in jest than anything, but any mariner knew danger lurked in every storm on the high seas. And this was potentially a storm of cataclysmic proportions.

In one intuitive swipe, his right arm lashed out and caught hold of the leather cord.

The girl reared back out of his reach, but too late.

She clutched at her breasts, attempting to smother the fall of the antique rings as the leather snapped.

In a flash, she swung her feet out of the water and rose, panting, hugging her cleavage in the towel.

Her eyes were dark and intense, not in the least panicked, as she glared down. An angel lit in an avenging halo by the candlelight.

"Madame Moonlight insists. The opera on Thursday. Or you'll be sorry. She says if you don't come, the only person sorrier than you will be the Countess."

#

The only person sorrier than you...

De Vile groaned as the masseuse's nimble fingers worked into his foaming scalp, fingers and thumbs flexing the slippery shampoo with a pressure that was just short of painful. Was he groaning from pleasure or from dread? He didn't know.

In the seconds after the girl disappeared like a vapor, he'd stared into the empty doorway, asking himself if he'd imagined the entire encounter. Then his eyes had dropped to the pulsing water, and he'd leaned into its depths, groping for something, anything, to prove to himself she'd really been there.

His foot nudged a small object. He'd leaned over and drawn out a dripping totem. A small bone ring, creamy with age, from which dangled a silver shield engraved with tiny letters.

He resisted the urge to race straight back to his house on Russian Hill and examine it with a magnifying glass. He'd paid for the full treatment at the Imperial Spa—shoulder massage, shampoo, shave, barber and a luxurious soak—and no courtesan, however dangerous and desirable, was going to panic him into going home.

Besides, the entire episode gave him time to think. Madame Moonlight, otherwise known as Sophia Morrigan, was a celebrated San Francisco hostess who owned this Imperial Spa premises beside the popular Imperial Club next door. She was famous; some would suggest notorious.

She'd appeared in San Francisco nearly twenty years ago, an almost twenty-year-old supposed European heiress with midnight-black hair and sapphire eyes that quickly earned her the sobriquet "Black As Night," *Nera Come La Notte*. And not just because of her hair.

She'd gained early infamy when an engagement to James Willoughby, a rich English heir, turned sour and her outraged "guardian" sued for breach of promise. They'd settled out of court for an undisclosed sum, and that perhaps had encouraged her to try the same trick a few years later with another overconfident rich boy.

She's like Bertha used to be when she was younger, Hector thought, as the attendant briskly towelled his hair and sprayed his locks with a fresh-smelling eau de cologne.

But a lot younger than Bertha was.

She must have been a girl—fifteen or sixteen—when I was taking Bertha out on the town and she was luring wealthy men into public humiliation. She was reckless with her own reputation. Couldn't care less.

Like Bertha in so many ways. A beautiful woman, seemingly not interested in a conventional life of marriage and children. Hungry instead for riches and having her own way.

And far too young to have had anything to do with Bertha, thank goodness.

Now in her thirties and still unmarried, Madame Moonlight operated in a twilight zone in the city's society. A brilliant hostess, she ran the Imperial Club and Spa with just enough audacity to keep her clientcle enthralled without alienating their wives.

She engaged controversial, entertaining speakers like Mark Twain. Held soirees with risky guests like clairvoyant physician Ephraim S. Taylor, who enjoyed a brief season of popular notoriety as the doctor to the city's rising social "stars"—excitable but bored young women with more money than sense.

She staged dance parties where society women couldn't resist showing off the latest in fashion. Sophia never failed to earn some mention in the society gossip columns, because of her own risqué ventures or the scandals of those who frequented her establishments. Above all, she was a consummate publicist whom local editors knew they could rely on for a tantalizing yarn on slow news days.

He'd have to be careful, because she was exceedingly clever. A dangerous woman for a politician to get on the wrong side of.

But why bring Elizabeth into it? She was threatening to sully her name by association?

He stepped out of the Imperial Spa into the dust and noise of Market Street, newly coiffed and immaculate, but not nearly as confident of his future as when he'd stepped through its perfumed archways three hours earlier.

Two

"So? Did you do what I instructed you to?"

As an answer, Isla Jensen proffered Sophia a clutched fist.

Morrigan flattened her palm to receive the item the Irish waif held.

Isla dropped the treasure she carried into Sophia's hand.

One child-sized bone ring trailing the leather thong draped over slender fingers.

Frowning, Sophia's painted nails closed over the smooth token.

"Only one? What happened to the other one?"

"He grabbed it." The child's face

creased into anxious lines.

"It… it…" she stuttered. "It fell in the water."

Morrigan nodded. One of Isla's near-white locks fell across her pale face. Her straight upper teeth nibbled at her lower lip.

"Don't worry, girl. If he grabbed it, he's rattled. That's good." The older woman tipped her hand and let the bone ring fall onto the table in front of them, her face breaking into a bright smile.

"Excellent, in fact. He wouldn't have lost his dignity if he'd been his usual commanding self."

She reached out and squeezed the girl's shivering shoulders. "Get yourself dried and dressed, Isla. Then go to the kitchen for hot lemon. And don't worry. All is as it should be."

The girl left with a patter of bare feet

and Sophia fingered the emblem left behind.

When she scrutinized it, her spirits lifted even higher. The one she'd retained belonged to de Vile's "son." The memento he'd be most desperate to possess. And that was the one still in her keeping.

She smiled grimly to herself and checked her appearance in the dressing-room mirror. The darkness in her expression softened to a self-satisfied smirk. She was looking imperious, in her deep crimson gown with the plunging neckline covered by a tantalizing paisley shawl, which revealed as much as it concealed. Her Queen of the Night hair bore the tiniest shimmer of à la mode, Empress Eugenie glitter.

She sank into the padded basket chair in the Imperial's private women's salon, one of several such rooms set aside for important female guests. Of course, the number of women using the facilities was much fewer than the men, but there were some brave souls who challenged convention in the name of self-indulgence.

The coffee she'd ordered from the kitchen was exactly as she liked it, hot, creamy, with a hint of spice, and she sighed contentedly. She'd cast the first lure, and like a trout just waiting to be tickled, the mighty and—for his age—remarkably virile Washington statesman had taken it, hook, line and sinker.

She massaged her hands, feeling them as smooth as the skin of the finest newborn kid, and a glow filled her.

She'd be Mrs. Hector de Vile, senator's wife and celebrated society hostess, before the year was out. Just see if she wasn't.

Three

His morning of being patted and pummelled like an indulged sultan hadn't left him with the anticipated sense of satiated comfort. Instead, Hector de Vile had a crippling headache and indigestion.

He went straight home to his house on Russian Hill and retreated to his bedroom, telling the sharp-eyed housekeeper Mrs. Crisp as he passed through the front hall that he was taking an early afternoon rest and was not to be disturbed.

No lie that, either. He felt as if a mallet-wielding fairground muscle man was hammering at his temples. As he loosened his collar and collapsed onto his four-poster bed, he couldn't ignore the clawing indigestion that hooked at his insides.

He lay like a beached dolphin for thirty minutes, musing on the morning's events, and fingering the heart-shaped silver token he'd retrieved from the Turkish bathwater.

The tip of his finger traced a faint engraving: three letters drawn in a flourishing script. F.R.C.

Obviously a child's initials, considering they had attached it to the bone ring. But what was the object itself? A christening bracelet? A teething ring? An anklet, even? Some mothers favored them.

A soft tap came at the door, and Mrs. Crisp's commanding voice penetrated the quiet, asking if he wanted tea. He barked an affirmative, and the full-bodied matron bustled in, her white hair pulled hard off her forehead under a starched cap, carrying a silver tray with teapot and cup.

"Black spiced tea for you, sir," she said in her Midlands brogue. "With ginger and lemon. Just the thing if you're feeling a little pasty."

She set the tray down with a clink of fine china and rounded on him, hands on hips. "You've been working too hard, Senator."

In her spotless white apron tied around her block-shaped middle, she resembled an army commander, or a hospital matron. If there was a waistline somewhere under there, it wasn't on view.

"Thank you, Mrs. Crisp. You're too kind," de Vile muttered, suitably chastised.

If only I could fix my problems as easily as she imagines.

"I need a rest. You're right."

She leaned in with a muscular arm and poured him a cup of steaming black tea. He breathed in its fragrance as she handed him the cup; spicy from the ginger, astringent from the lemon, and sweet from lavender honey.

"Here you are. Good for your head and your digestion, it is."

F.R.C.

"Thank you, Mrs. Crisp. Could you let Crawford know I'm to be undisturbed until I go out later this evening?"

She pulled the door behind her quietly and he sank back into his plumped-up pillows, depleted and seeking sanctuary.

He'd begun the day with such certainty that life was coalescing around him in just the way he'd long hoped. In his newfound son Kaleo, he'd located capable progeny who, with a modicum of luck and training, could take over the estate he'd spent his life putting together. Unlike his adopted son Alex, who, though a joy in his life, was an artistic soul with dreams of becoming the foremost photographer in the West. After years of hoping he'd change, Hector was finally accepting Alex was no businessman.

And after a lifetime as a bachelor merchant focused entirely on business, he was going to ask his friend and widow of many years, Elizabeth Westerhoven, for her hand in marriage. Beautiful, charitable, and wise, Elizabeth held onto a youthful energy and refined beauty well into her later years. His heart warmed at the thought of her. They'd make a good-looking couple, even if they were graying around the edges.

He lay back with a satisfied sigh, and then the pain clawed at his sides, as he remembered the chit and her delivery of Moonlight's demands.

Meet her at the opera or else.

Or else what? She tempted him to play dumb and ignore the message entirely.

He was escorting Elizabeth and his children to Platt's Hall on Thursday for a Farewell Complimentary Benefit for the Spanish Opera Troupe. Platt's, also known as the New Music Hall, was an acclaimed city venue for popular culture—musical extravaganzas appealing to middle-class tastes, lectures from fiery orators and fanciful divines, charitable fairs, merry dances and balls. The Spanish Opera Troupe had been playing a widely lauded season of comic opera amid much hilarity.

He'd find it darned awkward to attend a secret tryst with San Francisco's most notorious courtesan while he was escorting Elizabeth for the evening. The hand that held the charm cooled at the thought. They hadn't nicknamed Elizabeth the Countess for nothing. If she got wind of it, she'd demand a full explanation, and he wasn't sure he wanted to give one.

F.R.C. He scrambled his brain to recall what name Elanora and Rafael Castellanos had given to Alex's twin sister, now known to all as Sebastian Russell's wife, Isabella.

Alex had always been Alejandro—the Spanish version of the name he'd kept when de Vile took the boy into his care. He couldn't for the life of him remember what Huldah, Bertha's sister, had said about Isabella. Had she renamed the child, or kept the name she'd been christened with?

He didn't know, but the heaviness that weighed him down gave him the answer. The only reason this Moonlight woman could have for dangling the rings in front of him was because they'd once belonged to the Castellanos twins.

He'd snatched the one belonging to Isabella. Moonlight's messenger held on to the other one. The one belonging to his son "Alejandro."

Dare he ask Alex if he remembered if Huldah changed Isabella's name, and if so, from what? And how could he make it sound like a casual inquiry?

F.R.C. The "C" would stand for Castellanos. On that, he'd stake his life. What the other letters stood for, he did not know, but he had a sickening feeling he was going to find out.

Four

"Sophia. Come and sit. We're waiting for you for dinner."

Raizney Grigor watched with mounting irritation as Morrigan showed no sign of hearing his request. She drifted toward him, her glittering sapphire-blue eyes turned inward in satisfying private preoccupation.

He had been waiting for fifteen minutes. That Scottie O'Callaghan, the adaptable all-rounder who served as their house manager, stood at attention beside the carved oak sideboard, ready to serve the rapidly cooling fish chowder for the same stretch of time, appeared lost on her.

Her smooth glide as she crossed the dining room had a relentless quality which declared to the world that she'd never hurry for anyone. If ever there was a woman who kept her own counsel, it was Sophia Morrigan.

She slid into her chair at the candlelit dinner table in their apartment above the Imperial Club on Montgomery Street and flashed a smile in Scottie's direction.

"Sorry, O'Callaghan. I've got things on my mind."

They were two floors up from the hot tubs and steam rooms on the ground floor of the building, but the faint fragrance of eucalyptus and lavender persisted over the salty velvet of the chowder as Scottie served first Sophia and then Grigor with their opening soup.

Tonight, as on every other night, Grigor had carefully chosen the complementary courses and the wine. His childhood deprivation had left deep scars, and his enjoyment of the best available was his redress. Just as he'd ordered, the chowder Scottie was about to serve used locally grown oysters.

Ten Thousand Dollar Calf's Liver and Bacon, a recipe dreamed up by one of the local French chefs, would follow. They would finish with a dessert of Sicilian Rum Cake. He'd spent his boyhood as a slave in Welsh coal mines, eating rabbit stew he'd shot in the few hours he saw of daylight, and he was making up for those years of servitude now.

Morrigan flashed her startling blue eyes at him with a look that said, *Thank you. You've done it again.* She was back from whatever dreamland she'd been inhabiting.

He smiled grimly to himself.

Anyone looking in on this scene—an angel from heaven, say, fluttering above the candelabra—could easily take them for a settled married couple, eating their privileged food in companionable silence, with nothing important left to say to each other.

He corrected himself. The scene wouldn't fool an angel, because angels saw into the beating, bleeding hearts of men like him, and women like Morrigan.

He was forty-seven, old enough to be her father. Indeed, he'd played the role of father since she was five years old, and now she was thirty-five. He was dying, and she was pretending she didn't know it and making her secret plans for what came next, when he, like Hamlet, shuffled off this mortal coil.

"What did you get up to today,

Sophia? Anything interesting to report?"

She gave that nonchalant flick of the shoulders, which was another trademark gesture. Her way of spelling out that she was impervious to other people's opinions.

"I set a couple of lures. Found a girl who might be tolerable in the house." She paused, her spoon poised in front of her ruby-red mouth.

"How about you, Raizney? What naughtiness have you got yourself into?"

"Who's the girl?"

"You wouldn't know her."

She concentrated on her soup bowl, refusing to meet his eyes.

"I might. What's her name?"

She acknowledged him at last, flicking her eyes to meet his with a snap of annoyance.

I haven't gone yet, girlie. Remember that.

Her cheeks flushed the slightest extra shade of pink.

"Isla. Isla Jensen. She's got the most extraordinary hair. It's that white-blond shade that's common in children under the age of five, but usually dulls to butterscotch as they reach ten or twelve. Rather like your hair, come to think of it."

"Isla. Is she Scottish?"

She nodded. "Hebrides islands, I gather, but orphaned years ago. A story like mine. Came to America without her family and has had to make her own way."

Raizney snorted. "You hardly had to make your own way. You had me there at every turn."

"That I did, Raz. That I did. And sometimes I was the worse for it."

"I don't know what you're talking

about. You wouldn't be sitting like a queen on a muck heap as you are now if it weren't for me."

Sophia broke eye contact and beckoned Scottie, who'd remained standing like a dumb statue through their entire exchange.

"Tell the cook the chowder was delicious, Scottie. I think we're ready for the next course."

She wiped her lips with her starched linen serviette and took a sip of wine.

Her compelling blue eyes and waterfall-of-midnight black hair looked much as they had when he'd first seen her riding on her father's shoulders thirty years ago. Even then, it was plain for any man with eyes to see that she was of the tribe of Fianna, the ancient band of female warrior hunters, the banféinni.

What you couldn't see as a child,

when desperate with grief after burying her father, was the ice-cold tint that sometimes irradiated in the blue of her eyes, as it did now. Or the bitter edge that sharpened her voice and hardened the line of her finely shaped lips when her plans were thwarted. The frown that said she'd swallowed something foul.

They'd come to America together, refugees from British law, and he'd never, for one day, regretted the move, despite her calloused soul.

As he dug into the calf liver, his mind flicked back to her earlier comment.

"You say you set a couple of lures today. Tell me more."

She toyed with the stem of her glass, the fine column of her throat rising from tangerine silk with a ruffled neckline which didn't hide the sharp swallow his question prompted.

Not as impervious as she wanted to appear.

"I thought I'd amuse myself with Hector de Vile," she said in a throwaway voice. Like she could take or leave one of the most powerful men in the state.

"De Vile?" His ears buzzed with an instant warning. "Whatever could you want with him?"

She shrugged, still playing the frivolous coquette.

"He could be useful. He is a member. I thought it would be wise to get to know him better."

Grigor drilled her face, his eyes moving from her defiant brilliance to her wickedly amused smile.

"Why go seeking trouble?" Grigor said. "We're doing very well as it is. Hobnobbing with someone like him could backfire on us, like last time."

Sophia's face hardened into an unreadable mask.

"I know what I'm doing. Don't worry."

"Oh, but I worry," said Grigor, savoring the calf liver in his mouth, thinking of their flush bank accounts. "Most of all, about what you're not telling me."

Five

Maestro Campanone had all the hallmarks of an overripe comedy, and the capacity audience at Platt's Hall hooted and cheered and whistled appreciatively as the action progressed. It was a show within a show, built around a comic opera company staging a two-act operetta and running into a bucket load of problems: backstage feuds between tenor and bass, a chorus full of mistakes and a soprano mispronouncing her words.

De Vile's party was happy to enjoy the joyful vulgarity of it all and clapped and booed with the rest of the common crowd.

Elizabeth shone like royalty in gold satin with a draped cowl neckline set off by an embroidered shawl in Persian designs that hung from her elbows. Pearl drop earrings completed the stately look. De Vile couldn't help musing on what a dazzling splash she'd make in Washington.

His son Alex, and his Hawaiian-born twins, Kaleo and his sister Leilani, had all joined them for the night out, and it occurred to de Vile that it was the first time he'd entertained all three of his children in a public setting like this. The boxes at Platt's were modest in comparison with those found in other metropolitan opera houses, but they'd shared a fine sense of family bonhomie.

The cast completed the penultimate scene of the first act, where they go for a country picnic and get caught in a storm.

Elizabeth's eyes smiled over the top of her fan, which she dropped monetarily to whisper, "So lovely to have everyone here together like this."

He beamed in agreement, but his stomach coiled with nausea as he considered how he was going to escape to rendezvous with Moonlight at halftime.

He'd had a reminder dropped through his letter box yesterday, threatening dire consequences if he didn't pay his respects to the Madame in her box.

He hoped to get around it by calling in a favor from Bank of California president Bill Ralston and his wife Lizzie Fry; he'd arranged for the couple to visit their box, and then he and Bill would leave the women together and slip out "for a beer and boring men's talk."

The cast took their positions for the first-act finale—a fiery lover's quarrel between the soprano and tenor—and Elizabeth raised her fan, leaned over to his left shoulder and whispered behind it.

"Are you happy to meet William and Lizzie downstairs at halftime?"

The pit that was already making itself felt at the bottom of his stomach opened further.

He raised one brow and ducked his head toward her.

"They're coming here—but Bill and I have got a few things to go over on a deal—boring men's talk, so we thought we'd leave you ladies with Alex and the rest."

She raised a questioning brow in response and fastened her attention back on stage.

De Vile hid a covert sigh behind his right hand like a callow schoolboy.

What is wrong with me? I'm fidgeting like a schoolboy.

The usual halftime convention was for guests to do one of two things; either emerge from their seats to meet in the bar to "see and be seen" and gossip with friends, or remain in their boxes with refreshments brought in and entertain friends privately.

De Vile had planned for the second option, intending to slip away as soon as they served his group with pre-ordered snacks and refreshments. William would accompany him out, leaving the two women to happy gossip. Once clear, he and Bill would part company because Madame Moonlight had insisted he come alone.

As the soprano stamped her pretty feet and rose to a high C in protest at what she saw as her lover's shabby treatment, de Vile's hairline grew hot. He dabbed beads of sweat with his handkerchief before they dripped down his nose.

Elizabeth gave him a doubtful sidelong glance.

He silently heaped a litany of abuse on the head of the Madame responsible for his social misfortune.

He didn't deal with brothel keepers, no matter how sweetly she might present herself to a society willing to look the other way.

Six

Sophia Morrigan had chosen her attire for a night at the Spanish opera with careful thought, decked out in a black lace gown ruffled with diagonal frills and topped with a silver mantilla, the fall of glittering lace highlighting her flawless alabaster complexion.

She'd painted a beauty spot below her right eye at the apex of her knife-edge cheekbone. Her scarlet lips rested in a satisfied line as she spied him in the doorway of her box. She rose with a dramatic sweep of her right arm.

"Senator," she purred. "So glad you could make it."

She peered around his shoulder,

checking he was unaccompanied. She was tall for a woman, but he had a comfortable four inches on her. Her smile broadened.

"Alone, as I instructed. What a splendid fellow."

Blue smoke fogged the air. De Vile suppressed his quick shock when he saw she held a narrow cigarillo between her index and middle fingers. She raised it ostentatiously to her lips and drew deeply before tilting her head to the ceiling and exhaling in a long, thin stream.

Even in the liberal arts salons, they frowned on a woman smoking. In middle-class San Francisco, everyone understood a woman who smoked cigars was thumbing her nose at society.

She patted the seat behind her with a proprietorial air. "Sit." A pause. Then another irritated tapping of the seat. "Come, sit."

She's talking to me as if I'm her lapdog, de Vile thought.

The brazen gall of it.

He complied with reluctant inner grace.

"I suppose you're wondering why I've dragged you away from your beautiful Countess," she said with a single brow hooked up in a theatrical question mark. "Or have you already guessed?"

The sapphire-blue eyes were as hard as diamonds.

De Vile backed as far away from her as he could without being blatantly rude. Something about the malevolent posing offended him deeply, and he'd pulled plenty of similar acts in his time.

His mind flashed guiltily back to his last dealings with Bertha, and the way he colluded in the kidnapping of Graysie Russell's stepdaughter Minette. Graysie Castellanos, as she was then, but who was counting?

But it wasn't Minette's kidnapping that Morrigan was interested in.

He reminded himself that the ancient Morrigan was one of the Celtic gods of death, war, and discord, a phantom, a queen of demons, and he wondered if Sophia had deliberately adopted the name as a warning.

Ancient folklore said the predatory Morrigan hovered over a battlefield as a crow or a raven and could predict or influence the outcome. Deities and mortals who scorned her ended up dead on the field of war, with a raven perched on their corpse.

He cleared his throat and forced himself to lean closer to her porcelain cheek.

"I'm waiting to be informed by you, naturally. We take nothing for granted here."

Her blue eyes bored into him, narrowing into slits as she made her calculations.

Then her face split in a hard bark of laughter. "Playing dumb, I see. What? A clever strategy to draw the other fellow out?"

She transferred the cigarillo to her left hand and raised her right, the one furthest from him, and gave a sharp click of her fingers, as loud as the click of a castanet. The move was so much like that of a Spanish dancer, he wondered for a fraction of a second if a shape-changing ability to transform herself into something else entirely was another of her formidable talents.

But she didn't produce a castanet out

of thin air. Instead, a wiry, dangerous-looking fellow with a long scar stretching down one side of his face appeared at her shoulder. He'd been standing in the shadows, partly masked by a red velvet curtain, and Hector had failed to notice him on entering.

"Just so you know, Senator. I'm never unprotected. You might have been able to snatch a bauble from my girl the other day. In fact, I'm rather pleased you did. It saved me the embarrassment of having to spell things out."

She flicked loose the raven locks that de Vile was fast imagining as feathers over her back and touched her retainer's arm as she brought her hand down.

"It would be most unwise to underestimate me. My friend doesn't have any conscience. My wish is his command, as they say."

She took another long draw on the cigar and exhaled.

"Just so there are no misunderstandings."

She picked up a pewter goblet from the floor at her feet and took a long draught.

Then returned it to its place and licked her lips.

"Now, where were we? Oh, that's right. F.R.C. Have you worked it out yet?"

She gave him an interrogative look, as if delighted with the puzzle.

He stared at her, unsure how to respond. Acknowledge his suspicions? Or continue to act dumb? To his humiliation, she held all the cards. And whatever he did, he'd look stupid. He stayed silent.

"F.R.C." She rolled the initials on her tongue, savoring them. "Perhaps not the easiest one for you to recall. After all, it was a long time ago."

She lifted her hand to her throat and de Vile sensed the knife-man at her side tense.

She drew something out from under the near transparent silver lace at her neck.

He knew it immediately for what it was. The matching ring. Alex's ring. No longer on a single leather thong, but suspended on a silver chain. She'd made it impossible to snatch this one.

'Now this one. This one would have been so much easier for you to decipher."

She squinted down at it, mimicking trying to read the initials, although she obviously knew already what they were.

"What does this one say? Ah yes. A. Something C. Now don't disappoint me again, Senator. You know what that one stands for, surely?"

He remained stone still, withholding. She was taunting him, and he would not give her the satisfaction of responding.

"You can keep the other one. I don't want it back. Take it as a warning for what will happen if you don't do as I ask."

Finally, he found his voice.

"And what, may I pray, is that?"

She threw her head back and cackled with laughter.

"What may I pray? Yes, you will be praying if you don't follow instructions."

She tucked Alex's ring back into her cleavage.

"What do I want? Let's just say I've planned this like Queen Esther. You know her? The queen who saved the Jews in the Bible, though I don't know why she bothered.

"You don't get to know it all at one sitting. Like that hated Haman, you are going to have to come back a second time. We'll make it a wonderful banquet, just like Esther did. Then, and only then, you'll learn what you must do to earn your repentance. You've got—shall we call it a stay of execution?"

A gong sounded—the warning for the audience to resume their seats for the second half.

Morrigan took a last puff on her now well-burned-down cigar and vigorously stubbed the glowing tip out under her foot.

"Ah, there we are. You'd better trot back to your Countess, Senator. Wouldn't want you to get in trouble at home."

Seven

De Vile's face wore that far-off preoccupied vagueness she'd seen often when he was digesting major news. When he contemplated the vote on a bill he wanted to see get through—or conversely be defeated. Or mused on the price of certain shares—ones he wanted to either buy or sell—when he opened the morning newspaper and checked on the stock prices.

With Ralston's wife Lizzie Fry and Alex, Elizabeth had taken a stroll around the gallery to stretch their legs before taking their seats again. At the sound of the gong, Lizzie had hurried back to her seat, leaving her and Alex to return to theirs—and bumped straight into Hector, emerging from a box further around the circle.

His nimble son stepped sideways with enough speed to avoid a collision as theatergoers, keen to get back to their seats before the action began, streamed back into the theater.

"Father!" Alex's handsome face lit up with pleasure at his father's surprise appearance. "I thought you said you were going to have a beer talk with Bill Ralston. I didn't know his box was close to ours."

De Vile shot Elizabeth a panicked look, like a fawn caught in a hunter's flare.

"Just completing a bit of business, son. Nothing unusual."

"Madame Morrigan must have improved the status of her clientele since I last checked," Elizabeth said, surprising herself with her own bitchiness.

What has gotten into you? You don't conduct yourself this way...

De Vile's dark eyes flicked to hers again.

"I've been investigating buying into ownership of the club," he said with a shrug. "And she caught me for a quick chat when I was on my way back with Bill."

"A share of the Imperial? Why would you be interested in that, Father?"

Alex seemed to have entirely missed the undercurrents between them. He was taking the entire conversation at face value. Something you could rarely do with de Vile. He usually juggled multiple agenda in any situation.

"I didn't comment earlier, Hector, but you're looking especially smart tonight."

She dropped him an arch smile.

He pulled himself up self-consciously. "Why thank you, my dear. Not too different from any other evening, I'd think. When I'm accompanying you anywhere, I want to ensure I hold up my end."

She considered de Vile. The black superfine evening jacket, with silk facings on the lapels, narrow sleeves and a nipped-in waist, worn over a similarly neatly tailored waistcoat and slim-line trousers. An outfit designed for a younger physique than de Vile's, but he carried it with as much youthful vigor as Alex might have. He also carried one of the newly fashionable collapsible evening hats.

He was probably right. He always looked exceptionally well turned out. It was unlikely he was putting on any extra display for some other woman.

She dipped her head to de Vile.

She adjusted her Persian shawl and, with a slight forward motion, gave Alex the prompt to move on.

"I guess we'd better get back to our seats and see where that lover's quarrel is taking them."

Eight

De Vile's misery deepened when he stepped through his front door after his night at the opera and discovered a letter propped up in the wrought-iron letter holder on the hall table next to the coatrack.

The Imperial Club's Madame Sophia was inviting him to an evening of entertainment in two days' time. The same night that he was taking Elizabeth to Harkness's Oyster Cafe for one of the establishment's famed oyster and terrapin suppers, which were currently all the rage in the city. He'd have to lie to her again, and he was pretty certain she hadn't believed him tonight, so she was even less likely to believe him the second time around.

He held his hand over his eyes and massaged the pressure points at his temples to ease the ache that had developed over the second half of the evening.

The Spanish opera troupe had performed *Maestro Campanone* with a wonderful comedic flourish, but the encounter with Morrigan had put a damper on the evening, and de Vile's best efforts had failed to lift the gray cloud that enveloped them. Elizabeth had been unusually quiet.

He hated having to lie to her, but couldn't work out a reasonable alternative. Thankfully, the young people had carried the night, seemingly unaware of the strained communication between him and Elizabeth.

He sat down on the edge of his bed to pull off his evening boots and discovered to his comfort that Mrs. Crisp had already put his stoneware bedwarmer between his sheets. Good old Crisp. He needed extra comfort on a night like this.

He slipped into his nightwear and lay back, positioning the water bottle against his side.

He had to go along with Moonlight's tricks, because he had to find out what she knew and what she intended to do about it.

Only then would he be able to decide on his next move.

#

Elizabeth dallied over her toilette, giving herself time to go over the events of the evening. She sat at her three-mirrored dressing table and applied the cosmetic wash that celebrated Lola Montez had recommended as a beauty regime. Two parts white brandy to one part rosewater, applied morning and night, the celebrated theater star had said, protected a lady from developing the "dingy face of the desert-wandering gypsy."

Elizabeth smiled at the essential female lore passed down from one generation to another. Heaven forbid, no proper lady wanted to look like a desert-wandering gypsy. Lola, bless her heart, had passed away penniless in New York more than a decade ago, but her fame lived on in the Bay where she'd enjoyed a brief flare of fame.

She was another "Countess," her claim to the title as shaky as Elizabeth's own. Lola's lover, the king of Bavaria, had given her the honor before they spectacularly fell out of love.

At least Charles's family came by their title honestly, Elizabeth mused.

She recalled the guilt written across Hector's face when they'd intercepted him leaving Sophia Morrigan's box. Just what was going on there? Hector had never been susceptible to female enchanters like Morrigan. Over the many years she'd known him, a host of women had set their caps at him, but none had led him to the altar.

He deserved his reputation for ruthless business practice, of that she was certain. More than once she was sure he'd broken moral and legal codes in his restless greed to get rich. But she would never have picked him for a man entrapped by more sensual appetites.

And Sophia Morrigan was far too blatant a temptress to appeal to his ingrained European finesse. No doubt he'd acted rashly in his youth, but he would have been well aware he was doing it and hated himself for it. In short, Morrigan wasn't the sort of woman who tempted him. So why was he visiting her in her private box?

She examined her profile in her bedroom mirror. Stroked at her cheeks, minutely examining whether the fine lines around her eyes and mouth had deepened since she last peered at them a week ago. Even if she said so herself, she was holding up pretty well for a middle-aged, verging on old, woman.

She'd thought Hector might be considering marriage—to her. She'd toyed with the idea. She admitted it. Were her instincts so wide of the mark that he'd set his sights on another woman entirely?

She drew her mohair bed jacket up around her shoulders, suddenly shivering.

She really needed to get to bed, or she'd look a decade older than her forty-eight years in the morning, and with the competition she was facing, she couldn't afford that.

She climbed into bed, and as she did every night before she closed her eyes, she pulled a small painting set in a gold frame on her bedside table toward her. Gazed at it for a few minutes and whispered to the empty room.

Tell me, Charles. What am I to do?

Nine

De Vile arrived five minutes late for his nine p.m. invitation to the Imperial Club, twirling his walking stick and presenting a picture of the confident man about town. He doffed his hat to half a dozen fellows he knew as he walked up the stairs to the second-floor entrance, where he was met by a shockingly white-haired man he could imagine was Grand Vizier to Empress Sophia.

He was Raizney Grigor, Sophia's mysterious sponsor. He knew the man by sight and reputation, but surprisingly, considering they'd both been in the state for more than a decade, they'd never spoken.

As far as de Vile understood, he was not Sophia's father, but had acted as her guardian and godfather for all the time they'd been in America.

Grigor stood, hands behind his back, surveying the terrain with the piercing, sharply honed aggression of a falcon on a block, readying for takeoff, keenly surveying the terrain for prey. A one-man reception committee, de Vile determined, and his face was as icy as the Arctic fox hair that fell in a smooth pageboy to his ears.

He might not know me, but he already hates me.

"Senator de Vile." Grigor's voice carried the faintest melodic hint of his Irish birth.

Hector halted, tucked his walking stick under his arm, and extended his hand in anticipated greeting.

Grigor ignored it. Stretched taut on the balls of his feet, he glared like a medieval peer, fierce comprehension in his emerald eyes. He gave a sharp nod of acknowledgment.

"Follow me. Madame is waiting."

He wheeled on his heel and, without a backward glance, led de Vile through the crowded bar and gaming area to a private suite.

He paused at the curtained door and gestured. "Through there."

Then he turned and left, again without looking back, shoulders erect, his gait fluid and graceful.

De Vile pushed apart the red velvet curtain that obscured the room inside and stepped into a brightly lit gold and white room that sparkled like an Austrian palace. The panelled walls were painted white and edged in gilt, lit at intervals by crystal teardrop lamps which added to the sparkle of the overhead chandeliers. A circle of angels draped in cerulean blue, reaching toward a heavenly deity, decorated the Renaissance-style ceiling.

At a table brilliant with crystal and silver sat Sophia Morrigan in a low-cut cobalt blue gown, her neck draped in a halter of blue moonstones and sapphires.

Kashmir blue sapphires, de Vile detected in a glance, one of the darkest blue and rarest of the gems.

Momentarily, he didn't know where to look. At the low neckline, the necklace, or her matching sapphire-blue eyes.

He settled for the eyes, which were sparkling with amusement.

"Senator, come. Let the fun begin."

She sat at the head of a moderate-sized dining table set for a multi-course meal and gestured to a chair at right angles to her own. He noted there were two place settings only. So Grigor wasn't joining them. And an array of different liquor glasses marked each setting. So, she was expecting the meal to last at least five courses.

"I hope you like oysters," she said, with what she imagined was a seductive smile. An irrational conviction took hold of him; that she knew he'd been planning to take Elizabeth out for an oyster supper tonight, and was determined to upset his plans.

They ate their way through a spread fit for a queen—oysters in the half shell, shrimp salad, baked sole, filet de boeuf, roast turkey and asparagus, quail, Swiss meringue, candied fruits with Roman punch, champagne, sherry, claret, sauterne, liqueurs and coffee to accompany the food.

And all the while, not a word spoken of Morrigan's true intentions.

When they were close to finishing their meal, Grigor returned unannounced, and assumed the chair at the opposite end of the table from Morrigan.

"I suppose you're a-wondering why she's brought you here," he said in a strikingly soft Irish lilt.

De Vile appraised him, struggling to keep his face bland in a situation fraught with distrust.

"Naturally," he said with a wry smile. "I didn't think it was for my charm or good looks."

Grigor scowled. Wrong note to hit, de Vile surmised.

I need to try another tack

"We're concerned about the future of the club, should anything untoward happen to either of us." Sophia's voice sounded a regal tone, as if it was a given that she spoke for both of them.

De Vile felt blood flush into his temples, overheated and dizzying. His mind raced ahead.

The future of the club? She led me to believe it was about Alex and the fallout from that be-devilled stage coach smash twenty years ago. What's she playing at now?

He didn't know if he should be curious or terrified.

He feigned nonchalance. "The club? I don't understand? What's any of this got to do with the club?"

Grigor curled his lip in a smile that resembled the snarl of a wolf preparing to devour a tasty morsel.

"Madame Moonlight believes we need a new, respected backer to see us through the next thirty years. We've got these Johnny-come-lately competitors like the Pacific and Union and the Bohemian Clubs, all nipping at our heels. It's sound business to build ourselves a guarantee. Insurance against going broke, you might say."

"Oh? And what percentage share are you talking about?"

There was a pregnant pause. Sophia fussed with her serviette.

"Only twenty-five percent. Naturally, we intend to maintain full control."

It's sounding more like a shakedown every minute, thought de Vile.

"Mmmm." De Vile let himself sound noncommittal.

Grigor took over again. "We've spent a lot of time and energy getting it to where it is today, and it could go up in a puff of smoke tomorrow."

"What level of additional funds are you looking for?"

"Ohhh... Somewhere near $100,000."

Mirth gurgled up from deep inside. The sum suggested was so ridiculous, he decided despite his prudence he'd drunk too much wine.

"One hundred K? You're serious? I could buy the club outright for that, if I wanted it. Which I don't."

Sophia raised an imperious eyebrow.

"Oh, but I think you do."

She raised her scarlet lips in a quizzical smile, but the eyes were hard-edged icebergs.

"Tell me. Why would that be?" She looked at him knowingly.

"I very much doubt you want your son Alex..." She loaded the word *son* with caustic irony. "... for Alex to learn that his father didn't adopt a poor little orphan out of the goodness of his heart. That, in fact, his soon-to-be-ever-loving father was an active partner in his abduction," said Sophia.

De Vile's heart jolted in disbelief.

She wouldn't...

His face betrayed not a flicker of emotion. He'd brazen this one out.

"And where did you get this fanciful notion from, Morrigan? More to the point, who is going to believe the fantasies of an elevated courtesan against the word of a US Senator?"

The tension in the room bottomed out into North Pole frigid as the Arctic fox spoke in a rasp from which any trace of Irish melody had vanished.

"Alex will believe it, because Bertha was one of my molls. I was there. I saw what she did."

Ten

Any pretense of being a guest of honor at a sumptuous feast evaporated with Grigor's declaration, but Sophia was not ready to call it quits. She pushed her chair back in a decisive conclusion to the meal and offered de Vile her arm.

She darted a warning shot in Grigor's direction. A flash from under her long lashes which said clearer than words: *Careful. Softly softly, catchee monkey…*

"Come now. You must allow me to show you around. Let you sense the possibilities. You haven't been here for some time, have you?"

Grigor's disclosure had blindsided him. His head buzzed like a beehive.

He allowed Sophia to lead him back onto the main floor of the club. Coming up to midnight, men in varying states of inebriation filled the big room. Excited conversation rose from the well-populated bar. The click of cues on balls at the billiard tables filtered through the quieter talk at the scattered tables.

After the library-like quiet of a few members having pre-dinner drinks or playing chess when he'd entered hours earlier, the Imperial was warming up for a night which would go through till dawn.

The comfortable lounge, subtly divided into spaces for different activities, with a study-like area at one end, fitted out with deep leather sofas and occasional tables set up for conversation and chess or cards. On the central floor, a livelier crowd could gamble, play billiards, drink, and play their regular games of masculine one-upmanship.

And apart from Sophia, tonight it was only men who were present. They welcomed women as guests but not members, given entry on special nights when dances, music or other entertainments were on offer.

De Vile's emergence on Sophia's arm brought the talk to a faltering halt, the background buzz and clinking of glasses dying away as men took in the sight of Madame Moonlight under full sail with the Washington senator on her arm, his face flushed from several hours of attendance in her private suite. The pause was momentary, but the looks were knowing.

Charles Falmouth, a young blood said to be the heir to a title in England, was the first to break away from his circle and step across to greet him. Falmouth, a clerk in the Supreme Court in Sacramento, regularly visited the Bay to keep up with the latest political and business gossip.

"Senator. Can I be the first to congratulate you?" Falmouth stretched out his big soft hand, a broad smile on his face. Registering perhaps the streak of confusion that crossed de Vile's face, he added, "I hear you're to become a major investor in the club. Jolly good news, I'd say."

De Vile disengaged from Sophia and shot her a questioning look. She responded with a barely perceptible shrug. He turned his attention to Charles.

"You're up on the poker talk, old chap. Seems you've heard the news before I have."

Falmouth hesitated, and his face flushed pink.

"Oh, I hope I've not said anything to offend..."

Sophie reclaimed ownership of Vile's arm and said smoothly, "The senator always has been one for holding his cards close to his chest." She tinkled with playful laughter, and Falmouth flashed de Vile a confused glance and then joined in.

But as the Madame led him on, de Vile realized with a sinking heart Falmouth was not the only member of the Imperial to have heard the hot gossip. He was soon followed by George Seymour, one of the town's fashion plates, seen at all the desirable social functions looking as if he'd stepped out of London's Bond Street.

He'd made a fortune as a merchant supplying first the 49ers and then Nevada's silver mines, but had sent his family back East for their education on the grounds that local schools didn't match up. De Vile had always suspected it was so he could lead the life of a gay bachelor most of the time.

He too had "heard the news" of de Vile's investment.

The wires had been on fire. The next to congratulate him was little Joe Thornton, dubbed "Spanish Joe" or Don José to his friends, an American-born attorney whose highest ambition was to be a Spaniard and who spoke English with an accent. He'd married the daughter of one of San Francisco's founding Spanish families.

"Hola, Senador," said Joe, placing his left hand on Hector's right forearm as they shook hands.

"I understand we'll be seeing more of you here in future. Que bueno!"

"Who told you that, Joe?" Hector asked.

Joe's face wrinkled as he tried to recall.

He shook his head. "Not sure who told me," he said. He glanced around the gathering. "Maybe Romano."

Romano Bernardo Sanchez, a dark young Spaniard from Florida and one of the most popular bachelors at the city's annual Delphi balls, waved to them from a nearby billiard table.

"And I don't suppose you have any idea where he heard it?" De Vile smiled. Joe's face creased with concern.

"Don't worry," said de Vile with a shrug. "Just curious."

Hector allowed himself to be propelled around the members and their guests for another thirty minutes and then made the polite platitudes expected of a guest taking his leave.

The slow response and the heaving sigh. The right formalities, in earshot of the crowd who hovered, curious to watch the exchange between him and the beautiful proprietress.

"Thank you for the wonderful dinner, Madame Moonlight. It's been a very enjoyable evening, but I must be going."

Annoyance clouded her exquisite features for just a second before she regained her self-control.

"I understand, Senator. It's been our honor. A pleasure to complete our business."

She spoke loud enough to be heard two billiard tables away.

He moved purposefully towards the door.

When they were out of earshot of anyone loitering, he paused on the club threshold.

"We've completed nothing of the sort this evening, Madame, and well you know it."

He leaned down, close to her right ear, and spoke fast and low.

She smiled serenely, as if he'd been sharing some lover's compliment, and closed in on him, standing on tiptoes to reach his ear.

"You're quite right, of course, Senator. Your investment in the club is just the beginning. There's a lot more to come, including the wedding."

She brushed his cheek with her scarlet lips just below his ear, stared meaningfully into his eyes for a long moment, and then in a swirl of cobalt skirts and blue sapphire sparkle, she was gone.

Eleven

From Our Lady Correspondent *Daily Alta* California - June 1871

Seen Out and About This Week

The comings and goings at the Imperial Club in Montgomery Street always fascinate my readers. We all know this is where our metropolis's great and good meet for a well-deserved brandy at the end of a demanding day solving the problems of our fair and fulsome State.

None more so than our very own Senator Hector de Vile, whose wise hands are not so full of serious political business that he can't rest his pen and take time out to socialize and be entertained.

Regular readers of this column won't be surprised to discover that the senator was kicking up his heels last night. It's well known that he is a member, and he has said in the past that the club helps him keep in touch with the heartbeat of the city and with what "men who matter" are thinking.

Our informant reports there were plenty of "men who matter" in attendance last night including Willie Botts, son of Governor Botts of Virginia, Joe Thornton, who is married to Don Bolado's daughter, *and Supreme Court clerk and assistant to Judge Raymond, Charles Falmouth.*

Her niece, Sarah Wyndham, bustled in, interrupting Elizabeth's solitary breakfast.

"Sorry to be late rising today, Aunt Elizabeth. I had such a good sleep! Best for ages."

"That's marvelous, dear girl. I don't begrudge you an extra hour in bed, I assure you. You work very hard all week."

Elizabeth's eyes flicked back to the newspaper, and she noticed her hands were trembling. She put the paper down in a rustle of newsprint and devoted her attention entirely to Sarah.

"What are you planning for today?"

"Kaleo's coming in a couple of hours and we're taking a run out to Cliff House in Hector's coach. Depending on how we feel and what the crowds are like, we might stay for an early supper."

"That will be very nice for you, dear. The weather's nicely settled. You should have a highly enjoyable run."

Sarah glanced up sharply. "Are you all right, Aunt Elizabeth? You don't sound quite your normal self."

Elizabeth's mint green day dress, with a stand-up collar that perfectly framed her dark hair, also concealed the stiffening in her shoulders at Sarah's enquiry.

"Of course, dear girl. I'm just fine. Catching up on the overnight gossip. I see our friend and your current business partner, Hector de Vile, was out on the town last night."

Sarah halted the serving tongs holding a piece of breakfast bacon in midair and stared at her aunt.

"Hector was what?"

"Having a night out with the boys. And not just that. It appears he's about to invest in yet another business, although I don't suppose that should surprise anybody."

Hector's business interests were substantial and widespread—from Hawaiian sugar to Comstock silver, San Francisco and Sacramento real estate to railway stock. A few months ago, his old friend Bully Pike had left Hector and Sarah shares in his import-export agency. Bully was Sarah's uncle. They'd been in close communication over shared business interests ever since.

"What business? He has said nothing to me. And I thought you were out with him for one of Harkness's famed terrapin and oyster suppers last night?"

Elizabeth's heart beat so hard in her chest she thought it might hit her ribs.

"He cried off. Said he had an unexpected business meeting. Sounds like a bit more than that, though."

Sarah finished piling her plate with two fried eggs and toast and sat down in a shiver of skirts.

She raised her knife and fork in anticipation and smiled over her plate.

"You're talking in riddles, my dear aunt. What's going on?"

"According to the *Alta*'s lady gossip columnist, Madame Moonlight entertained him over a luxurious three-hour Imperial Club dinner before emerging with the news that he was buying up a substantial share in the club.

"He spent the next couple of hours

being congratulated by the punters before being farewelled with a touching little doorstep kiss from the goddess Morrigan herself."

Sarah set down her cutlery without taking a bite.

"I don't believe it."

Elizabeth grabbed up the paper and waved it to appear gay and unconcerned.

"The newspapers never lie, dear Sarah. You know that!"

"He's hurt your feelings... Oh, I'm so sorry, Elizabeth. But that's all it is, isn't it?"

She reached out and cheekily snatched the paper out of Elizabeth's fingers. She spread it beside her plate and skimmed it. And then she cast her eyes up, her fine brow crinkled in parallel lines.

"You're right to be worried. This is all

very odd. Not like Hector at all."

Elizabeth waited, her heart soothed by having her disquiet vindicated by someone like Sarah, one of the sharpest women in the Bay and also one who had got to know Hector better than most.

"The insinuation underneath it all is that there's something going on between Morrigan, the Celtic queen of death, and Hector. I can totally assure you, that won't be the case. He hates that sort of overdramatic, attention-seeking hetaera. So if he was there for three hours of private dining, there's something weird going on. Very weird indeed."

Elizabeth let out a long sigh.

"It's a relief to know I'm not going mad. But I'm disappointed. It's the second time this week he's lied to me. Not what I expect from him, not at all."

She shook her head and bit down hard

to keep Sarah from detecting her trembling lips

"Oh Elizabeth, I'm so sorry. I know Hector's been a rascal, but this is quite unlike him, to let down someone he cares for as deeply as he cares for you."

Elizabeth took in a breath, about to reply, when the front door knocker rattled vigorously.

They exchanged an understanding look and sat poised, waiting to see who was calling.

"Hope it's not Hector. He's probably got no idea he's in the dog box," Sarah whispered. Elizabeth hiccupped, Sarah giggled, and both turned to the door to see de Vile's stepson, Alex, enter, a whirl of energy and handsome good looks.

Elizabeth rose and clapped hands on both of his shoulders. She bent to kiss him lightly on both cheeks. "Alex! Lovely to see you, and rather unexpected. What brings you by so early?"

He stepped back, acknowledged Sarah with a wave of the hand and the newspaper he clutched in it.

"Countess. I had to see you."

He waved the newspaper again.

"I don't know what's gotten into the old man, but something's off here. Way off."

Elizabeth settled back down in her chair and gestured for Alex to take an empty one at the table.

She laughed as she did so.

"What makes you say that?"

"I know Hector and how he feels about you. The queen of death is the farthest contrast you could ever imagine." He stared from Elizabeth to Sarah and shook his head.

"She's gotten to him somehow. I don't know how, but it can't be good."

Twelve

Hector was scowling over the *Daily Alta* gossip column during his morning coffee the next morning when Mrs. Crisp knocked tentatively on the breakfast-room door.

He stopped chewing on his marmalade toast.

Her normally merry blue-gray eyes shifted nervously, and her lined face creased in anxiety.

"Senator, a gentleman of the press is at the front door. Says he needs to speak to you urgently."

He sighed and asked: "What does he look like?"

Her worried mouth softened.

"Tall, lanky feller with red hair and freckles."

Angus McLeod from the *Argus*. One of the most astute of the business reporters in town.

He wasn't just chasing social scandal.

A weight like the sails he'd hefted in his sailing days descended upon de Vile's shoulders.

One drawback of being a high-profile businessman and Washington politician was that his every move attracted notice.

Anyone else buying into the Imperial Club? It would have made only a mention in the social columns. But when a Washington Senator did it? They all went looking for ulterior motives and power plays.

He'd have to cool things down.

De Vile pointed to the coffeepot

cooling in front of him.

"Show him into my study and take a fresh pot and two cups in there. I'll be there in a few minutes."

#

When he entered his study a few minutes later, Angus McLeod was watching Mrs. Crisp pour him a steaming cup of coffee. The aroma of Java beans blossomed in the still room.

The reporter jumped to his feet as Hector entered, his eyes searching the senator's face to read his mood.

De Vile braced himself to play it confident and hearty.

"McLeod! This is a surprise! What's so urgent to bring you to my doorstep on a Saturday morning?"

The journalist laughed, a rusty hollow gurgle, as if it had to rise from hidden depths to make its way into the world.

"Not exactly urgent, Senator. It's just I don't like being pipped by the opposition, and I had caught no hint of your interest in the Imperial."

He hesitated, as much to give Hector time to get oriented as to choose his next words, Hector thought. De Vile slid into a chair opposite and pulled the coffee Mrs. Crisp had just finished pouring toward him.

"Thanks very much, Mrs. Crisp. That's all we need at present."

He gave McLeod a friendly grin and sipped yet more coffee, although he was already buzzing with caffeine.

He put down the cup and drew his hands up to his chest in a thoughtful steeple.

"There's nothing to miss, Angus. Whoever the 'Lady Correspondent's' source was for that piece of puffery in this morning's *Alta*, he or she has a vivid imagination," he said. "As far as I can tell, they saw me at the club—not an unusual occurrence when I'm over this side—saw Madame Moonlight doing her hostess thing, and put two and two together and got five."

He leaned forward. "Confidentially—and this is strictly off the record, you understand—I feel a little 'set up' by the lady Morrigan. She invited me there for what was supposedly a briefing on how she sees things as one of the business folk with many people going through her doors—influential people—and she seems to have created a little 'event' of it. All of no consequence, I can assure you."

When Crisp showed a mollified Angus McLeod out of his study twenty minutes later, de Vile slumped into grateful torpor. Just for ten minutes, he wanted to flop into his favorite fat armchair and rest. To answer no more questions. Provide no explanations. And especially give no account of what he had or hadn't done after a stagecoach accident on a dark night nearly twenty years ago.

He sat fending off a creeping fatigue that stole through him. He pulled at his collar irritably, although he was wearing a loose-fitting shirt under a velvet maroon breakfast jacket, the lapels faced with quilted satin.

Haman's noose. He felt it tightening around his neck. He'd been able to put off the nosy reporter, at least temporarily anyway, but satisfying Elizabeth would be a lot harder.

The thing that terrified him most about last night's encounter was Sophia Morrigan's last obscure comment about a wedding to come.

She couldn't possibly think...

She wasn't proposing...

He couldn't make himself confront the possibility. It was bad enough that he had to find the best way to defuse the ticking time bomb Morrigan had unloaded on him.

If his long-time son Alex and his newly discovered progeny Kaleo ever found out what he'd done... Well, all the trust he'd worked so hard for would go up in a puff of smoke.

And as for Elizabeth? He feared he might have already lost any affection she might feel for him because of his lies over the last few days. The Tenderloin Countess wasn't to be trifled with, as many a hard-nosed grifter had discovered to his cost.

After a few more minutes of reflection,

he decided his only option was to brazen it out. He'd tell Grigor and that woman he would do due diligence on the club and make an investment decision based on sound business principles. But no one was going to hustle him. He wanted time to examine the books and not be pushed into some knee-jerk settlement.

And that's as far as it would go. No further.

Thirteen

"I thought I should tell you. I'm considering meeting up with Dolphie in London in the fall." Elizabeth paused with an oyster on her fork and gazed at him across the table in Harkness's Second Street dining room.

De Vile's stomach lurched, and Elizabeth's face swam before his eyes.

Adolphus Westerhoven, Elizabeth's nephew by marriage, had spent most of the last year in California, where he'd been an invaluable ally in settling an attempted scam in silver shares.

He was a favorite of Elizabeth's, more like a son than a distant nephew, but he'd returned to Europe months ago because of his father's illness. Westerhoven senior had since died, leaving Adolphus a title of count but little in the way of a fortune.

De Vile clutched the sides of the table and squeezed his eyes tight. When he re-opened them, Harkness's Second Street dining room, with its starched linen tablecloths, potted ferns, and the string quartet in the corner, was undisturbed. Only his world was rocking.

He'd made good on his promise to take Elizabeth out for their delayed candlelit supper, but he'd detected her unusually cool mood from the moment he'd called to pick her up.

Terrapin – or turtle – soup had become the dish du jour for the moneyed set at the best restaurants from New York to Baltimore in the last few years, and San Francisco was not about to be left out of the craze. Cooked with butter, cream, onions, herbs and a healthy dose of Madeira wine or sherry, with egg ball dumplings added to the mix in the last five minutes of cooking, the San Francisco caterer boasted he served the "gold standard" in turtle dishes.

But the atmosphere between them was strained from the moment Elizabeth had stepped up into his new yellow-wheeled barouche with light blue satin interiors and sat down without comment.

"London?" He couldn't hide the shock in his voice. "With Dolphie?" Or the disappointment. "Why this sudden change of plans?"

Spoon poised over her soup bowl, she gazed directly at him.

"No sudden change. He suggested I might like to join him there before he left in January, and I'm seriously considering it."

De Vile rested his spoon on his soup bowl saucer.

"I see. But why now, Elizabeth? You haven't mentioned it before."

She made a little pouting movement with her lips and sighed.

"I think you've got a good idea why now."

She followed his lead and laid her spoon down. Dabbed the napkin to her lips.

A bolt of fear shot through him. She would not get up and leave in the middle of the meal, would she? Without giving him a chance to explain?

"I don't like being led on, Hector. Kept in the dark. It's not something I'm inclined to tolerate."

He stared at her, desperate to find the right words. He grasped at straws.

"You feel I'm keeping you in the

dark?" he said weakly.

Her eyes flashed with anger.

"You know jolly well you are. And you should know me well enough to understand that more than anything, I hate being lied to, Hector. I'm like Kaleo in that."

De Vile registered another tremor deep inside. His relationship with his son Kaleo came close to permanent rupture last year because Kaleo had believed his father was deceiving him.

He spread his hands in a helpless gesture and peered nervously towards the neighboring tables. He didn't like being drawn into such a personal conversation in a public place.

She put her hand back on her spoon, and he felt his tension ease by the smallest fraction.

She whispered, "No one is paying us

the least bit of attention, Hector. And some things simply have to be addressed."

He leaned toward her, his posture beseeching. The table was small, suited to two diners, so the space between them was limited.

"Elizabeth, please. Do nothing rash. I'm caught in a pinch. A bit of a bad loaf. I'll get out of it. I just need time, and I can't explain any more than that just now."

He placed both his hands flat on the edge of the table, as if reinforcing the gravity of his mood.

"You're extremely important to me, and that hasn't changed."

She stared at him, her expression set, her dark brown eyes uncompromising.

"Your boys have noticed something's wrong, Hector. Don't fool yourself. Alex and Kaleo are as disturbed as I am. And Leilani? She thinks it proves she was right about you all along."

"Right about what?"

"That you're not to be trusted. Old dogs and new tricks... all that. You know the score."

Hector's brow furrowed.

Leilani had remained more aloof from him than Kaleo, even though he'd given her a lot of support in the Manolo family's sugar business last year.

"So you're all talking about me behind my back now?"

He felt himself deflating like a leaking balloon.

"That's what families do, Hector."

She fixed her stern eyes on him, her mouth resolute.

"They're concerned for one another. And if you want this family, like you seem to think you do, you'll have to learn to handle it."

There was a finality in her tone he didn't like. A warning sign.

The hairs on the back of his neck bristled, like a dog defending its territory.

He picked up his spoon.

"Our soup's getting cold and it's very good. Let's not waste it."

"You'll have to explain yourself eventually, Hector. Or you'll lose us all."

Heat climbed up his neck and flushed his face. He was going to lose everything he'd fought so long to hold on to.

"Something unexpected has come up, that's all. It's very complicated. I'm sorting it out. I promise I'll explain to you all as soon as I can."

She arched one eyebrow.

"But just not now, is that it? The

clock's ticking, Hector."

He stared into the creamy broth on his half-full plate. Suddenly he'd lost his appetite, but he was darned if he was going to admit it.

"The soup," he said. "It's delicious. And we've still got the oysters to come."

Fourteen

The clock's ticking, Hector.

Elizabeth's voice rang in Hector de Vile's head as he stood in the Imperial Club third-floor lobby waiting to be escorted to Sophia Morrigan's private apartment.

After a restless night, he'd taken the bull by the horns and was delivering his response to Madame Moonlight with no further procrastination.

He'd decided he'd get there early, before she'd got involved in her daily rounds, whatever they were. It was unconventional, unexpected, but he'd back himself with the advantage of surprise.

He'd buy time by making it clear this was purely a business decision. He would insist on doing due diligence before completing the deal. That would be the beginning and the end. Any further proposals were off the table.

Deep in his heart, he knew he was acting as if he was bargaining from a position of power when actually he occupied the lower ground, but pumped up with pride, he refused to admit it to himself.

So when Raizney Grigor answered the oiled mahogany door with the air of a man who ruled the domain within, de Vile felt the wind knocked out of his sails.

"Grigor... How do you do..."

The Irishman's iceberg eyes drilled into him.

"And you're here because..." The Irishman's voice held a peremptory edge. De Vile had never heard Irish musicality sound so menacing.

The Arctic fox hair fell over one side of Grigor's grooved veteran's face, but the locks didn't conceal the fact that de Vile was an unwelcome visitor.

"I'm here to discuss Morrigan's business proposition. What other reason could I possibly have?"

Grigor stared him down. "You tell me."

A drawn-out, embarrassing silence followed. Time for de Vile to fleetingly reconsider whether it had been a good idea to call without an appointment. He hadn't expected Grigor would front up with such a possessive air.

He decided to re-set the barometer.

"Is Madame Moonlight at home? Your barman led me to believe this was her private apartment."

"*Our* private apartment," said Grigor sourly.

A female voice sounded down the passageway behind him.

"What is it, Grigor? Is there a problem?"

Raizney Grigor stepped aside, and Sophia appeared in the entryway, in rainbow-colored silk sarong pants and a loose top tied in an enormous bow at the waist.

"Oh Hector, it's you. What are you doing here?"

"I'm here to discuss the club proposition, Sophia. What do you think? It won't take long."

His voice was brisk, his tone suggesting he'd brook no opposition.

She hesitated and then stepped aside to make way for him. "Of course. Come into the library."

As she passed Grigor, she murmured, "Ask Scottie to bring coffee, can you?"

The library was a generously spaced room with windows down one wall and the other three walls lined with floor-to-ceiling bookshelves that were loaded with books, their spines printed in gold lettering that caught the light from four crystal chandeliers.

They settled either side of a large leather-topped table stacked with reference books—an antique atlas, Webster's American Dictionary, and a fine desk globe with meridian and equatorial rings of engraved brass, the mahogany base inscribed with the medallion of the French mapmakers C.H. Perigot.

A ginger-headed, freckled servant arrived with hot coffee within minutes and de Vile watched in silence as he poured two cups.

"Grigor not joining us?" he enquired.

Morrigan raised a finely arched eyebrow. "He is not."

"I wasn't aware you shared a home together."

She lifted one shoulder, her face unreadable. "Why should you?"

Her striking blue eyes flickered from her cup to the doorway.

De Vile's eyes followed hers. *He's not here, but he's listening in.*

Coffee dispensed, they were alone.

"So. We offered you a share in return for the suppression of certain information. I think we made it quite clear. What is there to discuss?"

"First, I demand to know what exactly the supposedly damaging information you claim to possess is. And what proof you have that it's correct."

She fixed him with an unyielding stare.

"Second, what satisfaction can you give you won't try the same trick again next year? And the one after that?"

She gave him the slightest nod of acquiescence.

"Third, if we settle the first two points to my satisfaction, I would expect to have access to your accounts before we finally agree, just as I do when buying any business."

She tossed her head so her black hair swung on her shoulders, and gave a silvery laugh.

"Really, Hector. You think you can buy the moon? We're the ones holding all the cards here. You talk as if you're in a strong bargaining position."

She shook her head with a mocking smile.

"Your hand is empty. A very good attempt at a bluff, but you've got no cards left to play."

She took a leisurely sip of her coffee.

"I do like your style, though. Bold as brass. Just what I look for in a man."

Hector's blood froze in his veins.

She licked her lips suggestively.

"As for your points one and two. I'm hardly going to destroy your reputation when I'm on your arm, am I?"

"On my arm?" De Vile suppressed a wave of dizziness that threatened to overwhelm him. "I'm not sure I understand."

"You didn't think this was just about hush money, did you, Hector? Not really?"

She tipped the corners of her full mouth up in unconcealed amusement.

He stared back at her, his brows pulled together.

"I'm not following. You've dumb-fogged me, Morrigan."

He wasn't sure if he was playing dumb, or if he just didn't want to follow where she was leading.

"We've got a long way to walk out together, you and me. It involves a lot more than money. Though the money is important."

Peals of silvery laughter filled the high-ceiling room.

"You really don't know, do you?"

"Know what?"

"I've got plans for you. Starting with the Delphi Ball."

"The Delphi Ball?"

He'd turned into an echo chamber.

The Delphi Ball was of the city's high social events of the year, and it was coming up at the end of the month. Organized by the leading ladies, they carefully scrutinized the guest list to ensure those attending were all of sound reputation. He'd never checked, but he doubted Madame Moonlight would have ever made the list.

"Yes. The Delphi Ball. You're going to ensure I am a guest this year, for the first time. They can hardly turn me down if I'm the senator for Washington's partner, can they?"

Fifteen

Grigor had heard enough to know what the Sophia was planning, and it stuck in his craw.

He slipped down the stairs and vanished into the empty Imperial Club with what felt like a billiard ball-size lump in his throat.

Even as a child there'd been something seductive about way Sophia gazed out at the world from under her long dark lashes, and when they'd escaped to America after the riots that killed her father, her precocity was frequently the only thing between them and starvation.

He steeled his heart to recall how

many times she'd lured a mark to her side, only to pick his pockets and flee with enough to keep them fed for another week. It had been a game with her, one she played with no compunction for her victims, and as she'd matured, she'd simply raised the stakes. Taking on the senator, however, was ramping up her extortion racket a thousandfold.

And what he'd overheard through the library door told him she had a lot more in mind than greasing a fat sow. She was lining up herself up for a Gee-gee dodge, selling horse flesh for beef, setting herself up for the post-Grigor era.

Alive or dead, she was leaving him behind without so much as a backward look to fulfill her dream of being a society star, as brilliant as Lola Montez had been when she'd arrived in San Francisco in the '50s. Montez, a king's consort, whose spotty reputation had not denied her entry to the best drawing rooms, when Sophia was a wide-eyed nymph watching from the gutter.

Sophia was going to use de Vile's status to hitch a ride into the best drawing rooms. She was going to take Grigor's dirty little secret and use it to buy her way out of his life.

Saliva surged in his throat, and he swallowed a bitter taste back down. A low ache in his groin confirmed that his hatred for de Vile had just got personal.

He slipped into a dark room off the big commercial kitchen that serviced the club, the servants' common room, and found the man he was looking for.

"Santana."

A wiry, muscular man with a lean, sharp-eyed look about him stepped away from the wall he'd been lounging against, flicking through a morning newspaper

"Got a job for you. Strictly sub rosa. You'll need your gun."

Santana grinned out of a pockmarked face through yellowing teeth.

"I want you to go after the slimy senator. A near miss will be good enough. Don't kill him just yet."

He gestured to the man to sit, and stood over him, one foot up on the chair beside him.

"He's giving Angel Face a bit of trouble. I want to scare him off. You know the score. A good scare. That's all we need right now."

"Sure, Boss. When would you like it done?"

"He lives up on Nob Hill and he's got a fancy new brown and yellow barouche. Take up a watch and go in after dark.

Make sure there are no witnesses.
Understand?"

"As good as done, Captain," Santana said. "My pleasure."

Sixteen

Elizabeth was up early after a sleepless night had given her plenty of time to go over Hector's words during their turtle supper. Her stomach felt heavy. The turtle dinner sat in an undigested knot. She couldn't face breakfast.

She dove into the back of her wardrobe and brought out the brown serge skirt, simple front-buttoned white blouse and loose blue Hessian dust coat which had been her Tenderloin uniform. She had made no calls in San Francisco's seedier parts for a year, and as she dressed, the memories of past encounters there came flooding back.

She wondered how Mamie's son Teddy

was doing. Mamie had died drinking poisoned wine, an innocent victim of a conspiracy against John Russell's Vino d'Oro wines. She made a mental note to call at the Occidental on her way back tonight to check on Teddy's progress with his stepfather Sam Morley, who was maître d' there.

As she passed the hall mirror, she halted for a quick check on her way out the door. If she slumped her shoulders a little, she was anonymous as anyone could hope to be… Just what she wanted.

In the dark hours before dawn, she'd come to two decisions. One, Hector deserved a second chance. And two, if he wasn't willing to tell her what was going on, she had her own ways of finding out.

Her heart beat a little faster, and butterflies fluttered in her stomach as she thought back to the previous night. She could admit to herself in the solitude of her bed that she'd grown fond, even more than fond, of Hector over the last six months. She'd known the hugely successful former rapscallion businessman for thirty years, going back to his early days in Hawaii.

She'd been good friends with his first and only wife, the ill-fated Abigail, mother of the twins Kaleo and Leilani, and she'd always regretted the role she played in deceiving de Vile, falsely confirming the twin's deaths in a measles epidemic when she knew they were alive and living with their hanai grandfather. At the time, Archie had convinced her it was in everyone's best interests if they sidelined de Vile, and she'd agreed.

He had been a rogue and a vagabond

then, and for a good few years afterwards, but he'd changed as his adopted son Alex matured, and now, with the addition of the twins back into his life, he was a new man.

Well, he had been, she corrected herself. Until the last few days, when he had lied to them all.

I said to myself I'd made two decisions last night, she reflected as her Rockaway coach pulled away from the Nob Hill house. But really there were three things.

Madame Moonlight, everyman's favorite hostess, was the source of Hector's problems. She was convinced of it. She'd known the woman at a distance for years now, ever since she arrived in town as a girl, probably in her early to mid-teens then.

Elizabeth had run a charitable work

rescuing abused women and children, and warning bells had rung when Sophia and Grigor first arrived in town. They made an unusual pair when they appeared in a Barbary Coast doss house, the mysterious white-haired Irishman and the pint-sized coquette with a precocious smile and long dark eyelashes.

The age of consent in California was ten—so Grigor couldn't be accused of child prostitution, but the relationship raised suspicions. He apparently wasn't her father, but he acted like one.

When he fixed Elizabeth with a filthy look as he and the girl walked by hand in hand, the young woman apparently happy and secure in his company, she'd left well alone. There were plenty of women and children in more urgent need of help.

As the girl matured into a dramatically beautiful young woman, rumors surfaced of hushed-up "breach of promise" settlements made by the young scions of prominent merchant houses caught in her tentacles, and Elizabeth had almost felt sympathy for the unsuspecting swains.

And now? Did she have Hector in her sticky claws? If he'd become a target, she was certain it was because of some vulnerability in business, rather than any susceptibility to her beauty, voluptuous as it still was.

She knew where she could find the answers, and this time she wouldn't allow herself to be distracted from discovering what she needed to know.

#

De Vile returned home from meeting with Sophia, cut down with a debilitating nausea. He stumbled up the stairs, straight back to bed, muttering orders not to be disturbed as he passed through the entry hall.

He sprawled on his back on the fine counterpane, clutching his abdomen as the dizzying sickness gradually faded away. A feverish sweat across his brow cooled. His ears, minutes before blocked by a cotton wool deafness, cleared.

He stretched and luxuriated in his private sanctuary, his mind blissfully blank. The familiar liquid notes of the songbird that occupied a station in the cherry trees poured in through the open window.

He knew if he looked out into the fresh late morning, he would see small buds on the bare branches, preparing to burst forth in a pink and white storm of blossom in the next few weeks.

As if he'd sent a message to the outside world, the pure melody poured forth, music one could interpret as a song of praise to some heavenly creator, but which he reminded himself was simply a creature marking boundaries, warning other birds off its patch.

He groaned. Was that what life came down to? A contest for a few inches of ground? And if he was being a pragmatic man, what would be so awful about resigning himself to Morrigan's demands? She was a sensual creature, capable, he was sure, of creating music just as alluring as the bird's outside the window.

A gorgeous young woman in his bed? He might even beget more children and fulfill his fantasy of a late-in-life family. And as she had suggested, she'd be far less likely to expose his past sins if he was introducing her to the highest circles of society on the Coast and in Washington.

They could make a business deal like any other. Weren't many of the marriages he saw around him nothing but embellished business arrangements?

He flattened his back against the soft goose-down pillows and watched the light filter through the open shutters.

He took an audit of his state of mind. The fogginess in his head was evaporating with the calmness and song, and he could feel hope rising with the crystalline notes. But a closer check showed him that under the flickering elation was a foggy doubt.

Accept the temptation of Sophia's blandishments and rid himself of his murky past? Or stay on a steady course of winning Elizabeth's hand and accept the inherent consequences? He was risking losing everything—Elizabeth's affection, the respect of his sons, maybe even his Senate seat next time round.

Fifteen years ago, he'd have settled for the obvious immediate benefits without a backward glance.

But now? He rolled on his bed like a horse casting about in soft sand, and guffawed in self-mockery.

I'm spoiled for such duplicity now, aren't I? What do you know? I've developed a conscience.

He shook his head, parodying the man of integrity he was becoming.

Nothing for it but to get out there and fight for our future. Mine. Elizabeth's, Alex's, and the twins... I've got people who need me to do it right.

With a sudden decisive urgency, he sat up and pivoted to the edge of the mattress. His feet hit the floor with a thump of reality. He would not pay for Sophia's silence by accepting her as his mistress or—God forbid—wife. He was going to find another way to fight his way out of the mud.

And at the end of it all, he hoped he'd still keep faith with those he loved.

As he pulled the rope to summon his valet, he was still deep in thought.

What will Elizabeth think? And will I ever tell her the truth?

Seventeen

Alex was swinging out of his Market Street house on his way to get more darkroom supplies when a smart mahogany-panelled barouche with yellow spindled wheels pulled up right outside.

Hector's new coach. He'd heard his father boasting about its imminent arrival.

He waltzed down the steps, smiling at his father's graying temples. His father's hair was longer than usual and a few straggling locks waved in the afternoon sea breeze that swirled up Market Street.

"Hex," he said, using his affectionate sobriquet. "What are you doing here in the middle of the afternoon?"

He tapped the coach side. "Showing this piece of art off, are you? It's gorgeous."

He stretched up into the open coach—its canvas roof folded back to catch the afternoon sun—and pecked his father's cheek.

De Vile squeezed his shoulder with answering emotional warmth.

"Want to come for a ride?" he said. "Wherever you were going, you can delay by twenty minutes, I presume?"

"Certainly," said Alex. "I'd love to test the suspension. Besides, I haven't seen you since the opera…"

"Ahh yes,' said de Vile. "About the opera. I wanted to explain…"

He moved across to allow Alex space to get in and settle opposite him in the facing bench seat.

"Out to Seal Point," he called to the

driver. "We mightn't make the entire distance, but let's get some wind in our hair."

Alex chortled. "Looks like you already have. Elizabeth will send you off to the barber any day now."

He grinned across and saw the cloud that skittered across Hector's face at the mention of Elizabeth's name.

Oh dear. Wrong thing to say. Should I dig a deeper hole or shut up?

De Vile sucked in his breath.

"About Elizabeth too…" he said. "I've got a bit of air to clear, don't I?"

He patted the seat beside him. "Sit here," he said. "It'll be easier to talk."

As the two iron-grays got into a glorious rhythm on the Pacific Coast out of the city, de Vile turned to his son. Alex noted de Vile's handsome features cross-hatched with worry lines.

"Can I ask you something that might seem rather strange, Alex?"

Alex dipped his brows and gave a short laugh. "Of course, Hex. Anything."

"Did Isabella or Graysie ever mention anything about items that were found with you on that dreadful night of the coach accident? Baby toys, or teething rings, or any personal kiddie items like that?"

Alex sparked with excitement. He'd lucked into a charmed life as Hector's adopted son, and he gave thanks every day for his good fortune. But he still wondered about the events that had led up to his adoption. His mother's death in a stagecoach smash. He and his twin sister Isabella spirited away before rescuers came, even though his father was still alive and capable of taking care of them. Well, maybe only marginally capable, but still alive.

Rafael Castellanos had lost his children and died a broken man, not knowing they'd survived and were being well cared for.

"Only the little fir cones dipped in gold," Alex said. "Did anyone ever tell you about them?"

De Vile shook his head. "I don't think so. Remind me."

"Isabella and Graysie both had these little souvenir cones they wore on gold chains around their necks. Apparently, in the early days of the Gold Rush, when miners made a strike, they often dipped a souvenir cone from the mountain firs in liquid gold as a keepsake. The girls both had one, but if I ever had one, it disappeared a long time ago. You saw nothing like that?"

He peered into his father's eyes.

"I think I've asked you before, and I'm sure if you had seen anything like that, you would have told me."

De Vile agreed with a nod.

"Not gold cones, no, but something else rather strange has come up. It's one thing I wanted to talk to you about."

Hector told him about Grigor and Morrigan.

"They got a bone ring, a bracelet or a teething ring, something like that. Too small to fit an adult wrist. Someone clearly designed it for a small child," de Vile said. "I've got a suspicion it might have belonged to either you or Isabella. The one I saw had a silver nameplate with the initials F.R.C. Does that mean anything to you?"

Alex's heart quickened. "It does. It's almost certainly Isabella's. Graysie told me Huldah renamed her. The 'F' would be after our Scottish grandmother. Fanny Rose. She married Marqués Angel de Castellanos."

His father's eyes grew thoughtful.

"There's something else," he said, turning to face Alex. "I suspect that Grigor, the guy who runs the club with Sophia Morrigan, knows more about your mother's crash than he's saying. I suspect the bangles might have come from that crash."

Alex's throat felt dry. "You don't think…"

He struggled to speak, suddenly hit by the implications of what his father was saying.

"You mean he might have been there? He might tell us more about what happened? That would be amazing…"

He sensed de Vile bristling.

"Even if he was, there's no guarantee

he'd tell the truth about it. Those two are simply out for what they can get."

He fixed Alex with his dark gold-flecked eyes.

"You can't believe a word he says."

"I understand, Hex, I do. It's exciting news."

"Don't go poking around, Alex, I beg of you. There's all sorts of stuff going on I can't talk about right now, but part of it is they're trying to extort money from me for the story, and I'm not paying."

Alex felt his warm enthusiasm cool. "What? That's not right."

"You're darn right it's not. But leave it to me. I'm handling it."

"Is that why Elizabeth is peevish with you? I was up there yesterday and she didn't seem her usual bright self. I thought it was because of Thursday and you going to see 'that woman.' You could have just come clean about it rather than telling lies…"

"Yes, Alex. I see that now. I'm kicking myself, but I'll make it up."

They sat in chilly silence as the coach sped on, parallel now with the long beach that stretched up the coast from the ferry wharves to the rocky outpoint where hundreds of seals basked below the popular restaurant Cliff House.

Alex's bright mood had dampened at the reminder of the sad events of his babyhood.

His father seemed equally sobered, and sat beside him, lost in thought.

He tapped de Vile's hand, and when his father met his eyes, he felt a surge of new hope.

"Father, would it be all right if I told Graysie about this? She was older than us, and she was there. She might remember something new if I jogged her memory."

"Go ahead, son. It can't hurt. But apart from her, keep it to yourself for the moment. You never know. People can get the wrong end of the stick."

Funny thing to say, Alex thought as his father drew his fob watch out of his inner jacket and checked the time. "We'd better be getting back. I don't want to delay your important work," he said with a sly grin.

He's always happy to take a poke at my photography, Alex thought. *To him it's just playtime, but I'll let it go this time. No point in stirring things up.*

They turned and headed for home. A cool wind had got up, and it contented them to snuggle under a heavy seat rug and watch the sun sink low over the Pacific Ocean as they sped back to town.

He turned to his father with one last thought: "It's all so long ago, I'm sure no one but us would be in the least bit interested."

Eyes soft with affection, Hex gazed at him for a few seconds, then nodded and smiled.

"Let's hope you're right."

Eighteen

Santana lowered his eye along the barrel of his shotgun and lined up the brown and yellow coach in the crosshairs. The driver perched in the front box seat was slowing down, preparing to turn into the driveway, which was presently shut off by massive wrought-iron gates.

He'd followed his instructions to the letter.

Wait till dark and there's no one else around.

Done that.

Don't kill him. Just scare the heck out of him.

Yesseree. *Here we go.*

With careful precision, he lined up his

quarry one more time, and then squeezed the trigger with consistent force. The roar pierced the quiet suburban night with a velocity loud enough to even surprise him.

Before he'd moved his head from the barrel, the driver slumped over and tumbled off his perch with the dead weight of a sack of potatoes, barely missing the coach wheels as he crashed to the cobblestoned street.

The fancy white horses reared. One screamed. And the fancy dancy cart made a dizzying two-wheeled turn as the horses bolted.

Scare the heck out of him.

Job done.

Nineteen

"I tell you, Graysie, it was terrifying."

Alex contemplated his half-sister over the length of his bandaged knee resting on an overstuffed footstool and waited for her reaction. But before she drew breath, he continued in a rush.

"It's lucky they killed neither of us. We got off lightly."

In the terrifying seconds after the driver fell from his perch in front of them and the barouche had lurched wildly, Alex acted on instinct. He'd lunged forward against the mad swaying of the cabin to take Jeb's place.

The angels must have been at Hector's shoulder, because Alex grabbed for the lead reins as they were slipping out of reach. For a heart-stopping second or two the iron grays had hurtled onwards, ignoring the gentle pressure he was bringing to bear. He knew another shock of a sudden hauling on the reins might be too much, and thankfully he'd guessed correctly.

After the dizzying two-wheeler turn, the barouche thumped four wheels back to solid ground, and the horses slowed.

As he poured out his story, Graysie's eyes never left his face. She curved her lips in a worried question.

"How's Jeb?" she asked, her voice husky.

"Bruised and concussed, but that seems to be the worst of it. Father's given him a few days off to recover. The bullet missed him by a hair. It grazed one of the iron grays' haunches. Their sudden bolt threw him out."

Graysie perched on one edge of the fat footstool next to Alex's resting leg, and she gently stroked his ankle as he talked.

She was in town from her Grass Valley home for two weeks, performing at the Imperial Club with her sister-in-law and dear friend Pania Russell, Sir John's wife. Alex felt it the ultimate luxury to pore over the previous night's extraordinary accident with her.

"Thing is, Father seems intent on making light of it. He's brushing it off as the antics of some lushington crazed with booze."

Her emerald eyes flashed with understanding.

"But you don't think so," she observed.

He shook his head, and the jag of pain

down the side of his face reminded him he sported an egg-sized lump above his right eye.

He winced, and she regarded him keenly.

"How did you come by the lump on your head?"

"I honestly can't recall. I think my head and knee got slammed against Jeb's seat when the horses were going crazy. It all happened so fast it's hard to remember."

He gave her a sheepish grin, and she responded with an affectionate pat to his foot.

"You're not overdoing it, are you? Should I let you get back to bed?"

"No Graysie, please, don't. There's something I want to talk to you about, and Hector said it was OK, so I'm not breaking any confidences."

She moved from the footstool to a

full-sized armchair close by and fixed him with her full attention.

"We're all just so grateful that you brought those horses back under control before they hurt or killed anyone else. You deserve a medal."

He laughed, but resisted shaking his head again.

"Anyone would have done the same," he said. "No heroics involved."

"Hector's got to drop this habit of needing his sons to save him, that's all." She smiled up at him approvingly. "Kaleo last year. Now you."

"Something's going on with him and that woman from the club. Madame Moonlight."

"Sophia Morrigan? Really? What kind of thing?"

Graysie's brows drew into a skeptical question mark.

"You don't think he'd get muddled up with her?" Alex gazed into Graysie's exquisite emerald eyes. The fine mouth turned up at the corners in disbelief.

She hesitated, drawing her fingers into a triangle, pressing the tips together.

"I don't think she's his type. Not at all. However, she might have something to ensnare him. She's got a reputation for…" she hesitated, "shall we say, extracting favors from high-powered men. It's how she got where she is, I understand."

Alex's jaw dropped. "You mean extortion?"

Graysie nodded, silent.

"And where has that got her?"

Graysie shrugged. "Running one of the most successful men's clubs in the city. Enmeshing herself with and influencing the chaps who run the city. Usually rich men."

Alex nodded. "Do you mean blackmail?"

"She wouldn't call it that, but you know the old saying, 'If it walks like a duck…'"

Alex joined in… "'walks like a duck, quacks like a duck…'"

They both gave a soft huff of laughter.

"That sounds about right. And what about her offsider? Gregory or someone? Father seems to think he knows something about the stagecoach crash when our mother died."

Their mother, Elanora Castellanos, was married to his father Rafael at the time of her death, but she'd been pregnant with Graysie before Rafael had married her, so they didn't share fathers.

He could see from the flash in

Graysie's eyes that this new piece of information interested her.

"Grigor? It's Grigor, not Gregory. He's the Irishman who's Sophia's foster father. I think her father died in some political riots in England, and he fled to America with Sophia and her mother. Somewhere along the way, the mother died too, and left them to make the best of it."

She gave a wistful smile. "A story many of us share, isn't it?"

From their previous heart-to-hearts Alex knew Rafael had remarried, but Graysie and her stepmother never got on and her father had slowly faded away, never regaining the joy he'd known before Elanora's death.

Graysie cleared her throat. "But I digress. Why does Hector think Grigor is involved?"

Alex frowned. He was getting a headache, and when he tried to recall exactly what Hector said, the throb deepened.

"Honestly, it was vague and confusing. But it was part of the excuse for why he went to Sophia's box at the opera the other night. You heard about that?"

She shook her head. "Not really. Some vague mention..."

"Elizabeth's in a knot about it."

Graysie nodded understandingly.

"That was when he mentioned about these bangles, or bracelets. He thinks Grigor picked up some keepsake on the night of the stagecoach crash. He didn't exactly explain the significance."

Two vertical lines formed in the middle of Graysie's forehead between her elegant brows.

"You know, I seem to remember Mother got you both these cute little ankle rings with your initials engraved on them. It upset me because she didn't get me one. She said my ankles were too big."

She gazed at Alex and laughed. "Aren't we funny, the things we remember?"

Graysie was two years older than the twins, and for years after they'd disappeared, she'd blamed herself for their loss, for not looking after them better.

"If those bracelets have turned up, that would be amazing, although I don't know what it proves," she said. "He might have found them in a pawnbroker's, for all we know."

"Mmm. He might have," said Alex. "But from the funny way Hex was talking, I somehow doubt it."

Twenty

De Vile slouched on the Cobweb Palace's long mahogany bar, sipped his German ale and fed peanuts to one of Abe Warner's parrots. He looked to all the world like he'd just stopped by for a lunchtime drink, but he had an ulterior motive for visiting the San Francisco landmark frequented by all classes.

Hector did not know if the green-and-red-feathered bird eating his peanuts was Grandfather Warner, the creature famous for occasionally spouting off phrases like "I'll have a rum and gum. What'll you have?" and swearing in four languages. So far, the bird had remained silent.

A quick glance around told any visitor that this was no ordinary waterfront bar, situated as it was on the disused Meigg's Wharf at the corner of Francisco and Powell streets. To begin with, curtains of silvery fine spider web festooned the walls and ceiling, because the owner heartily admired the eight-legged creatures and refused to kill them.

And in the way of oddity, the parrots weren't the only live creatures to be seen at the Palace. Monkeys and other furry animals scampered between tables, entertaining patrons with their antics. And on the street outside, a menagerie of caged animals and birds, including kangaroos and bears, were on display for tourists and idle wayfarers.

Hector wiped his hand across his nose. The musty air smelt of bird dung and insect dust, but visitors extolled the food—simple seafarer fare in keeping with the location, like sweet and succulent Dungeness crabs, clam chowder and mussels with excellent French bread.

De Vile wasn't here for the food, or to enjoy the eccentricities of the owner. He had it on good authority: the Cobweb Palace was one of Raizney Grigor's favorite haunts, and he was staking the place out, hoping to catch the Irishman unawares.

The Palace's owner, Abe Warner, sidled up to him and grinned through yellowing teeth.

"Slumming it today, are you, Senator?"

The housekeeping standards of his establishment might leave a lot to be desired, but except for the state of his teeth, Abe was well-groomed, with clean collars and neatly trimmed beard.

Hector leaned in to him and shook his hand warmly.

"Just like to go incognito, now and then, Abe. Bend my ear to the local gossip."

The two men eyed each other with warm respect. Both had once been seamen, and they knew the wrench of settling on dry ground.

"Anything worth reporting down here?"

Abe grinned and shook his head. "Not unless you consider another scrap between Emperor Norton and the cartoonist news," said Abe with a twinkle in his eye. A gifted local artist had drawn a cartoon of the city's eccentric Norton with two equally notorious dogs, Bummer and Lazarus, which Norton took exception to as not being "respectful" enough.

De Vile laughed and took another sip of his ale.

Abe stepped back and considered the old politico with a shrewd glint in his eye.

"From what I'm reading, you're the one in danger of losing his sanity. You're not considering going into the hospitality business, are you, Hector? Thought you'd have more sense than that."

"Don't believe everything you see in the paper, Abe. Thought you'd know that by now," Hector replied with a cheeky grin.

Abe leaned in close. "I reckon old Grigor wouldn't welcome someone like you on his patch," Abe observed, eyeing the room as if this was a throwaway line. De Vile recognized it for what it was—a warning.

He leaned in even closer, so Hector could smell the whiskey and fish on his breath. "Word is that Grigor's not long for this world, and he's frantic to secure his place before he goes."

"Speaking of which…" He stood straight up and cast a significant glance to the door, where Grigor had paused on his way in to talk to the peanut seller, who occupied a permanent spot just outside.

Hector followed his gaze, and his heart kicked into a higher gear. He clamped down on an odd rising excitement.

"Where did you hear that?" He spoke slowly and in a low voice, but his studied ease wouldn't take Abe in.

"Same place I heard he's got a bairn he's been feeding all these years. When a man knows he's about to die, he likes to leave things tidy for the ones he's leaving behind."

He fixed his gaze back on Hector. "I bet a man like Grigor does, anyways."

And with that, he lumbered off, as if he'd been doing nothing more than exchanging the day's pleasantries with a customer, leaving Hector transfixed.

Now that would explain a lot, he thought.

Maybe Grigor and I aren't that different after all.

Twenty-one

Elizabeth directed her driver to stop right outside her destination near Union Square. As she'd instructed, Bert jumped down from his driver's seat and took her arm to escort her to the front door of the glorified Morton Street boarding house her old friend Kate Buchanan ran as a "parlor house."

She peered nervously up and down the street and started up the path to Kate's front door. Respectable women rarely ventured into this area. A police officer was often stationed at the start of the street, warning 'respectable' women away. She didn't want to be mistaken for anyone, or anything else other than what she was: a righteous widow.

Bert's vigilant gaze turned back to their curbside horse and coach as he thumped on the stout door for entry. When Kate herself answered, looking as round and blousey as usual, he scarpered back to the black mare.

"Well, well…" The steely questioning in Miss Buchanan's stormy gray eyes softened to surprise and then delight when she recognized Elizabeth on her doorstep.

"If it isn't the very Countess herself. Long time, no see. Come in. Come in."

They hesitated, shoulder to shoulder, and peered up and down the quiet working-class street, as if fixing the moment in their memories. At this early hour, the only folk about were the clerks and tradesmen who occupied many of the modest Victorian cottages, heading off for work.

When Elizabeth had first made the acquaintance of the denizens of the St. Mark's Place neighborhood, as they called it in those days, these villas had nestled along a quiet dirt lane which absorbed the noise of the passing traffic.

Now renamed Morton Street, St. Mark's had become a planked thoroughfare, and the soft thud of men's boots and the grinding of coach wheels on timber formed part of the daily background noise.

"It's changing fast," said Kate, subtly acknowledging the fact that they hadn't seen one another for more than a year, when they'd used to meet much more frequently.

She stepped aside and ushered Elizabeth in before closing the door behind her. Once inside, she raised her arms around Elizabeth's back and drew her close.

"So wonderful to see you, Elizabeth. Do come in and share a café au lait and croissants with me. I sent Jake out early. To Boudin's, of course. I must have known you were coming."

The French family bakery was one of their shared delights, operating in the Downtown area since early Gold Rush days.

"You must have." Elizabeth removed her soft-brimmed hat and smiled. "Just like old times. I'm delighted to join you."

They stepped into the house's central rotunda and, as always, the serene beauty of the place momentarily took Elizabeth's breath away. A high stained-glass dome over the foyer threw a kaleidoscope of rainbow splashes across the white walls and onto the wide mahogany staircase which curved out of sight, rising like a stairway to heaven.

Upstairs, as Elizabeth well knew, Miss Buchanan had fifteen rooms, all fitted out with elegant rosewood furniture and antique gilded mirrors. According to city records, Kate Buchanan ran a superior boarding house. All of San Francisco knew, however, that Morton Street was at the heart of the Barbary coast's red-light district, and Kate's house was one of the most popular high-class brothels.

She was a muscular woman, with the strong build and handsome fresh face of a horsewoman or gardener, with a prominent Roman nose, wide dark brows which stood out from her light brown hair, and a mobile, generous mouth. Her skin had the golden sheen that would usually signify a woman who spent a lot of her time outside.

Elizabeth smiled into her steady gray eyes with affection. She did not know how Kate maintained the tan, because her working hours were mainly nocturnal, overseeing her highly profitable but demanding business.

Kate disappeared to the kitchen to search out the coffee and Elizabeth sank into a padded chair at a wrought-iron corner table and breathed in the fragrance of a posy of spring bulbs, yellow jonquils with pointed orange hearts displayed in a simple glass jar.

She'd met Kate at the start of her charitable activities in the years after her husband's death, when she'd entered an entirely new world after one of her maids had asked for help in rescuing her sister from an abusive de facto partner.

Horrified by what she saw of the threadbare lives many of the women lived, enduring mental cruelty and physical abuse with no avenue of escape, she'd become more and more involved.

She couldn't help it. First, it was Emily's sister. Then Emily's friend Matilda, and within months she'd become a mistress of mercy to destitute and despairing women, some of whom had been driven to prostitution by the men who controlled their lives or by their own desperate need to feed their children.

And then she'd met Jack again. Jacob Mortimer Cabot, to give him his birth name, the son of wealthy Methodist merchants who were family friends back in her hometown of Boston, and the heartthrob of her girlhood.

He was also the reason her mother sent her to her aunt in Hawaii all those years ago. To get her out of trouble. Or rather, to keep her out of Jack's reach. Because everyone in church knew the devil incarnate resided in Jack's restless nature, his mischievous eyes and sparkling smile.

Kate returned and settled herself into the chair opposite her. She gazed at Elizabeth over big square hands drawn up in front of her face. "Tell me, how have you kept yourself busy without your girls to look after?"

She gave a tinkling laugh that seemed at odds with her staunch form. "I know you'd never be the sort to play bridge at Regina's."

"You are so right there," Elizabeth chortled. Regina Overington, wife of one of the city's leading bankers, was a celebrated hostess and self-appointed guardian of public virtue.

"I've had plenty of excitement from new arrivals in town—young folk who are children of friends, acquaintances I knew years ago, that sort of thing," Elizabeth said. "They've got themselves into this and that spot of bother, and I've been able to help."

Kate's faced sobered. "Ah yes, I heard something of that. My condolences on Bully's death." Bully Pike, a businessman who was also a close friend, had been murdered last year, and she was involved in the administration of his will.

"Thanks, Kate. Yes, that was an awful shock."

"That and Cyrus May and his wife Misty dying. A terrible thing."

They allowed the moment to stretch, as if paying tribute to those who were gone forever.

Kate shifted in her chair. "And I hear the honorable de Vile is on the scene again. Are you enjoying his attentions?"

It was a rhetorical question, lobbed

over the sweet table posy with a knowing smile.

Elizabeth laughed. "I haven't seen you in a year, but you have missed little in the meantime, haven't you? I'm not sure that I even need to visit. You already know all my news."

Kate shook her head while she continued to chuckle.

The soft footfall of Kate's housekeeper, Jemima Hudson, interrupted them. She came padding across the intricately laid mosaic floor with a laden tray, as proudly as if she might come bearing a crown for a queen.

"Countess Elizabeth," she crooned. "It's been too long since we saw you last."

"It has indeed, Hudson," agreed Elizabeth. "I don't know where the years have gone."

They waited for Hudson to slip back to her work, then sipped the creamy brew and tore at the flaky soft pastries for a few minutes in silence.

Elizabeth asked sotto voce: "Who's running the underbelly these days?"

"Mostly the Tongs these days. The Suey Sing and Hip Yee Tongs," said Kate. "You would have heard of the two shipments last year? Hundreds of Chinese women brought in on each voyage, basically as slave labor. It took the full force of the metropolitan police force lined up on the docks to protect them from sex-starved men who were ready to pounce and tear them away like Romans abducting the Sabines."

"I saw something of it in the *Daily Alta*," said Elizabeth.

"I'm sure they would've been in better hands with the men looking for wives than with the Tong masters who bring them in as sex slaves. Ironic, isn't it? The police protected them as 'privately owned goods.' Made sure they made it to the cribs unmolested. Can you believe it?"

Elizabeth shot her a wistful smile. "It's a complicated old world, isn't it?"

"It doesn't affect my business. We don't have any Chinese girls," said Kate with unaffected frankness.

They chatted on in a similar vein as they finished their coffee. Then Kate pushed back her chair and stood.

"Come with me," she said. "I've got something to show you."

She led Elizabeth around the back of the staircase and into a fine study kitted out much like an office, with all the accoutrements of a masculine owner—leather-bound books, antique maps, and a big ashtray beside a packet of cigars.

"Still smoking?" said Elizabeth.

Kate grinned. "Occasionally. Mainly when I want to stamp my authority on a situation. Always works like a charm."

She sat down behind her desk with a satisfied sigh.

"So. Why are you here, really, and how can I help?"

Elizabeth's eyes fluttered in part confusion, part embarrassment.

"I… I thought you said you had something to show me," she stuttered.

Kate's face creased in one of her shrewd, lopsided grins.

"I still might have. But for now, you sit down and tell me what's going on. You're not here on a courtesy call for old times' sake. I can tell you that."

Elizabeth spotted a chair poised in exactly the right spot to talk over the desk.

She reluctantly slipped into it, drawing her Hessian frock coat around her protectively as sat.

"It's Hector," she said, dropping all pretense of a long introduction. "I think he's in trouble with the Angel of Death. Or Grigor. One or the other. And he won't tell me what kind of trouble."

Kate's eyes sharpened. "Which one is it? Morrigan or the Fox?"

"I don't know, exactly. Morrigan is involved, I'm pretty certain. I'm not sure about Grigor."

Kate's mouth tightened. "Pity. I'd rather deal with him than her any day."

Elizabeth gave a wan smile. "Oh? Why's that?"

Kate's already tight mouth hardened into a grim line.

"The Fox is just your usual Grade A blackguard. The Angel of Death? She's a different proposition altogether."

Elizabeth's insides chilled. "In what way?"

"There's something missing with her. I think it's her heart. Don't know what keeps her blood circulating."

She reached out for one of her thin cigars.

"Even talking about her makes me want to smoke. She's scary, Elizabeth. Behind the facade, which can be as sugary as she wants, there's a dark hole. She'd stomp over, torture, kill those closest to her—her own mother, if it suited her purposes."

She paused with a grim smile. "I say her own mother. From what I recall, she hated her mother, so killing her would have come easy."

She lit her tobacco and blew a satisfied plume into the air above her head.

"I'm not sure even Grigor knows what she's up to. She's got several brothels she's managing around the state. She's servicing them with poor devils she's trucking in from back East who are as badly off as the Chinese gals they're landing on the Queen's Field. The worst of it is I hear whispers she's trading children as well."

Elizabeth clasped her hand to her mouth in reflex as her stomach heaved.

Kate regarded her with soft, understanding eyes.

"I know. I've got no proof, only rumors. And I do not know how or where she's getting them, or what she's doing with them. Perhaps selling them as kitchen slaves and chimney sweeps. Or worse. As catamites and cab-molls. Who knows? None of it's against the law, unfortunately, or someone might do something about it. But it's totally against any human feeling."

She gazed into Elizabeth's eyes, understanding lightening her masculine features.

"She's much worse than she looks, and if Hector's somehow fallen into her clutches, he'll be lucky to get out a whole man, in soul if not body."

Elizabeth felt an ache at the back of her throat. Her mouth filled with sourness.

Kate pressed on. "Have you got any idea what kind of thing she could have over him? I mean, he isn't stupid."

Elizabeth shook her head, unable to meet Kate's eyes. Her face was burning hot at the thought that Hector might be with Sophia in any but the most appropriate way.

"He's been so attentive these last few

months. I thought we'd got close." She was talking to the desktop. She raised her eyes to meet Kate's searching gaze.

"He'd even been hinting at the possibility of marriage. Very slight hints, but I don't think I was imagining them. And then suddenly, he's off spending opera breaks with Morrigan in her box at Platt's Hall and lying to me about it."

She shook her head, perplexed. "It's so out of character. I know he's a scoundrel, but he's always been a pretty straight up and down sort of scoundrel, if you know what I mean. Not a shifty-eyed, knock-kneed one, like he is at present."

There was a long, pregnant silence. The fire at Kate's back crackled. The curtains on the garden side of the room weren't fully closed, and birdsong floated in through the gap.

"I've threatened to go to London and

join Dolphie, to give him a bit of a wake-up call," she said, bringing her gaze back from the window to Kate's face.

"I think that gave him a shock." She examined her fingers, which felt icy cold, even though the room was warm.

"And then I decided that was just giving in. I'd rather see if I can find out what's going on, and help if I can."

"Just like last time," Kate said, with a dreamy note in her voice. "And look how that turned out. Does Hector know the contacts you've got in the dark underground? In Sophia's world?"

Elizabeth laughed throatily. "Of course not."

"Are you sure about this, Elizabeth? You mightn't like what you find."

There was another pregnant pause.

"Like last time," said Elizabeth. "That's what you mean, isn't it?"

Twenty-two

Graysie woke with a thumping heart. Her skin was clammy, the remnants of the dream so real that for a few moments she couldn't remember where she was. She rolled on her side and with a flood of relief saw Nathan's precious, sun-tipped mussed-up hair. She reached out automatically for his love, for the reassurance he represented that all would be well, and he stirred and pulled her to his chest.

His eyes flickered open. "Everything OK?" he murmured. His long, feminine eyelashes fluttered. He was still half asleep.

She buried her face in the masculine

fluff of his chest and breathed in his salt and spice maleness as images from her dream flooded her again. The black cave mouth, and the white wolf glimmering in the moonlight. An alpha male wolf, she was certain, and he'd been calling to her, but his bone-chilling howl wasn't the thing that frightened her the most.

The arms she'd drawn around her husband stiffened under the soft sheets.

"The children. George. Minette. I've got to see them," she muttered into Nathan's chest. She was mumbling, but he seemed to hear her anyway, because she felt his languor dissolve.

He stroked her hair.

"They're fine, sweetie. You needn't worry..."

She struggled up onto her elbows. "No... no, I've got to see them..."

Nathan let her go. "Of course... Of

course, my darling." His eyes were hazel bright and alert. He was fully awake now, like she was.

"I understand... You've had another dream?"

She nodded. When they'd first married, and then again after their son George was born, recurring nightmares had destroyed her sleep.

She'd never understood why, but they haunted her.

On the night the twins disappeared, the night she'd failed to look after them for her dead mother, there'd been this white wolf. She'd never known whether she'd imagined it, dreamed it, or truly saw it in the hours they waited for rescuers to find them.

In the weeks and months after the crash, the adults whispered predators had taken the children—mountain wolves or bears. They acted as if the children couldn't hear their murmurings, but of course she wasn't deaf. She'd suffered from nightmares for years after, tortured by the thought her little brother and sister had been eaten alive.

But the strange thing was, the wolf in her dream seemed to be her friend, not her foe. And he tried to warn her of the presence of real danger.

She rolled out of bed and tiptoed to the adjoining room to check on her precious children. Here in San Francisco, they were sharing a suite in Lick House while she fulfilled the concert engagement at the Imperial. She only did two of these concert seasons a year nowadays, and when she did, they travelled together as a family.

The months she'd tried to maintain her singing career with her five-year-old goddaughter Minette after Minette's mother died now seemed like a nightmare of a different kind. She loved keeping some professional life, but she and Nathan agreed it was never to be at the cost of leaving the children at their Grass Valley home without them.

She tiptoed into the children's room and stood between their beds, breathing in their tangible peace. Two darling little bodies, George, coming up to his second birthday, a sturdy round little chap with his father's tawny blond hair, twinkling eyes and strong physicality, always ready to laugh at life.

And Mimi, her best friend Francine's treasure, with her mother's French flair even though she was California born and had not set a foot outside its borders. Dark-haired, graceful, with her pixie features and a faraway look in her eyes.

She adored her little brother and was Nathan's girl even more than she was hers, but Graysie knew from firsthand experience the yawning gap a mother's death left.

George lay on his back, arms and legs splayed out in abandoned confidence that he was safe, his chest rising and falling in a perfect gentle rhythm. *Come on, world, I've nothing to fear,* his posture declared.

Mimi, in contrast, lay on her stomach, her head buried in her pillow, as if to say, *If I don't look, the boogie man won't come.* She wasn't an anxious child, but the horror of losing her mother in a gambling hall fire had left its mark.

Graysie stood perfectly still, letting the peace that filled the room seep into her bones. When her racing heart slowed and beat at its normal cadence, she returned to her husband's arms.

A few hours of good sleep later, they lingered over their breakfast coffee while Nathan's sister Marigold took the children to feed the ducks. Whenever they could, they spoiled Minette with croissants as a reminder of her heritage, and the crumbs of croissants and apricot jam from the French patisserie in Dupont Street lay before them.

Graysie picked at the leftovers.

"Do you want to talk about it?" Nathan asked.

She fingered the rim of her coffee cup, revisiting the phantasm, a visitation from another world, shrouded in mist and yet crystal clear at the same time.

"It's so hard to explain," she said. "I know I've tried before."

She gazed at Nathan, but she wasn't really seeing him. She was lost in the memories from last night, drawing on every resource to recall what she'd seen.

"It was different this time. The same Papa wolf was at the cave mouth calling. The man appeared out of the trees with the gun, just like the other times. But this time..."

Her heart jolted. "Oh, my goodness."

Her hands froze, and her heart pumped hard.

"I think in the past, even though I never saw the man's face, I believed if he showed himself, it would be your brother John, or my father Eustace."

She made an apologetic little dip of her mouth.

"I'm sorry to say that. But it's true."

Nathan nodded smoothly, taking no offence. He knew John and Eustace had both been implicated in the disaster, because of a madcap scheme Eustace had taken on to persuade his onetime fiancée, Elanora, to run away with him.

"It's understandable, sweetheart. We know they were there that night. I know they've both claimed that they didn't take the twins, but they've admitted they played a stupid trick. They were partly responsible."

Graysie clutched at Nathan's wrist, as if his words were in danger of carrying her away.

"I've just realized what was different this time. Just now. It wasn't John or Eustace with the gun. It was him."

She stood up, her face pale, her breathing fast and shallow, seeing something deep within. And he stood with her, stroking down her spine in soft, consoling waves.

After a long pause, he said quietly, "Who was it, Graysie? Who did you see with the gun?"

She snapped her eyes to his, and he understood in that instant that she was back with him in the real world, in their Lick House hotel suite, with the destroyed breakfast in front of them.

"Grigor," she whispered. "He had the gun. Raizney Grigor. And there was the stink of gun smoke in the air."

Twenty-three

When a man knows he's about to die, he likes to leave things tidy for the ones he's leaving behind.

De Vile gazed absentmindedly into his ale, as if it was the most normal thing in the world for him to be just chilling out on a sunny winter's afternoon at the Cobweb Palace, not expecting to see anyone in particular.

It wasn't a busy day, so it was easy for him to pick up, as if by a sixth sense, Grigor's approach from the door to his stool.

He timed his act perfectly, raising his head and staring right into Grigor's face when the Fox was ten feet away. He focused his eyes on the fall of white hair and then moved down his brow to make eye contact.

Grigor's face froze in a mask of equal proportions of dislike and disbelief. A fraction of a second before he made contact, Grigor slanted his eyes away to the floor, scratching at his jaw as he did so. He circled behind de Vile's stool as if he hadn't noticed him, and continued on to lean in at the farthest end of the bar.

De Vile allowed his own eyes to slide away as if he didn't know the Irishman was there, and turned his attention to the parrot. He parodied the bird's speech: "Good day, Grandfather Warner. What'll you have?"

A couple of old tars gathered at his table, sniggering as the brightly feathered creature strutted up and down, gazing about with beaky eyes.

Within minutes Grigor joined them, holding a handle of ale, a belligerent scowl set on his handsome features. De Vile glanced away from the bird at his approach and masqueraded surprise at seeing him.

"Well, stone the crows, if it isn't Raizney Grigor. Just the man I was hoping to see."

Grigor's jaw jutted suspiciously. When he spoke, de Vile noticed for the first time a flash of gold in his mouth.

"What business do you have with me? Or here in the Cobweb Palace? I've never seen you here before."

"Always a first time, old chap," de Vile said with sanguine confidence. "If we're going to be partners, we need to get to know each other better. Wouldn't you agree?"

Grigor regarded him in stony silence.

De Vile considered the other two old tars who dallied looking at the parrot, then gestured toward an empty table in the corner next to the smouldering fireplace.

"You can come and talk to your friend here later," he said, gesturing to the parrot. "Why don't we find a seat over there and have a little chat?"

Grigor stood with a mutinous expression and followed him to the table.

"It's not my idea to get you involved. You should know that, for starters. I do not know why Sophia's in such a fizz."

De Vile gave him plenty of time to finish before replying.

"Is that why you sent your man over to scare the hell out of me last night?"

Grigor's face paled. He bit down on his bottom lip with his gold eye tooth, making him look even more vulpine that usual.

"I don't know what you're talking about." He glared at de Vile, as if challenging him to contradict.

"Come on, Grigor. I know it was your man," he bluffed. "I recognized him from the other night at the club. I only saw him for a moment, but I've got an excellent memory for faces."

"Then maybe you'll take the hint," he snarled. "We don't need you. We're doing fine on our own."

"That might very well be true," de Vile said. "But two things need to be said here, Grigor. First, it seems your goddaughter—or whatever she is…" He paused suggestively. "She doesn't seem to agree. And second. I don't take kindly to having my son threatened. You can do whatever you like to me. But when you endanger by own, I get mad."

He didn't have to pretend when he

stared into Grigor's face. He knew his eyes were blazing with fury.

"Have you got kids, Grigor? I mean, offspring you see as your future. The ones you're doing it all for. Got anyone like that, Grigor?"

He stayed silent, watching Grigor's face. Saw the eyes flicker, a slight wince of his right cheek as if he could not suppress an involuntary reaction no matter how hard he tried.

"I see you do," de Vile said. "So you'll know what it's like. When you get to our age, you know you haven't got too much longer. It's all about preserving and passing on."

"You know nothing about me," Grigor said. "What I want, what I like, what I've got. Nothing." He turned and spat into the fireplace. "So don't make assumptions."

"Point taken," said de Vile, "if that's how you want it. There's more than one way to play this game, Grigor."

As they approached the evening hour, a few more drinkers were piling in looking for an early clam chowder supper. The place was filling up.

"Just so you know, if you set that hulking brute on me or anyone close to me again, I'll make sure the city fathers come down on your little club so hard you'll be lucky to have a business left at the end. They'll be in there checking licenses and fire escapes and goodness knows what.

"There'll be so many coppers in every night your clientele will get windy. Their wives will hear all kinds of things they don't need to... and start objecting to them going out. By the time I'm finished with you, you'll be lucky to have your doors open." Grigor was watching him closely, drumming his fingers uneasily on the table edge as he did.

Good. I'm getting to him. He's not stupid. He doesn't want to buy trouble.

"I'm going to tell Sophia I'm willing to do due diligence on the club and treat it like I would any other investment. But I'm not willing to go along with the rest of it."

Grigor frowned. "The rest of it? Like what?"

De Vile pondered his response. How much did these two confide in one another? Could he even assume they were on the same side?

"Like the business of Sophia being accepted in society. Me taking her out and about."

"She said she wanted you to do that?" Grigor's voice carried a sharp pitch of disbelief.

De Vile spread his hands in a gesture of acquiescence. As much as to say, *who can understand what women want?*

"That's what she said."

"Never bothered her before." His eyes glinted with suspicion. "What else?"

De Vile shrugged, as if he had trouble remembering anything else.

"What else?" said Grigor with more determined emphasis. "I know there was more. What was it?"

It occurred to de Vile in a flash that Grigor would be most unhappy to hear the full demands Sophia was making, and that a house divided would play very much in his favor.

He took a deep breath and blabbed the rest.

"She'd got this crazy idea that I'm going to marry her. Take her back to Washington and make her some sort of society success. I don't know where she got the notion, and I'm not interested."

He stared full into Grigor's chiselled face, which even in his fifties was still relatively unlined and attractive. His iceberg-blue eyes glittered with a strange pleasure.

"She did, did she? The little tramp."

De Vile narrowed his eyes, disturbed at the transformation in Grigor's demeanor.

Grigor was in another space, staring past him, as if seeing some other scene in his head.

De Vile reiterated, "I'm telling you. It isn't happening."

Grigor curled his lip, displaying his gold tooth, and then smiled a bitter smile.

"The conniving little cow," he muttered under his breath, as if he'd forgotten de Vile was there listening. "She's making her plans for when I'm not around."

He kept staring at the Cow Palace carpet, once an Oriental floral pattern but now so threadbare the design was barely recognizable.

"Do your due diligence," he said in a choked whisper. "Just remember, whatever she tells you, we've got equal shares in that place. We might not have any written agreement, but half of it is mine, and she'd be wise not to forget it."

De Vile jumped in on what he hoped might be a weak moment. "Why can't we work together on this, Grigor? We've got interests in common."

He reached out his hand to take Grigor's arm, but pulled back when he saw Grigor's body stiffen.

"I'm only dragged into this because of

this damned blackmail claim. Why don't we forget all about everything, and you and Sophia go back to running a nice little business as even partners. No skin off anyone's nose."

The Irishman pushed back his chair and thrust himself upright in a rush of furious energy.

"Too late for that," he said. "You and Sophia both. You're going to pay for this."

#

He stumbled along the Meigg's Wharf pier, not registering the animal exhibits in their cages—the monkeys especially—that he usually liked to dawdle among, and feed with the organ grinder's peanuts.

He clasped at his heaving chest, unable to think of anything but the betrayal that was being perpetrated right under his nose. And he hadn't seen it. He shook his head in wonder. He was on his last legs, a blind old man.

He well knew the flinty nature that lay hidden beneath Sophia's bewitching beauty. Many a man over the years had tasted that remorseless cut to his cost. Over a lifetime of intimacy, he'd become convinced she'd been born with a heart of stone, but he'd never expected to have it turned against him.

As he plodded, panting and unseeing, up the pier that stretched from the wharf to the North Beach shore, he recalled the impish sylph she was the day he'd first met her. At first glance, it was hard to tell if she was boy or girl, with her cropped midnight hair hanging over a pixie face, and waif's body clad in loose pants.

He felt again as if it were only yesterday; the damp warmth of her wiry little arms clamped around his neck, hanging on for dear life, refusing to release until he'd hoisted her onto his shoulders. There she'd fastened herself like a tick on a wolfhound, her stick-thin legs locked under his armpits. Even at five years of age, she'd had an indefinable but irresistible allure.

That was the day her father Jamie died, and she'd transferred her affection to him in the blink of an eye. He'd understood. Her mother, his sister Maive, was an enchanter like Sophia, but without her inner steel. And even as a tiny tot, Sophia had an unerring instinct for her own advantage.

He'd been her magnetic north in the storm for nearly three decades. Now she was resetting her compass, in a much more calculated and devious way than the five-year-old had grasped for safety. Now she was a woman on the cliff's edge of passing from full blooming womanhood to overblown maturity. She appeared at the peak of her beauty, but he knew she feared the chill winds were blowing the petals off the rose.

He came to a halt at the Powell Street curb, grabbing at his ribs. He'd forgotten to compensate for his condition. He'd allowed de Vile's revelations to disrupt his composure. The miner's curse. Black lung disease, they called it back in the homeland. The doctors might still not be willing to recognize it, but to the men underground, it was a constant companion.

He'd been an underground slave for nearly twenty years, from the age of ten. From the day he quit the mines, the day

Jamie died, he'd never gone underground again, but all these years in the fresh air of California had not cured him. The black death was closing in, and he and Sophia had found it impossible to talk about it.

He couldn't walk in this state. He'd die of a heart attack on the street. He waited patiently for a free hack up Montgomery Street to the club, but eyes turned inward, he missed the passing landscape, the proud arched frontage of the four-story Cosmopolitan Hotel, the silver shares shysters hanging around outside the Bank of California exchanging the latest Comstock tips. Grigor saw none of them.

He saw Lochie O'Riordan when he was a sparky fourteen-year-old with his father's platinum hair and ice-blue eyes, desperate to get out of boarding school and into the world. He was twenty years old now, shaping up as a brilliant artist like his mother. Lochie O'Riordan knew nothing of Sophia, and Sophia nothing of him.

And that's how it's got to remain.

He tumbled out of the hack, paid the driver, breathed in the eucalyptus and lavender fragrance leaking out into the street from the spa, and surveyed their own impressive three-story facade, built, like the Bank of California, from Angel Island local stone.

He'd achieved the unimaginable in the days since he'd fled the Old Country, a political rebel and a fugitive for his role in organizing worker demonstrations. He wasn't about to see it all slip away into the hands of a Celtic witch at the expense of his own son.

Twenty-four

Kate moved aside the dirty dish that sat on the ottoman between them to make room for her ashtray.

"What you need, my dear friend, is someone who knows the inside workings of Morrigan's mind. And then have someone who could help you turn that inside knowledge into a practical strategy."

They'd squirreled themselves away in Kate's library for a couple of hours, and they'd moved from facing each other across the desk to sitting side by side in front of the fire.

Jemima had brought them a delectable brunch of French bread and soft white cheese with more coffee, and in between fireside chatter where they got entirely off the topic at hand to discuss what had happened to this and that one, they'd followed through on nutting out how to best investigate de Vile's troubles.

They'd come to the obvious conclusion that if Sophia Morrigan was threatening Hector, the most straightforward solution was to dig up dirt about her he could use as a defence.

And Kate was supremely confident there were incriminating details to be found, if they knew the right places to look for them.

"It won't be easy. And it will almost certainly be dangerous," Kate said, shooting a worried look between drawn eyebrows.

"I think I can help with the first step—

finding someone who's got an idea of Sophia's secrets. I'm afraid I come up short with the second. A pity Dolphie isn't back already. He'd be eager to help—it's just his line of work."

Elizabeth nodded her head slowly. "You're right, but he's not due back home for another couple of months. And I absolutely do not want to put Hector's two sons in danger. They've already been in some rough and tumble for Hector's sake. I wouldn't want to risk them in anymore."

She stretched out her legs toward the hearth and soaked up the warmth of the flames.

She picked up a poker that was hanging from a firedog set at her feet. She pushed a couple of charred remains aside and placed new logs on top.

"Who did you have in mind to help

with the inside knowledge? It would be good to have a place to start…"

"Sam Morley's an obvious one. Occupying that central job at the Occidental, he hears a lot of gossip… And of course there's Mamie's friends too. They keep in touch and send him a pie and pudding now and then."

Mamie Bilouxie had died in a tragic poisoned wine scare last year. A dressmaker in the downtown area who knew a lot of the local women, she'd been a big help to Elizabeth's charitable work.

"Yes, I thought of going to see Sam. I wanted to have a clearer idea of what I might look for before I went, though. Anyone else that comes to mind?"

Kate struck a match to light another cigar. She took her first leisurely puff before answering, staring into the flames with a faraway look in her eyes.

"There's this young girl, Isla. Her mother was one of my women. When Isla got to be around eight, she couldn't stay here any longer. She's a beautiful girl, and I didn't want the visitors getting any wrong ideas. Her mother, Saffron Sue, died, and she got sent to live with her mother's sister. But then her aunt died too, and the last I heard she'd disappeared.

"Now I hear she's turned up, working for Sophia as a personal attendant. A 'maiden of the boudoir,' if you will. If you paid her well enough, she might be a useful source."

Elizabeth felt a heaviness around her heart. "Mmmm," she said. "How would I know if what she told me was true? She might be lying for money."

Experience told her this was exactly

what some of the bordello women did with their policeman consorts and escorts. Anything to keep the cops happy without causing trouble for their fellow hookers and the brothel owner—and ultimately themselves.

Kate nodded sagely. "You would need someone with enough undercover experience to confirm if you were getting the right story. I can see that." She tapped the ash end of her cigar into the ashtray.

"There is one rather obvious name neither of us has mentioned. I've been waiting for you to do it, but I'm plumb out of patience."

She glared playfully at Elizabeth. "And I suppose you haven't got a clue who I'm talking about?"

Elizabeth burst into spontaneous laughter.

"Oh boy, so here we go. Is this where I ask, 'So how is Jack Cabot?' with a casual inflection that shows I haven't given the fellow a thought in years?"

Despite herself, Kate laughed, half choking smoke at the same time.

When she'd cleared her throat and got command of her breath, she spoke again.

"He's one man in this town who can move easily between the two worlds. You know exactly what I mean, Elizabeth. It's useless to pretend otherwise. He can sup with the biggest Barbary Coast boss at night and breakfast with a bank president the next morning."

Elizabeth let out a slow breath that accepted everything Kate was saying.

A confirmation, too, of what she'd known from the moment she'd set out this morning.

The whole point of coming here was to find Jack.

Nausea rose in the pit of her stomach at the thought.

He must be alive. Surely I'd have heard if he wasn't?

Followed immediately by the next thought.

What if he's alive but refuses to see me? What will I do then?

She pulled her legs away from the hearth and turned to face Kate full-on.

Suddenly, the warmth that had been pleasantly comforting a minute or two ago was suffocatingly hot.

"Okay," she said, with a rising intonation. "How is Jack? Or should it be 'Where is Jack?' Have you heard anything of him? Is he still here?"

"If you mean 'here' as in San Francisco, then yes, I believe so."

Kate's brow furrowed, and she took another drag on her tobacco.

"But what? What aren't you telling me?"

"I hear he buried himself in Chinatown after your fiasco a couple of years back. Disappeared in an opium cloud. I don't know about his state of mind. He might be on this planet, but not entirely of it, if you know what I mean."

"Are you saying he's fried his brain?"

His brilliant brain, the little voice in her head chanted.

The corners of Kate's lively eyes turned down in sympathy.

"I suppose that's exactly what I mean," Kate said. "But if there's anyone who could pull him out of opium hell, it would be you."

Twenty-five

"Why, Grigor? Aren't I your family?"

Sophia's sapphire eyes gazed at him from an emerald-green gown which enhanced their sparkle—they were the color of an ocean wave rolling onto a forested shore.

Grigor closed his eyes to shut out the image, and her powerful influence, from his vision.

"I'd like to think so, Morrigan. I've devoted myself to little else these last twenty years. And yet, I'm led to wonder..."

The marine orbs widened in astonishment.

"Why, Grigor? Why would you doubt it?"

"Be straight with me, Morrigan. The 'business deal' you are plotting with de Vile. What's the genuine point of it all? And how do you see it affecting our current fifty-fifty distribution of the shares in our business? What are you proposing?"

She batted her long black lashes like bird wings.

Raven's wings, thought Grigor.

Appropriate. Harbinger of death and life. My death. Her rebirth.

She opened her mouth to speak, but he interrupted.

"Before you say anything, you should know. I've been talking with de Vile."

Her eyes widened and the blood-red lips drew into a tight line.

"Is that some sort of warning?"

"You decide. What are you proposing with this deal?"

She straightened her shoulders, as if preparing to take unpleasant medicine.

"All right. I was proposing he buy twenty-five percent of your shares."

Grigor's heart beat harder, swelling into his chest cavity so he suddenly, once again, was gasping for breath.

He bent over, elbows on his knees, and focused on breathing slowly and deeply.

When his eyes met Sophia's, she was staring into his face, her own showing no sign of emotion.

"And when I die?"

"When you die? I'd expect to inherit your share as your sole beneficiary. That's fair, isn't it?"

He ignored the question.

"Because I am going to die. You know that, don't you? It's plain to see and you're not stupid."

She shrugged her shoulders lightly, and the front of her low-cut dress moved, displaying the swelling of her firm melon breasts.

Not quite on the downward slope yet, but soon....

"We all die, Grigor. That's the sad fact of life."

She sounded strident. Irritated.

"That's not what I mean, Sophia, and you know it. And aren't you assuming rather a lot? What if I have other plans for my shares? What if I believe that if we are pursuing this plan of yours, that we should each take an equal cut? Say fifteen percent each?"

She stared at him with Queen of Death eyes, like wedges of ice.

"What has got into you, Grigor? What has de Vile been saying?"

He shook his head, denying her the

abrupt change of subject.

"I'm not a horse to be changed in the middle of the night, Sophia."

Her face paled.

"And he's not marrying you, so you can forget that fancy."

She flushed bright red and her hands came up on her hips in fury.

"Who else have you got to leave it to? What difference does it make once you're dead?"

He took a step backwards as if she'd struck him. The gruelling pain that had lingered in his chest ever since he left the wharf twisted like a knife.

"You really are a prize, Morrigan," he hissed in one trolling breath.

"True to the old warrior queen myths. Circling the battlefield, waiting to carry off the dead."

He took another step away from her,

gathering up the coat which he'd laid across the back of the nearest chair when he'd come in.

"Well, I'm not ready to lie down and let you carry me off just yet, inconvenient as that may be to your empire-building plans."

She took a step toward him, her mood agitated.

"No, Grigor, wait. You don't understand. I'm not…"

But he didn't stop to hear the rest.

Twenty-six

Elizabeth left Kate's house equipped with the sturdy services of Bert, her own coachman, and Kate's house manager Jake, who Kate had "lent" to her for half a day. Her mission was to find Jack and see if he would help in digging dirt on Sophia Morrigan, because she knew it was a task impossible for her to accomplish alone.

The only other option to taking a muscle escort was to go in the company of a police officer, and she knew Gentleman Jack would regard that as a serious breach of Chinatown etiquette.

She'd lose any chance of winning his support if she did that, even if he hadn't lost himself in opium dreams.

Between them, Bert and Jake had done a fine job of banging on doors and raising the ire of the managers and madams of numerous boarding houses and brothels in the warren of streets and alleyways that ran north of California Street around Portsmouth Square, the area Kate suggested they'd be most likely to find Jack hiding out.

"Close enough to Chinatown, but not actually in it, and just enough distance away from the Barbary Coast to avoid some of the worst random gang violence."

Kate gave a wry laugh. "You know the score. The Sydney Ducks hate the Mexicans, who hate the Irish, who hate the Chinese."

Elizabeth hadn't seen it firsthand, but had heard enough about it secondhand not to want to get mixed up in it.

Nothing they'd done had produced Jack himself or any word of him. Everyone they questioned was surly and non-communicative, or wide-eyed and loud in their denials of knowing anyone matching Jack's description.

After two hours of searching, with Elizabeth waiting in the Rockaway as they'd moved from block to block, she was ready to give up and go home.

"Maybe I will have to get the police involved," she said to Bert, as he returned to her yet again to report no joy in the search. "He'll hate it, I know, but it might be the only way I've got to find him."

Jake followed in Bert's wake and leaned against the front of the Rockaway cab.

"We've given it an excellent shot,

Countess. He'll sure as the dickens know you are looking for him. Someone in this godforsaken place will whisper in his ear that a fine lady was here asking after him. I'm sure he'll guess who that was likely to be. Maybe he'll find you when it suits him."

Elizabeth gave him a pale smile. "Sound advice, Jake. We'll drop you back to Kate's."

"Don't worry about it, Mrs. Wenderhoven. It's only a hop and a skip and a jump away."

Kate suspected he might have some private business he wanted to complete on the way home, so she smiled and indicated she was letting him go. "Thank Kate for me, won't you? We've done the best we could."

She turned her attention to Bert. "We may as well head home, Bert. Let's not waste any more time here."

Bert gave Jake a friendly shove as a gesture of farewell and climbed up, ready to depart.

He was waiting for the right moment to pull out into the traffic flow when a man off the street wrenched the carriage door open and brought a foot up to climb inside.

"Whoa there, driver," he called. Bert swung around in alarm. Elizabeth stared, frozen.

Then she waved a hand at Bert. "We're all well here, Bert. Just wait a minute for the gentleman to get on board." She scooted across to the far side of the bench seat and gestured for the new arrival to get in.

Her hands tightened around her waist to stop her sudden rolling nausea. Was it from fear or dread, or excitement? She hardly knew.

She let go of her middle and put her gloved hands on the seat on either side of her body to brace herself.

Bert eased the cab out into the busy laneway, dodging other vehicles and pedestrians.

Her passenger settled with a thump.

"Jack," she said, her throat tight. "We've been looking for you."

"So I gather." He regarded her steadily with the penetrating green eyes she knew so well. "And I can't, for the life of me, fathom why you're bothering now."

He glanced out into the teeming street, and back to her with studied resolution, as if he could barely stand to look at her for more than a few seconds at a time.

"I can only conclude you want something, though what I could have that you would want, I do not know."

His finely shaped lips curved in a light, droll smile that exposed his straight white teeth, but the words carried a bitter edge.

"You haven't forgiven me, then?" She avoided his eye. He was right. It was painful to meet again.

"Forgiven?" The word came out as a soft explosion. Ever the courteous Bostonian, he was keeping in mind Bert's close presence. "Not in a million years."

She stared at Bert's back and told her racing heart to slow. She brought her hand to her mouth and swallowed hard behind it, masking her breathless dismay.

What else could I have expected? I knew how desperately he wanted to rescue Cordelia.

Tears sprang to her eyes. Her lips

were numb, and it took all her willpower to break free of the paralysis.

She nodded her head in an ungracious jerk and turned to look him full in the face, challenging him.

"You're right. I don't deserve forgiveness. And I want something." His green eyes flashed like jewels. He bit down on his jaw, determined to remain silent.

She wanted to reach out and grasp his arm, but she suppressed the impulse. She was certain he'd rebuff it. Her eyes flickered from meeting his, to his stiff mouth, and back to his eyes again.

"No excuses, Jack. I have none. But I beg you, give me a chance to explain, before you refuse me."

Twenty-seven

She sat next to him, their thighs close to touching, looking as serene and wonderful as she ever had, and the pain cut so deep in his chest he could hardly bear to look at her.

"No excuses, Jack. I have none."

You bet you don't, he thought angrily. *And why should I give you the time of day?*

He maintained a stony silence.

"Can I have a chance to explain, before you refuse me?"

"That's rich, coming from you."

He clamped his lips together as he regained control of himself. The last thing he wanted to do was show her how much he still cared.

She was wearing the "slumming it" outfit she'd adopted for her charitable work, but her transcendent beauty shone through the drabness. He shot her a covert look, and his gut cramped. She might have a few more lines around her eyes and mouth, but the faded baggy jacket and dirt-colored shapeless skirt were a laughable disguise.

They travelled in silence for some minutes, and he noted with a jolt that they were close to her Nob Hill home. He really did not want to go in there and be reminded of the gulf between them. Her, with her proper society airs, and him, a useless dropout.

He took a deep breath. "If we're going to talk, I want it to be somewhere else. Somewhere free."

Somewhere free. Do you realize how

pathetic you sound? Like some wet-behind-the-ears kid, not a responsible middle-aged man.

He thumped the side of the carriage with his hand in frustration.

Perhaps that's because you're not acting like a mature man.

She turned to him with the liquid eyes he'd so often seen in his drugged-up dreams.

"Whatever you want, Jack. I realize I'm the supplicant here."

"I want to walk the beach at Seal Point. Do you want to change your shoes or anything?"

Her eyes widened, surprised by his consideration, perhaps. And then she dipped her head in assent.

"Good idea." She braced her arm against the door on her side as Bert drew into the Nob Hill driveway.

As soon as the carriage had stopped moving, she slipped out.

"Don't leave. I won't be a moment."

Twenty-eight

"Tammy loved this coast."

His soft voice was barely audible above the sound of the coach wheels and the sea breeze, but Elizabeth didn't miss the tang of longing in Jack's voice.

"She did."

His face was full of yearning as he flicked his marine blue-green eyes to meet hers.

They filled the silence with memories neither of them wanted to recall. Then Elizabeth spoke. "It reflected her character. She was a free spirit."

Jack nodded and turned to gaze out to the open gray skies where seabirds floated on the afternoon thermals.

"I know you don't want to see me, Jack, and I'm sorry it's necessary. But if it's any comfort, I wanted to ask you about experiences that may relate to Tammy. That still might throw light on what happened to her. I'm not sure."

His head jerked sharply back toward her. His eyes narrowed. He focused all his attention in a piercing gaze.

"How? And what about Cordelia? Have you heard anything?"

She shook her head, her mouth squeezed up in an urgent plea.

"No, no. Nothing like that. I'm sorry."

His head dropped, and he turned once again to stare out at the deserted beach.

"It's about Morrigan," said Elizabeth.

He didn't respond.

"How well do you know her, Jack? Or did you know her back then?"

"Back when my sister was alive, you mean?"

The words cut like acid.

His shoulders took on a challenging set, but he spoke into the open air.

"I knew her pretty well. I have had little to do with her recently, but as far as I know, my stocks are still good. Why?"

Elizabeth felt rising butterflies in her stomach.

He's going to hate this. Do I have the nerve to even introduce the topic?

She stared after his turned-away face, pressuring him subtly to respond.

"Because it seems as if she's got Hector de Vile in her sights, and I want to know why."

The space between them charged with emotional energy. Jack's posture seemed to freeze for a few seconds, and then he expelled a long, resigned sigh.

When he met her eyes, the old bitterness was gone, replaced instead by a glow of admiration, and perhaps even a hint of amusement in his lifted brow.

He let out a nervous, breathy laugh.

"You really are incorrigible, Contessa. All part of your irresistible charm."

He'd drawn back into protecting detached irony, and she was grateful for it.

"Tell me all. Don't spare the details."

She laughed. "I will. But first, I think we've got where we want to be. Let's unload the basket and eat on the beach."

#

They walked across the sand, scooping up in their hands the ice-cold waves that came all the way from China, Elizabeth lifting her skirts high to avoid a drenching.

Then they found shelter behind an outcrop of rocks, laid out the picnic blanket, and she served up cold pigeon pie and ginger ale in sturdy pottery mugs.

"Nothing like eating outside to give you an appetite." Jack leaned back on his elbows in supine satisfaction.

Elizabeth smiled as she tidied the remains back into the picnic basket.

He returned to an upright stance. "So out with it. You've served a man his last meal. Now tell him his sentence."

He gazed at her with a tired, drawn countenance so different from how she remembered him. On that last night, when he'd stood in despair on a railway station platform at the end of a fruitless chase, his skin still bloomed with an expectation of life's goodness.

Now, it was as if the starting energy

had switched off. Unless they sparked with anger, his eyes were dull, hopeless. She studied him, and noticed fine lines that weren't there before, edging his eyes and mouth.

Elizabeth hesitated, reluctant to spoil the comradely feeling that had developed between them as they'd walked and shared the lunch. How to start this tale and pay regard to his feelings?

"Come on. Spit it out." He attempted to grin, but his eyes were desolate.

Best to tackle it head-on. Jack always did respect forthrightness.

"Morrigan is attempting to blackmail Hector, and he won't tell me what it's about. But I know it's serious. It could be career destroying. I wanted to dig around a bit. Find out what she might have on him. Or find something equally damning on her."

He regarded her with calculation. "And you care why? When I knew you before, you had nothing much to do with the fellow."

She felt herself blushing. "We've become close."

She took a deep breath and gazed directly at him. "We've been skirting around the idea of marriage."

She didn't miss the sharp flinch around his eyes.

"The merest hint, nothing more," she said, with the suggestion of an apology.

"Thing is, I'm wondering if Morrigan has ever had anything to do with child trading."

She saw his body go rigid at the suggestion.

"Was there ever... Did you ever... Before... When we were searching for Cordelia? Did Morrigan's name ever feature in the people who might have been involved?"

He came up onto his knees and stared into her face. "Are you suggesting Hector's somehow involved with selling children?"

His voice was raw, urgent.

She came up on her knees to mirror him. "Nooo. Nothing like that. I'm just searching for potential lines of inquiry." She broke eye contact and focused on the rocky face that sheltered them.

"I'm just trying to imagine the worst possibilities. Maybe even something to use against her. To fight back with. Because Kate Buchanan hinted Morrigan might have got her tentacles out in selling children into slave labor—or worse. That's all."

Jack stood, as if propelled by an

energy that no longer allowed him to stay horizontal.

He paced a few strides out, and then back. Out, then back.

"No one mentioned her name, but that doesn't mean Kate's wrong. She'd have good intelligence, would Kate."

He whirled to face her. "And if she's right, Elizabeth, you shouldn't get involved. Morrigan is dangerous, especially over something like this. It would be lucrative, so she wouldn't want to lose the trade, and damaging to both her other business and her reputation if word got out."

Elizabeth stood too, uncomfortable at sitting so far below him.

"I'm not necessarily going to 'out' her. I just want to stop her from threatening Hector."

He stopped in his tracks and wheeled

on her, his face thunderous.

"Oh. So you discover enough to blackmail her into taking her claws off of your boyfriend. But you leave her free to ply her loathsome traffic for profit?"

She cried out. "No. Jack, that's not what I meant. Not at all."

"I honestly thought better of you than that, Elizabeth." His face had flushed an angry red, and he was panting.

"Jack. Listen to me. I didn't mean for it to come out like that. If there's any chance she's involved, then I'm happy to do anything I can to stop it."

She hung her hands at her sides in a pleading gesture. "Honestly, Jack. I'm already way out of my depth here. Kate may be wrong. I didn't know where else to turn. And it's too much for me to handle on my own. I know that."

He continued to stare, his eyes the

color of a stormy sea, but peculiarly vacant.

"Jack. I know we failed with Cordelia, and that knowledge will eternally ravage me. But maybe there's still a chance…"

"Cordelia is gone," he said in a voice like thin ice. "And there's no chance of getting her back. Ever."

Twenty-nine

"So Graysie, tell me, when did you first meet my father?" Alex lay sprawled across a sofa in Graysie and Nathan's Lick House suite, while Graysie sat on the floor with her back to the sofa edge.

She set two-year-old George down on the fine Persian rug and pushed a smoothly polished wooden train into his fat little fingers.

"Here we are, Georgie. You play with that while Mummy talks to Uncle Alex."

The sandy-haired cherub with his father's mischievous twinkling eyes dropped the train and clapped his hands in delight, grinning up at Alex as he did.

"Dex. Georgie wants Dex."

Alex laughed in his face. "You play with your train, little fella. Dex will read you a story later."

"You'll never live that name down now." Graysie laughed with him. "I almost wish Nathan hadn't started it in his typical Aussie affection for nicknames. Hex, Dex. He thought it was funny…"

"It's appropriate. Hector's Hex to me. So I'm Dex to Georgie. I'm honored to rate in Georgie's affections…"

"Our mother's blood coming out," Graysie said with a warm smile.

"More coffee?" She reached up to the coffeepot on the low table beside her and refilled both their cups.

The room was cozy, and they were comfortably full from a fine Lick House dinner—roast beef and Yorkshire pudding, followed by pears with meringue and vanilla ice cream delivered on room service.

Nathan was out on Russell family business and she was enjoying a rare rest night from her concert program with Pania Russell.

"Now where were we?"

"Your first meeting with Hector. Do you recall it?"

She frowned as the memory surfaced. She'd never forget it, but she wasn't sure how much of it she wanted to relate to Alex. He adored his father, and she didn't want to be the one to spoil the image.

"I do. It was here in San Francisco. And I was performing at Maguire's—just like now." She chuckled. "Haven't moved very far, have I?"

Alex grinned. "You've added Nathan and George to the retinue. That's a good thing."

"Yes, well. First time I met Hector it was the last night of an exhausting season. I didn't even know Pania then. I was doing it on my own. And I'd had Minette with me for a few months. Mimi was having trouble settling and my third nanny had just quit on me. Hector strode in as if he owned the place, and all he wanted to talk about was buying some mine shares my uncle Eustace had left me."

She raised her eyebrows, inserting meaning into the gesture.

"You know what he's like. Thinks he can take over the world? He's mellowed a bit since then. He got irritated when I had to bring our conversation to a quick close because Minette was howling so loud we couldn't hear ourselves think, let alone talk."

Alex laughed. "I can just imagine."

"Hector couldn't believe I put a child ahead of him. I don't think anyone had given him such short shrift in a while."

Minette—who'd become Mimi under George's lisping talk—was now aged eight, and was having a bath under the nanny's watchful eye next door. Graysie had stepped in when Mimi's mother, Francine, Graysie's best friend, died in a gambling hall fire.

"He followed me up on it a week later in Grass Valley. It took another uncomfortable confrontation before he understood I wasn't interested in selling," Graysie added.

"Sounds like Hex," said Alex. "He usually gets what he wants, so that would have been a surprise for him."

He nursed his chin in his hands and bit the side of his lip in contemplation.

"I've been wondering some more

about that business with that fellow Grigor. You know I mentioned it to you? About the crash which killed our mother?"

Graysie nodded, a sense of dread forming inside at the mention of her mother's death. She reached out and stroked Georgie's neck for reassurance. His well-padded little shoulders comforted her. In one hand, he held the train and sucked on it, while he waved his free arm in joyful excitement.

"Sure. What about it?"

Alex hesitated.

"We've never talked about that night. Not in detail. I've never wanted to upset you."

He tensed his mouth in anticipation. "I mean, do you remember much about it? I know you were only little, and it was dark."

He made an apologetic moue with his lips.

"I've wondered though, since we talked last time. What do you remember of it, if anything? I'd be interested to hear, if it's not too upsetting."

She gathered Georgie into her lap and hugged him close.

"Funny that you should ask, Dex. I had terrible memories throughout my childhood. Nightmares, and the feeling that somehow I should have saved you and Isabella, that it was my fault they found me, but not you."

Alex frowned. "How ghastly for you. It must have been so confusing for a child…"

"It was. All I remember really was darkness. I was warm. Safe. Snuggled into Mother's side. She had her arm around me. And then this terrifying crash. She kept hold of me. We were flying. And then when I woke, she didn't move and the babies were gone." She gave a wavering sigh while her insides churned.

"I remember nothing else until our father arrived, an age later."

Alex's mouth dropped open. "Father came? He came to the crash? I never knew that before."

"He did. Looking back with adult eyes, I realize he was distraught. But back then, I was just so happy to see him. He held me tight and kissed the top of my head, over and over, while he cried."

Her eyes filled with tears as she spoke, and she smiled through them, watching Alex.

His cheeks were wet, too.

"And the nightmares?" he whispered tentatively, as if fearful of causing more pain. "Dare I ask? What were they about?"

She shook her head. "Oh, they started a few days later. When we were back in Sacramento. I've never known if they related to something I actually saw, or just imagined."

She shifted as George wriggled and tried to put his fingers in her mouth.

She laughed and tossed her head out of his reach.

"You know, I've been thinking about it all again these last weeks. Georgie is about the same age you were when all this happened. It breaks my heart to think of how little and vulnerable you were. If anything like that happened to him..." More tears spilled over as she gazed straight into Alex's soft brown eyes. "I can't bear to think of it."

A flurry of action from next door

interrupted their conversation. Mimi, damp and sweet smelling from her bath, came into the room smiling in a pretty flowered nightgown, with Nanny Blanchet trailing behind.

"Mama! Time for my story!"

Graysie grinned. "Albertine, if you take Georgie for his bath now, I'll do the story duties."

She gave Alex a wry smile.

"To be continued."

#

An hour later, with the dinner dishes cleared and another hot pot of coffee between them, they resumed. Graysie draped herself at one end of the deep blue, luxuriously cushioned sofa, while Alex slouched at the other end. Both nursed freshly poured coffees. Alex had done his uncle's duties reading to

Georgie, and both children were now tucked up in bed.

"They're both gorgeous. You're very lucky." Alex smiled, immersed in a deep sense of gratitude for family.

"I am." Graysie sighed contentedly. "Not a day goes by when I don't give thanks for them."

She contemplated him, her face glowing with affection. "We're both so fortunate, aren't we? I mean, that crash was terrible, but somehow we've both survived and prospered."

"We have," Alex agreed. "I've got Hex to thank for that. When I think where I could have ended up…" He shuddered. "In some freezing orphanage, living on spuds. And that's if I was lucky. I hate to think."

He shook himself, as if to shatter a noxious spell. "But if you can stand it, let's pick up where we left off."

He fiddled with the handle of his cup. "I don't want to encourage more nightmares," he added, as a tentative afterthought.

"You already have," she joked. "But, hey? Anything for you." Graysie was flicking the hair back from her face, working her fingers through her red-gold locks, with a faraway look in her eyes. She wriggled into a more upright position on the sofa and stared directly at him.

"Funnily enough, talking about it last time seems to have sparked off further memories. You never know, maybe the same thing will happen again."

"How so?" Alex was curious.

"Well, you recall you mentioned something about Grigor having inside knowledge?"

"Possible inside knowledge," he

corrected. "Hex didn't make himself entirely clear."

"Well, I had another episode of the dream a couple of nights after we spoke. Maybe the same night... I haven't had one of them since Georgie was born. And this time, it was different. Grigor was in it."

She put her cup down and stared at him.

"I don't know if you prompted that with our discussion, or whether it really happened. It all seems real in the dream, but who knows?"

"Grigor?" He felt interest surge inside him. "What was he doing?"

"In the dream, there's a white wolf, howling at the moon. He's always been there, and he always seemed like he's a friend, even though the idea of you being taken by wild animals petrified me. He's a big alpha male wolf, his head raised, howling. And then a man steps out of the black night and fires a gun at him. It was Grigor with the gun.

"The wolf honestly didn't scare me. I was terrified of the man. I wanted to warn the wolf. Tell him to run. But when I tried to scream, nothing came out."

She gazed at him, deeply immersed in her own thoughts.

"If Grigor really was there, I wonder why? And honestly? If I trust my childish intuition, he's scarier than the wolf."

Alex chuckled. "No offense, but we probably put the thought in your mind with our previous talk. I don't think you can put too much stock on the fact that he's popped up now."

He could see, though, that Graysie's thoughts were gathering momentum.

Her face flushed pink with excitement.

"Just think, though, if he really was there. That might explain why he's got something over Hector. I don't know exactly how, but it lends credibility to the idea."

She put her cup down and tapped Alex's free arm.

"Why don't we ask Hector about it straight up?"

She gazed at him, eyes shining.

"You know. Explain about the dream. Ask him if he knows if Grigor was there and see what he says?"

A crawling sense of unease worked its way up Alex's backbone, starting at the base and finishing with the bristling of the hairs on the back of his neck.

"Why would Hector know anything about it? He wasn't even there..."

"How do you know that?" Graysie slapped her hand over her mouth the moment the words were out.

"I'm sorry. I didn't mean…"

"Graysie. What are you thinking?" Hot anger surged through him. "If he was there, he would have told me before this. Besides, then he would have known who Izzy and I were. He would have shared responsibility for us going missing."

He shook his head. "That's not possible. When we discovered our link with Rafael a few years back, he was just as surprised as we all were."

Graysie's jaw sagged, but she didn't back down. "Maybe there are things…" She faltered, watching his face.

He felt as if he was blowing up inside.

Hector de Vile, the man who'd given him everything, was being accused of what? Child abduction? Lying to everyone, including him and his sister Isabella?

He couldn't believe it.

"It would insult Hector to suggest such a thing. I'm certainly not willing to be a party to it, and I ask you not to do anything like that either."

Graysie stared at him, her face mutinous and unrepentant.

"I know it must be hard for you…"

He didn't let her get any further.

"Hard? You're attacking the man who's given me everything, and you expect me to just go along with it?"

He stood up in a rush.

"I'm really sorry, Graysie, but this conversation is over. Thank you for a wonderful dinner. I'm sorry to end it like this, but I'm going. I don't want to hear any more about it."

He stood up, the pain in his chest so sharp he had to bend over momentarily to ease it.

"Alex... Are you all right?" Graysie's face creased in concern.

He pushed himself upright with an act of will.

"Perfectly fine, thank you, Graysie. Now I'll be going. Goodnight."

Thirty

Jack woke the morning after he'd seen Elizabeth with a new sense of purpose. He stumped early morning downtown streets, fizzing with fury at Elizabeth's presumption.

She was asking him for help to save a man she intended to marry. When five years ago she'd refused his proposal?

What was going on in the woman's head? He had no interest in doing anything to "save" Hector de Vile. None whatever. But if Sophia Morrigan had any involvement with the child traffickers who had stolen his niece from right under his nose, he would give his life to see her businesses—all of them—shut down forever.

Cordelia…

He thought of the last glimpse he'd had of his eight-year-old niece on the Oakland Wharf platform, stretching out her spindly arms for him before the nanny scooped her up and boarded the transcontinental train as Cordelia howled, "Uncle Jack."

Why had he given up? Why hadn't he continued fighting to get her back?

He recalled the pain of those days, his hopes extinguished for the life he'd pictured. He and Elizabeth married and bringing up Cordelia as their daughter.

When Elizabeth had refused his proposition, he'd seen no way to continue alone. A reprobate bachelor, bringing up a little girl by himself? He couldn't see it.

He'd submitted to his new reality and lost himself in a haze of opium.

But now?

If Kate was right... if Sophia Morrigan had any links into networks that sold children, even if she had nothing to do with Cordelia's sale, he'd do anything— forfeit his life, even—to see them closed down. Starting now.

As he stumped the teeming streets, he stopped now and then to take in the sights and sounds around him: the gritty aggressive sound of the Cantonese street merchants competing for customers, the earthy buttery smell of boiled rice and cabbage from hole-in-the-wall eating houses, the ammonia-cloud of steamy wetness from the Chinese laundries on every corner. He'd lost himself in this world for the past few years, but suddenly he felt the need to emerge from his lair.

He headed to the barber's shop near

his boarding house. First stop, get himself cleaned up and presentable. And then he was going to confront the Queen of Demons in person.

Thirty-one

Once upon a time, a bar like the Imperial Club's would have been Jack Cabot's natural habitat. But not anymore.

He leaned on the walnut edge and listened to his old classmate Philip Addison rattle on about his latest real estate deal. Philip was now one of the city's leading realtors, but as Jack's eyes gazed around him, he felt as if he'd stepped back through the looking glass into *Alice in Wonderland*. He'd read the popular Lewis Carroll story to Cordelia many times—it was one of her favorites—so it was appropriate he was filtering his view through it, he thought with an inner chuckle.

He was here as Philip's guest, never having bothered to renew his membership when he'd disappeared into the netherworld of Downtown's back streets. But he guessed Philip would be happy to take him there—the man was always on the hunt for new business, and there was no better hunting ground than the Imperial—so when he'd turned up at Philip's office in the early afternoon and proposed they go out for a drink later that night, his old buddy was surprised, and happy, to accept.

That was one good thing about being one of the Boston Cabots. He might be a renegade son, but he'd never gone to gaol, so when he surfaced freshly shaved and barbered in a new suit, they welcomed him with open arms back into the old aristocracy. Money talked, even if it was all inherited.

His brows tightened into a frown at the thought, as Philip held up his whiskey to chink glasses.

"Not changing your mind about being here already, are you, old chum? You don't look exactly happy…"

Jack cleared his expression in a flash.

"Fleeting thoughts, Phil. Everything's fine. It's very good of you to introduce me back to the old scene. I've been away for too long."

He hoped he'd injected enough enthusiasm into the last statement to convince his friend he really wanted to turn over a new leaf, get back into business, make something of his life.

The big room where they sat was filling fast. The older men—like them—favored hanging out at the long, polished bar, backed by tiers of fancy multicolored glass bottles offering anything that took your fancy. Golden brandy, green absinthe, the orange bottles denoting Cointreau and dark rum, all sparkling with good-time promise.

The young bucks gravitated to the center of the room, where they congregated at waist-tall tables, perched on stools or standing shoulder to shoulder. And further down the long narrow space, half a dozen green baize-covered gaming tables attracted those who liked to wager at cards or billiards as they drank.

Philip Addison waved his glass in an all-inclusive gesture.

"Word is Hector de Vile is buying a share of the ownership here. That will bring the tone of the old place up a bit. Wouldn't be too soon, hey?"

"Really? Now that is interesting," Jack replied, suddenly a lot more engaged.

"Why do you think he'd be interested in a place like this? He can come here anytime he wants without needing to own one brick. Probably doesn't even have to pay for a membership."

Philip shrugged. "Maybe he sees it as a wonderful investment."

Mmmm. And maybe not.

"So presently it's owned by the Morrigan woman and her guardian. Grigor, or whatever he calls himself. Is that correct?"

Jack feigned casual interest, but his insides danced.

Why is de Vile even interested? Perhaps Elizabeth's right. Morrigan has something over him.

Philip nodded.

"Think so. It's a good pile of real estate, that's for sure," he said approvingly. "Right here on the corner of

Market and Montgomery. Couldn't get a more central location."

Jack nodded, as if satisfied to end that topic. "How is the real estate business, Phil? Doing all right?"

"Great," said Philip Ashton. "Since Leland moved to Nob Hill that area's gone crazy. The rest of the Big Four are hunting for bigger and better plots to build on near him to outdo him. They're lording it over everyone else, and then you've got the housing for ordinary folks on the flats."

Jack grinned. "You real estate guys just can't lose, can you?"

Leland Stanford—one of the four magnates who got rich building the transcontinental railway—had bought a two-story house on the hill before his first term as California governor ten years ago, and quickly added two more stories and expanded it by dozens of rooms. It was widely touted that his fellow directors were jostling to outdo his extravagance.

"And where does de Vile live?" Jack asked.

"Oh, he's got a nice place on Russian Hill. Plenty of building going on up there as well. But it's really the commercial real estate I'm more interested in. Sites like this one, to be frank."

As they'd been talking, Jack kept a roving eye on the comings and goings at the tables spread before them.

He recognized some men who circulated around them. William Ralston, president of the Bank of California, for one. You saw him everywhere about town, so it wasn't too surprising he'd drop by.

General David Colton, the lawyer for

the Big Four railway tycoons, was drinking with his private secretary Charles Green, and nearby rancher and racehorse breeder James Haggin supped with his mine partners George Hearst and Lloyd Tevis.

Mainly, though, he was casting about for a glimpse of Sophia Morrigan. His plan for tonight was to make sure he caught her eye, but make no approach. Beautiful women always hated being ignored or invisible. They couldn't resist insisting on being noticed, and he didn't think Morrigan would be any different from a dozen others he'd come across in his checkered career.

"There's Grigor there," Philip Ashby said suddenly, giving a sideways glance toward a silver-haired chap in an immaculate suit with a high Mandarin collar, which lent him an extra air of distinction.

"He's the power behind the throne, I believe. Been the Warrior Queen's guardian ever since she was a tot."

Jack remembered Grigor from the days when he'd been active on the Downtown scene, and it shocked him to see how he'd aged since he had last seen him in Kate Buchanan's parlor.

They were much the same age. He knew the years had not been kind to him, but his face was nowhere near as ravaged as Grigor's. He looked two decades older than when he'd last seen him.

"Is he in good health?" he asked Philip. "He's aged a lot since I saw him last."

Ashby shrugged. "As far as I know. I've heard nothing to the contrary. He's got a tidy portfolio tucked away himself."

"Separate from the club, you mean?" asked Jack.

"Right," said Ashby. "Been a good client of mine for years now."

As if to confirm the statement, Grigor spotted Philip and made his way across the busy floor to join them.

#

Half an hour later, Philip had left them to go hunting for new clients and Grigor and Jack had moved to a private corner table.

"He tells me you've got a few investments yourself," said Jack, feeling his way into the Irishman's confidence.

Grigor gave him a wolfish grin, but his ice-blue eyes were devoid of emotion.

"The city's been good to me. I can't deny it," he said. "When I think of what I came from, it's a miracle I'm still standing. I'm living like a king compared to what my folks had to endure."

He gazed at Jack, eyes shining with meaning. "Raised for a future of slavery in the Welsh coal mines, I was. Three generations died with black lungs, and looks like I'm going the same way."

A shock wave of painful disclosure sat in the space between them.

My instincts were right, thought Jack. *He's fast about to leave us.*

He met Grigor's gaze without flinching. Ravaged by time and illness as he was, Raizney Grigor had a dignified composure, an aura about him. The similarity to Elizabeth struck Jack. They shared nobility. Sinner as Grigor surely was, ratty as his reputation might be, he'd clawed his way to a place in the world. There was a sense of implacable honor about the man which Jack treasured.

He slowed his quickened heart before

speaking again. The man didn't want sympathy. He wanted a witness to his passing.

"It's a bugger when time catches your heels," he said. "Bad lungs or broken heart, something always gets us in the end, doesn't it?"

He allowed the pain of the last five years to shine in his own face, the grief he kept masked most of the time. The unshed tears for Cordelia, for Elizabeth, locked deep inside and exhaled in blue smoke.

Grigor nodded in understanding.

#

They sipped their drinks without saying another word, watching the passing crowd. They understood each other. And then, with no fanfare, the atmosphere in the big room changed again, supercharged with a different hum. They both felt it, because with no prompt, they lifted their eyes in the same direction.

Making her way toward them, the eyes of the room on her hip-swaying progress, was Sophia, in a gold off-the-shoulder gown revealing an eye-watering expanse of creamy neck, dipping to a deep V between her breasts. The gold satin bodice tucked to a nipped-in waist, and then flared into a looped overskirt in iridescent pink, green and blue silk that covered half of the gold satin. She moved on a rainbow.

A necklace featuring impressively sized pearl droplets drew the eye to her décolletage and completed the picture of radiant elegance.

Grigor's face, which moments before had been vulnerable and grief-stricken, set in an icy mask of resignation.

Sophia, too, had her game face on. Jack could see it the minute their eyes locked. The siren's face, the one he'd wager she'd used many times over the years to hook men and lead them by the nose, was on full display. And in this moment, he sensed that he, Jack, was her target.

"Gentlemen," she said in a playful chiding tone. "You've got together to have a fascinating conversation and you've left me out."

She pouted her full red lips a fraction to show her displeasure.

Jack grinned at Grigor and responded in kind. "Fascinating? Would you call it fascinating, my friend?"

Grigor glanced up at Sophia, impatience creased in his brow.

"Haven't you got enough going on

elsewhere, Sophia? Is it really necessary to come and intrude on me?"

She pouted some more.

"Now Grigor, that's not very nice. I'm sure I recognize this new friend you're so determined to keep all to yourself."

Grigor gave a heavy sigh. "Jack Cabot, meet Sophia Morrigan," he said with the minimum of ceremony.

"Gentleman Jack?" She leaned familiarly into Jack's space. "It's been far too long between drinks, Jack."

Sophia lifted her finely curved brow in an ironic jest. The sapphire-blue eyes were sparkling with mischievous humor, and Jack could see how easy it would be to be drawn into her orbit. He was suddenly glad he'd taken the trouble to sharpen up his appearance, to at least play at being the Don Juan he'd once been.

"Have we finally lured you out of your

lair? What's made you emerge now?"

Jack humored her with one of his most brilliant smiles.

"Who knows?" he said, switching his attention back to Grigor. "Perhaps the rumor that a share of the club may be up for grabs." He saw the flash of surprise in Grigor's eyes, though the rest of his facial expression gave nothing away.

He returned his gaze to Sophia. She was regarding him with cool calculation.

"Anyone who reads the gossip columns will have heard that bit of chitchat. It's hardly a secret."

"Ahhh. But I'm interested in the rest of it."

"The rest of it? And what would that be?"

Sophia sounded irritated. She was fast losing interest in the game she instigated.

She glanced up, responding to yet another subtle shift in the surrounding energy. Heads had turned to the entry as Hector de Vile strode in, swinging his walking stick as if he already part-owned the place.

Her eyes flashed in surprise, then her mouth curved into a satisfied purr.

Jack felt the snap of tension in his companion. Grigor's face had thawed from icy resignation to a palpable loathing.

Now that's interesting. Sophia thinks she's got Hector de Vile hooked, good and proper. And Grigor loathes them—both of them—because of it.

Thirty-two

"We're more than halfway through," said Pania, giving Graysie a warm smile. "Only a few more nights to go."

They stood together in a quiet sitting room lined with books—the closest thing the Imperial Club had to a "Green Room" for artists. Usually this room was a quiet zone for club members who wished to read, play chess or write letters, but for a few hours each night while they were performing in the cabaret space next door, Sophia had commandeered it for their use.

The show—which was open to sisters, wives, girlfriends and the public—had been a complete sellout, so no one was complaining about them commandeering the smoking room for an hour before and afterwards.

"The family holding up all right?" The older soprano drew a caring arm around Graysie's slender shoulders.

"Yes, thanks, Pania. They're enjoying the change. What about you? How is little Robert coping with traveling?"

Pania's face opened up in undisguised delight. "He seems to thrive on change. Just like his parents."

Robert was an unexpected late blessing in Pania's life, after a long childless marriage to her first husband, the impresario Harvey Miller. Both she and John had turbulent lives before settling into happy family life together nearly three years ago.

Pania patted the seat beside her.

"Let's face it, Graysie. We're building

up good capital for another run at this next year if we want to do it."

Graysie gave her fellow singer and sister-in-law a weary grin. Their husbands were the oldest and youngest of the Russell brothers, John and Nathan, and they'd originally met through the Russell family connection.

"Yes. If we want to. Fitting in music gets harder every year. As the children get older, they seem to need more attention rather than less."

She sank onto the sofa with a happy groan.

"Are you feeling OK?"

Pania's full dark brows drew together in concern. The New Zealand-born Maori opera star was Graysie's cherished friend, and the younger woman gave a self-conscious laugh and patted Pania's resting hand.

"I'm fine." Graysie chuckled. "I've just had a lot going on and I haven't been sleeping well. Why? Do I look frazzled?"

Pania laughed. "Not in the least. I'm just concerned. You don't seem your usual effervescent self, that's all. Nothing anyone else would notice, because you're such a professional. But I can sense something's not right with you. What's the problem? Can I ask? Anything I can help with?"

"Oh, Pania, if only you could. I've had an awful argument with Alex, and I don't know what to do about it. I think it upset us both."

She fiddled with the hot chocolate that was waiting for them with some oatmeal cookies on their arrival.

"It's really upset me. It's the first time we've seriously disagreed about anything." She sighed. "Trouble is, I don't want to back down. It's a matter of principle and I know I'm right."

Pania turned her palm over and squeezed Graysie's hand, offering solidarity.

"Tell me all about it. From the beginning."

Graysie summarized her disagreement with Alex, the half-brother she'd only discovered was still alive a year ago.

"I suggested we should ask Hector straight whether he knew more about our mother's accident than he was letting on. I mean... It was Alex who said his father had hinted Grigor knew something about it. He was vague about what exactly. I was just following up on that."

She blew out a frustrated air that inflated her pink cheeks, then tugged at a loose lock that hung over her face.

"He just lost it. He declared it would insult Hector to question him. That if he knew something, he would have already said." She bit her lip. Her eyes glazed over, lost in faraway memory.

"The thing is…" She hesitated.

Pania watched, motionless, sensitive to Graysie's every word. "Since I've had that talk with Alex, I've felt more anxious about Hector, rather than less."

She gazed into Pania's face, her sparkling green eyes narrowed and troubled.

"It all came back to me. That awful time when Minette disappeared. Do you remember that day?"

Pania's heart froze, and for a half a minute she couldn't breathe.

As she recalled it, the day at Sir John's Grass Valley house when Mimi went missing was the first time she'd met Graysie, and it was one of the worst days of her friend's life.

She'd given up her singing career to take better care of Mimi and get her settled into home life after months of touring.

"Of course, Graysie. How could I ever forget?"

Pania, an old friend of Sir John's, was staying as a guest at Gold House—she and John weren't married then or even thinking of it—when the little girl had disappeared from her bed in the middle of the night.

No one had come up with a feasible explanation for how she'd got out. The outside doors were locked, and the handles were too high for the four-year-old to reach, anyway.

The plucky four-year-old turned up

the next day in a Grass Valley hotel run by an old battle axe named Madame Ring, whom a howling mob had blamed for the child's abduction. She'd been tarred, feathered and run out of town. As far as the town was concerned, the case was closed, but Pania accepted nothing was ever properly proven.

Madame Ring surely knew of the child's whereabouts, but had she had any part in abducting her?

Graysie interrupted Pania's recall.

"Hector was there, in town, when Mimi went missing. Do you remember? And he behaved terribly. He was hounding me about selling him those mine shares when I was distraught about her disappearance. Do you recall that?"

A shiver ran up Pania's backbone.

"I do, Graysie. He acted abominably. I always thought there was something sinister about the whole incident. Irish Red is convinced Madame Ring was planning to sell Minette. He claimed she'd been mixed up in stuff like that before."

Irish Red was the mines manager who'd freed Mimi from the cellar.

Graysie visibly paled. "Oh please. No. I didn't know that!"

"I think at the time we were all too worried about your state of mind to even mention it. But there was a suggestion of that. And as you recall, de Vile owned that pub she managed. They were buddies from way back."

Graysie chewed at the knuckle of her right hand. "I'd forgotten that, if I ever knew it. I was so overwhelmingly grateful to get Minette back unharmed. I let the rest of it wash over me, I think. And then when Madame Ring died a few days later—well, I thought it was probably all related, and she'd got what she deserved."

Pania gazed at Graysie, considering her response.

"I agree something seemed a bit 'off' about the entire business, her being shot in a bar."

Pania's deep voice was thoughtful. "Hector has mellowed a lot in the last few years, though. You recall he and John were sworn enemies back then. They get on a lot better these days."

Graysie gazed into Pania's face, considering her words.

"Maybe so," she said. "And I've never told Alex anything about that incident. Imagine how that would go down…"

Graysie put on a silly falsetto voice. "'Oh, by the way, I suspect Hector of being involved in abducting Minette.'"

She continued in her normal voice: "He's already upset. And I've got no proof Hector's done anything wrong."

She rubbed the back of her neck, as if easing tight muscles.

"But neither can I act as if everything is hunky-dory. I just can't."

She leaned forward and drew her hands down both sides of her face.

"Oh Pania, what should I do?"

Thirty-three

I'm like a cat in a bed of catnip. I can't help myself, I'm rolling in it.

Jack Cabot allowed himself a self-aware grin as he settled back into a hack for the ride to the Imperial Club for the second night running, togged out this time in a crisp white tuck-fronted evening shirt, black tie and a formal black jacket.

He'd checked his appearance in the mirror before picking up his silver-topped cane to stroll out of his modest rooms in Post Street, and noted with satisfaction that his shoulders and chest filled out the jacket in a manner likely to attract approving female attention.

But under the black superfine jacket, his skin prickled. He didn't belong in this world he was re-entering. One part of him wanted to return to the cave and hit the pipe.

But something had come alive in him last night, talking to Grigor and observing the drama that was playing out around him. He felt like a man in the refreshment break halfway through an engrossing play—*Hamlet* or *Macbeth*, something dark and fraught. He had to return for the last act to find out how it ended. Though, as he recalled them, no one won. Everyone died.

Despite that, the last thing he'd done before he'd slipped away last night was to organize with Sophia for a ticket to see Pania and Graysie Russell perform tonight. Sure, they'd already sold out. Everyone told him that whenever it came up in conversation, but Jack had flirted outrageously to charm one of Sophia's complementary tickets out of her.

As he did so, he noted Grigor didn't seem to mind him playing Romeo to Sophia's Juliet. He didn't know whether to be insulted or relieved by that. The wily old fox saw him as no threat at all, when he so obviously loathed whatever Sophia had going with Hector de Vile.

The hack pulled up in a parking spot a few doors up from the Imperial, and Jack was smiling to himself as he slipped out and paid the man. Tonight's Act Two was going to be very interesting.

He had an excuse to return without Philip Addison on his elbow. He'd satisfy his curiosity about whether the Russell women were as good as everyone said they were. And he'd make sure he had time to skulk and roam and sniff out further gossip about was going on with Grigor and Sophia—business or otherwise.

And perhaps—after all this self-indulgent entertainment—he'd be closer to the serious end of the business: understanding what happened to Cordelia, and preventing it from happening again to some other child.

#

The seat Sophia had gifted him gave him an enviable position for surveying his fellow theatergoers while protecting him from being snuck up on.

The moderately sized room served as either a theater or cabaret venue, with a wide flat area for a dance floor or café setting—filled tonight with round tables, each with eight chairs. Beyond that, where he sat, rose an outer ring of tiered seats.

He counted eight rows which overlooked the tables and gave the occupants a view of a stage closed off by thick red velvet curtains.

He gauged when they opened, he'd be almost eye-to-eye with the performers. The audience seated at the tables had arrived in plenty of time to order light snacks: oysters in their shells, and a range of French-influenced San Francisco hors d'oeuvres—Spanish-style tomato toasts with garlic and oil, mini Beef Wellingtons and burritos and crab cakes with lime chive mayonnaise. The usual fare for these occasions.

His mouth watered as he recalled the days when his life comprised such parties. He watched as waiters hurried back and forth with trays laden with drinks and food, serving the thirsty, well-dressed patrons before the show got underway.

Nicely thought out...

Morrigan ran a fine-tuned ship. Ten packed nights like this, with all the wine and food sales on top of the ticket prices, would bring a sweet profit.

Maybe de Vile really is simply interested in the Imperial as a business proposition. Nothing more complicated than that.

As if his calling the name to mind had summoned the man himself, de Vile sauntered in and positioned himself at the other end of the row from where Jack sat. He doffed his evening hat to various acquaintances and took his seat, placing the hat on his lap as he did.

Here alone?

Jack reluctantly acknowledged he'd been holding his breath, expecting Elizabeth to appear at any moment. His feeling of wound-up tension gradually faded as the seconds ticked by and no one appeared to fill the empty seat next to the senator.

Not tonight, anyway.

The house lights dipped, giving a universally recognized sign that the show was about to begin. Waiters moved with greater urgency, seeing through last-minute orders and refilling glasses. And just as the curtains rose, an elderly lady and a raw-looking young fellow with a red face pushed their way past his neighbors to take the two empty seats beside him.

"Sorry, dear." A wrinkled dowager leaned into his space and addressed him in a loud stage whisper as the curtains finally opened. A sweet floral perfume assailed him as she put her finger to her lips in a shushing gesture, as if he'd been the one doing the talking. And then a smoothly coiffed impresario stepped forward to ask for "Quiet, please," because the show was about to start.

From that moment, Jack lost himself in the make-believe world on stage, no longer aware of anything around him until the curtains fell, signaling the end of the first half, and the house lights came up.

"My word. They give a fine performance, don't they?"

Jack turned to the elderly matron on his left, and took in apparently genuine diamonds sparkling at her neck, and a pair of jewel-encrusted opera glasses dangling from one white-gloved hand.

"They do indeed," Jack responded. The women's eyes twinkled kindly through her heavily powdered face. He offered his hand. "Jack Cabot. Do you need any help to get out?"

"Daphne Partington. Pleased to meet you, Mr. Cabot."

"Jack, please."

"Jack then. But no." She patted the knee of the well-dressed, ruddy-complexioned young man next to her.

"My nephew Buster is on Great-Aunt duties tonight. Anything I need, he can get for me."

She fixed Jack with a shrewd eye.

"Cabot, you say? Not one of Mr. Justice Cabot's lot, I suppose? Andrew Cabot?"

Jack's heart fell to his boots.

He nodded reluctantly. "I'm afraid so. But I'm no chip off the old block, I can assure you. Quite the opposite."

She gave him a big smile and patted his hand. "You look like a fine young man to me. I might be old, but I'm not blind yet."

He grinned. "Appearances can deceive," he said.

"Can't they though? Wish someone had told me that before I married my last husband."

By the time Aunt Daph—as Buster insisted on calling her—had entertained him with a wickedly funny account of her recent life and times, and he'd collected her a generous tumbler of sauterne from the bar to prepare for the second half (Buster didn't approve of her drinking but had disappeared to the bar himself with alacrity), Jack had made himself a fast new friend.

She was regaling him with another of her funny stories about a friend who nearly married an Austrian count when she stopped mid-sentence, staring to the other side of the room, past de Vile's currently empty seat to the outer aisle.

She squinted through her opera glasses in the same direction and lowered them with a satisfied pursing of her lips.

Jack followed her line of sight but saw nothing worthy of notice. A couple of young men idled there, minding their own business. They weren't talking, but apart from mildly inconveniencing others by blocking access to seats, they were innocuous. Just a few concert stragglers, waiting perhaps for their partners to return to their seats.

"What kind of fun and games?" he asked Daph, humoring the old girl.

"The sort that can bring down houses," she said in a low tone, her face serious.

"See the copper-headed young man with the shy look, the one with the red bow tie?"

"What's wrong with him, apart from his abominable taste in bow ties?" joked Jack.

Daphne shook her head.

"He shouldn't be here. That's what's wrong."

Jack glanced down at her wizened complexion and saw she was not joking. Something crinkled her eyes at the corners, and long worry lines extended down her cheeks.

He was suddenly uncomfortable at the possibility someone might overhear them.

"Should we even be talking about this?" he said in a half whisper. "Are you going to get us in trouble?"

She gazed up at him in surprise and patted his cheek with her white-gloved hand.

"Why, what a well-mannered fellow

you are, Jack. See, good blood will out."

On the same impulse, they both stared back to where the fellow under her investigation had been standing, and discovered he'd gone. Jack scanned the room. He'd apparently vanished. The house lights dipped, and Buster came bobbing along the row, returning to his seat just in the nick of time for the second act.

"That was Grigor's son, Lochie," Daphne whispered. "And he's not supposed to set foot in here. Grigor won't be happy if he finds out. And as for Sophia…"

"What? You mean he's Sophia's son with Grigor?"

Aunt Daph's amused pale blue eyes peered at him from under puffy hoods.

"No, silly," she whispered. "Sophia knows nothing about him. That's the problem."

Thirty-four

As he made his way out, Jack congratulated himself that he'd decided he'd stay for the second act. Ever gallant, he'd offered his arm to Daph as they slowly progressed toward the open doors and fresh air, letting the gorgeous notes of the final number, the "Jewel Song" from *Faust*, seep into his soul.

Unusually, the two sopranos had shared the song, giving both an opportunity to display their different but equally sublime voices. He recalled the words of the aria.

"Achévons la metamorphose, Il me tarde…."

"Let's complete the metamorphosis, I am late…"

Marguerite was talking about trying on Faust's jewels, but he fleetingly wondered whether he too had missed his opportunities, far more important ones than trying on a necklace. Had he allowed disillusionment to poison his soul?

His newfound companion was silent as they made their halting progress to the open foyer, where a welcome gust of fresh air diluted her overpowering perfume.

Buster had led the way out, but as soon as they got free of the foot traffic, he gave them a good view of his back.

"He likes to drink with his friends," said Daphne understandingly. "And you must do the same, Jack. I can take care of myself. He'll be back to collect me when he's ready to go home."

"I wouldn't hear of such a thing," said Jack. "I'm glad to take you home. But first, some champagne. The night is young, *n'est-ce pas*?"

Daphne giggled. "If you insist."

He was gazing around for a place to park Daphne while he ordered a bottle, when Sophia Morrigan descended on him, arms wide open in greeting.

"Jack," she said, her voice serious and low, contradicting the expansiveness of her gestures. "How did you enjoy the performance?"

"Exceeded my wildest expectations," he said with a genuinely wide grin. "It was truly wonderful, Sophia."

She leaned forward and pecked him on each cheek, in the French manner.

He didn't return the favor.

"I've made a new friend as well," he

said, detaching himself from Daph, who had remained latched onto his arm during the exchange.

"You may have met before? Mrs. Daphne Partington?" he said, part query, part introduction.

Sophia raised one brow imperiously. "Daphne? Yes, we have met." She loomed over Daphne and said sourly: "Trust you to latch on to the most attractive man in the room."

If Jack had been drinking, he'd have choked on his glass. He stared at Sophia, shining like Venus, the morning star in a low-necked gown of emerald-green satin, her decolletage draped with a magnificent emerald and pearl collar.

Sophia's sapphire eyes were for Daphne only, and they were sparking daggers. Daphne was not in the least phased by Sophia's rudeness. She certainly wasn't taking it as an insult.

She raised herself to her full five feet in height and met Sophia's glare full-on.

"That's a fetching gown you're wearing, Sophia," she said. "Such a pity Dahlia didn't get a better fit around your cleavage, though. Gappy, isn't it? You wouldn't want the view to go to waste, now would you? So many men, so little time."

Sophia's hand clutched at her throat, a gesture of impulse and protection. Her blood-red nails hung off the necklace, fingering the pearls.

Jack fought to suppress a surge of laughter that threatened to erupt from deep down in his belly. Daphne the Undaunted knew how to give insults as well as take them. He hadn't had so much fun in a long time, and the night had barely begun.

"Now, now, ladies," he said, looking from one to the other as they scowled like circling dogs. "I can see you're old friends. What say you find a table?" He nodded to Sophia. "And I'll get the champagne."

#

When he returned five minutes later with a bottle of French champagne and three glasses, Daphne sat alone, her lips curled in a self-satisfied quirk.

"Your friend had somewhere else to be?" he asked cheekily. "Couldn't take the heat? That last exchange? I nearly choked on my beer."

"You didn't have any beer," she shot back.

"Only reason I didn't choke," he said with a laugh. "You've got some explaining to do. What was all that about?"

"Oh, nothing really. The battle of the frocks."

"The battle of the frocks?"

A guilty shadow cast a shroud over her normally open face.

"Wouldn't do to be overheard," she said. "Perhaps a story best left till later."

Thirty-five

How dare she?

After Jack left to get the champagne, Sophia had wasted no time in telling Daphne, the fat sow, what she thought of her, but it gave her little satisfaction, because the old bag obviously didn't care. She'd perched there, looking mighty pleased with herself.

Sophia stalked off, putting on a good show of not giving a damn, but inside she was seething.

When she'd delivered her ultimatum to Daphne three years ago—"either she goes or I do"—she hadn't for one minute expected Daphne would take Ashling O'Riordan's side against her.

Ashling was a nobody, a social recluse, never on the scene, so Daphne's fashionable salon dresses were wasted on her. San Francisco's style-setters never got to see them. Whereas she, Sophia Morrigan, was at every big show, every party, ball and dance that counted, with a new stunning model to show off every time. Daphne's business had increased a hundredfold with her as the model client.

So what had possessed her to choose Ashling over her?

And once she did, once she made her choice plain, there was nothing for it but to desert Daphne's salon. She'd had the satisfaction of taking Dahlia, her top dressmaker, with her. But still it rankled.

Sophia halted her blind progress toward the bar and surveyed the scene. The audience from the Golden Queens show was moving to the bar for after-show drinks. It was going to be another memorable night at the Imperial Club.

And the galling truth—that Daphne was right, Dahlia wasn't nearly as good on her own as she was when she worked under Daphne's keen eye—was one she just didn't want to deal with right now.

Why was that, anyway? She'd been brilliant when working for Daphne. On her own? Her work was coarse and overblown, lacking the finesse, the "je ne sais quoi" that always lingered in one of the Mode Salon creations.

Sophia's face twisted in triumph. At least Ashling wasn't getting Daphne's frocks any longer because she was dead. And good riddance.

The "other woman's" austere, willowy form, her tiny breasts, mesmerizing green eyes and tumbling copper hair…

She'd only ever laid eyes on her once in her life, but the image burned in her brain.

Grigor's love. The woman he would put ahead of her, if she ever forced the issue. Just like Daphne had.

She stroked the pearls at her throat and swung on her heels, searching the room.

Aha. There he was. Her womanly pride needed a boost tonight after that nasty fiasco of a few minutes ago. And Hector de Vile was the man who could provide it.

#

She sashayed across to stand alongside the senator, adjusting her expression to one of adoration, noting as she moved just where the newspapermen who were present tonight had stationed themselves. She could see the gossip sheet headline the next morning… "Love Is in the Air." Yes. He would be her consolation prize for tonight.

Hector stiffened as soon as he sensed her by his side. Not exactly the reaction she'd been hoping for, but she ignored it. She draped a familiar arm around his neck and kissed the side of his face nearest to her. His shoulders went rigid, and he drew infinitesimally away. Not so far as to embarrass her publicly. But enough to send her a silent message. She ignored that, too.

She hoped that the stuck-up Countess would read the gossip columns in the morning and realize she'd met her match.

"Senator." Her voice hummed with delighted surprise. "Back so soon," she crooned.

"We must be doing something right." She gave him one of her intense 'I only have eyes for you' stares and sensed his resistance weaken.

He turned and pecked her mechanically on both cheeks.

"Madame Morrigan, nice to see you again." The inevitable hangers-on who materialized wherever he went were already gathering around him.

"Our hostess has put on another fine show tonight. She's to be congratulated."

Sophia gave him one of her modest "oh, not little me" false wiggles.

"It will soon be your ship as well, Senator, so we want to be sure we're sailing in smooth waters."

Hector's face flushed. He took a step back to distance himself.

"Now, now. No counting chickens,

Madame. We've a long way to go yet, if at all."

She seized his upper arm and drew him back into her orbit.

Hector's eyes flickered to his right, and he swiftly tore himself free and regained his distance.

She saw immediately why. Grigor loomed into view, his gimlet eyes fixed on her, his mouth a hard line.

"Aren't you supposed to be looking after the talent?"

She dropped her eyes to the floor so he wouldn't see the charge of fury that went through her like a lightning bolt.

Grigor continued. "They're in the Green Room, waiting to say goodnight. The least you could do is thank them."

With a baleful stare, he dismissed her. Turned his back. And walked away.

"Better do what he says." Hector's

baritone was muted. "He's not a man to be thwarted."

It took all of her strength not to shoot Hector de Vile a venomous look.

You've got a thing or two to learn, but there's time.

She turned to go to the Russell women in the "Green Room."

As she did, she saw Grigor had moved in the opposite direction, to the head of the stairs, which exited to the street outside.

He was talking to a young man with the elegant build of a racehorse, holding him by the shoulders and leaning in, making a point with vehemence. She strained to hear what he was saying, but she was too far away.

The helpless fury she'd felt so recently in her exchange with Daphne rose and hit her in the back of her throat, so that she had to double over to stop herself retching bile.

A younger, masculine version of Ashling was standing there, with the same thoroughbred form and gold-copper hair, such a contrast to Grigor's Arctic white. Even the languid movement of his hand as he reached up and stroked his hair back off his face. His graceful fluidity was all Ashling's.

She couldn't see his eyes. But she bet they were the same brilliant green as the woman she hated above all others.

For the first time, she comprehended something she'd been blind to. Grigor had a son.

Thirty-six

Sophia slept badly, haunted all night by images of deep copper hair and green eyes. The realization she'd missed something so deeply personal opened up a cavern of uncertainty deep within. She'd always imagined she was the apple of Grigor's eye until she'd discovered his unfathomable infatuation with Ashling.

The very thought of that woman made her stomach cramp.

She stared down at the strong black coffee going cold in the cup in her hand.

Ashling was the only woman who'd ever threatened her lifelong, exclusive relationship with Grigor.

She no longer recalled the faces of either of her parents. Her only childhood memories were of Grigor. His reassuring, powerful arm around her skinny back in teeming New York, so overwhelming to her after their quiet Welsh village.

Grigor, when she was much older, waiting awkwardly in the reception area of Daphne's salon as Dahlia measured her for her first handmade gown. He was the one who stood his ground over the breach of promise claim which set them up in business together when she was nineteen. The upper-class lawyers and rich boys underestimated a tough, canny miner with the will to beat everyone else to a pulp.

The hacking cough that bothered him every morning announced his arrival for breakfast, and his stooped shoulders and heavily lined face told her he too had tossed and turned all night.

She set her expression at her most sweetly accommodating and gazed into his glacial blue eyes.

"Gosh, Raz, that cough sounds nasty. Shouldn't you be seeing the doc?"

He scowled, and she had to admit she sounded as tinny and false to her ears as she obviously did to his. Playing the compassionate nurse just didn't ring true with her, and she should have had the sense to know it.

"You know as well as I do there isn't any fixing it," he barked. "We've pretended nothing else. Why start now? And what's with the 'Raz' business? You haven't called me that in years."

He gave her a slow, wolfish smile. "Not since you infuriated Bertha by stealing her diamond earrings and needed me to play the concerned Papa."

She flushed at his nerve at bringing up something they'd buried long ago and shrugged irritably.

"I was just playing nice. I can go the other way if you like."

"I'm far more used to it," he said, with no trace of malice. "At least then I know where I stand."

"Oh Grigor, that's not fair," she cried.

"Isn't it? When was the last time you gave a moment's thought for what I want?"

He was standing at the head of the small table, leaning over, fixing her with a hard eye.

"Oh, for goodness's sake. What's wrong with you? Get out of bed on the wrong side this morning? Sit down and have some toast. It might put you in a better mood."

"What will put me in a better mood,

and I shouldn't have to mention it yet again, is for you to drop this ridiculous idea of marrying de Vile. It will not happen. I've already told you."

She twisted the napkin in her lap in tight frustration.

"I saw you draping yourself over him last night. It was humiliating. The man's not interested. It's obvious. You can go after him for the money. No problem. But for goodness's sake, forget the rest of it."

He dropped into the chair at the other end of the table and poured himself a cold coffee.

"You'll need to get that topped up," she said. "It's cold."

"It'll do. I've spent half my life not being able to afford coffee. I can stand drinking it cold."

"And that's my fault too?" she

whined. "That you were so poor you couldn't afford decent coffee?"

"You're sounding more like a spoiled brat every day, Sophia. You'd better watch it or you'll be hard-pressed to find my replacement." He gave her another wolfish grin, as if savoring the unpleasantness.

She fiddled with the handle of her coffee cup, watching as he reached for a slice of toast from the silver toast rack.

"Since you seem determined to be gnarly this morning, let me reply in kind," she said, her voice dangerously soft. "Who was the devastatingly attractive young man you were talking to on the stairs last night?"

His eyes shot up, and a nasty smile that mirrored her own flickered on his lips.

"The one with the deep copper hair

that resembled your own in every measure except color."

He stared back, his face not revealing so much as a flicker of surprise.

After a long minute, he bared his sharply pointed teeth.

"You mean you don't know." His inflection was downward. He wasn't asking her a question.

"Of course I don't know, Grigor. Never in all these years have you mentioned you had a son. Not once. So how could I know?"

He was on her like a hound to prey.

"Who said he is my son?"

She made a scoffing sound in her throat.

"You only had to take one look to see the resemblance to you," she said. And, added as a quieter aside, "And to that woman."

His deeply grooved face tightened. His eyes narrowed to slits.

She pushed her chair back from the table to give herself more breathing room.

"No wonder you were talking about family the other day. About the de Vile deal. You're planning to leave your share to that boy. Someone I've never even met. And if he's Ashling's spawn, you can bet he won't have a business bone in his body."

"Maybe not," he said with deadly menace. His normally pale complexion had drained to a ghostly white.

"But he is my blood. Which is more than can be said for you."

The thing she dreaded the most. Finally expressed. Her tongue was lead in her mouth. They stared at each other across the table, consumed by a mutual,

white-hot hatred that had emerged
without warning but seemed unlikely to
melt away. Ever.

Thirty-seven

Brunch was the earliest social engagement Daphne could countenance, so brunch it was. Jack sat in the Italian coffeehouse on Davis Street, huddled over a steaming hot café au lait and waiting for Madame to arrive on her cloud of sweet earthy patchouli.

He found it a surprising place for Daphne to suggest they meet, filled as it was by stock exchange clerks and hard-nosed businessmen, but he was discovering that Daphne was nothing if not a woman of unexpected surprises.

She'd happily partied on until Buster came to collect her, and the breadth of her acquaintances and friends—she was

on first-name terms with everyone from
Bill Ralston to King Neptune, it seemed—
left him in awe. If anyone had a good
grip on what was going on in San
Francisco's social circles, it seemed it
would be Daph Partington.

He was about to conclude she'd slept
in when she appeared in the doorway
swathed in an extravagant white fur
coat, twinkling her fingers at him as if
she was a fairy godmother out of Hans
Christian Andersen.

*You really know far too much about
children's stories for a man with no wife
or children,* he scolded himself as he rose
with a smile to greet his visitor.

"They've reserved a nice private table
for us upstairs," he murmured in the old
lady's ear and saw her flush pink with
pleasure. The maître d' who stood
behind a stand nearby acknowledged

them with a nod. "Take my arm and I'll lead the way."

"Sooo," he said once they installed themselves and ordered coffee and French lemon cake.

Daphne beamed. "This was the earliest French bakery in the city, and their lemon tart is every bit as good as their excellent sourdough."

"We can get some sourdough for you to take home for lunch, if you like," said Jack with an answering smile.

She sat back, clasped her hands together on the tabletop, and savored the moment of anticipation. Then her sharp eyes locked on Jack.

"Now, what can I do for you in return for this delightful outing?"

"I want to pick your brains on Sophia Morrigan. You know I do."

Daphne gave him a soft, warm smile.

"I'll tell you as much as I can, Jack. But there's an awful lot about her I don't know. Information, I suspect she doesn't want anyone to know."

He felt a quick warning check in his spirit.

"I'm not sure I understand what you mean by that," he said. "Care to explain?"

She nodded. "I suspect there are two Sophias. The public one and the private one." She gave him another quick, wry smile. "I know that can be said for most of us. But the gulf between public and private is a lot bigger for her than most people. To be fair, that's only a guess, but I'd wager it's a pretty good one."

He pursed his lips, digesting the implications.

"I'll take that as a warning," he said. "Just tell me what you know."

The waiter arrived with their order at that point, so it was another few minutes before they returned to their conversation and Daphne related what she knew.

Grigor and Sophia had arrived in San Francisco in the early '50—about 1851, Daph thought, because she remembered Grigor ordering Sophia her first ballgown sometime around then.

"They were a stunning couple," she said. "Even with the age difference. When she turned it on, she could look incandescent."

She punctuated the line with her raised brows. "You could see that brain ticking over, always calculating, not so attractive in a woman, but when she wanted to, she glowed like fire.

"Grigor was always restrained and respectful, as if he took his guardian's duties seriously. And she had a rather unnerving precocity, as if she knew far more than a young girl should. She had a real 'knowing' look about her. You'd never mistake her for an ingenue. That's why I always felt rather sad for the young men who got caught in her web."

She took up the silver tongs and dropped a second lump of sugar into her coffee. "Like the James Albert Willoughby, firstborn son of an Irish earl or marquis or something. He came visiting the West like it was some exotic foreign country. Treated it like he was on African safari, where the normal rules didn't apply. I suppose to him at that time, they didn't."

Daphne paused and delicately forked another piece of lemon tart. Savored another mouthful of coffee, enjoying Jack's rapt attention.

"He was six years older than her, but he was ripe pickings, a bald coot just waiting to be scalped, stupid infatuated with Sophia. He was hers for the taking."

"And take she did," Jack said with a cynical grin.

"Take she did," Daphne concurred.

"He was free of Daddy's coat strings for the first time in his life and thought he could get away with anything out here. But Daddy had his spies, and when word got back to the ancestral manor that the family's son and heir was betrothed to an Irish shyster... Well, you can imagine. We heard the cries of wrath all the way across the Atlantic."

Daphne shook her head and reached for her cup.

"The ensuing breach of promise case made it sound like she was an innocent, led astray by the promises of a more worldly, experienced man, and she played the role to the hilt."

She drained the last of her coffee.

"I'm pretty sure if this was a fairy tale, he'd have been the babe in the woods, and she'd be the ruffian uncle, if you know what I mean."

He gave a nod of understanding. "I do indeed."

"Anyway, Grigor devoted himself to her. Maybe he set her up for it. Who can say? Willoughby wasn't the only one, just the most spectacular. I could never decide if they worked together as a highly sophisticated con team or not."

Daphne waved her hand in an airy gesture of 'who could know?'

"I know some people thought they did. But after the second or third sting, the suitors got wary. They did well from it, and Sophia seemed perfectly happy as a single woman with Grigor as her protector. All went well until the 'other woman' appeared."

Jack's curiosity pricked. "Oh, I see. Who, and what then?"

"An artist called Ashling O'Riordan. She had some vague connection to them from back in Ireland. She and Grigor were like two harp notes in harmony. A Mick, like him of course, though very different in temperament.

"Grigor was relentless, intense. Ashling was ethereal, dreamy and artistic. You couldn't have imagined anyone more different from Sophia if you'd tried. She was a thoroughbred, a finely tuned racehorse, unaware of her own beauty, and a brilliant watercolorist." She forked the last piece of tart and paused as she raised it to her mouth, gazing across the table at him.

"Even with her, in public at least, Grigor maintained his stern propriety at all times."

She gave a self-conscious laugh. "Well, at all times that I saw him. I only knew they had a mad love affair because Ashling confided in me. She drew my gowns for my catalogues, so we had a lot of private moments to gossip."

"And Sophia? How did she take to Ashling?"

"Sophia was both dismissive and madly jealous. She may have had an instinct about what was going on, but Grigor never acknowledged it. Not that I knew of, anyway. Why did he act like that? Really, I don't know.

"From what I understood from Ashling, Grigor feared Sophia's reaction, and Ashling didn't care about a traditional life as a wife and mother. Her art completely engrossed her, so it suited them both to maintain their distance in public."

The waiter reappeared offering coffee refills, which they both happily accepted. Jack waited for him to depart before eagerly resuming where they'd left off.

"You said Ashling was an artist who wasn't interested in a traditional woman's role. If that was the case, how did she cope with a child?"

"Grigor took in a widow with a child of a similar age to Lochie to keep house and look after the baby while Ashling painted. He paid for everything. When Ashling died suddenly of a brain hemorrhage when Lochie was six or seven, the arrangement continued without her.

"Nan Waters cared for the two boys and kept house. She provided a family life and Grigor paid the bills. It worked fine for both of them. I gather the boy—he's a young man now, as you saw—has his mother's gift. He's an artist too."

Jack tapped the edge of the table with his fingers in a jittery rhythm, clearly on edge.

"That's a touching story, and gives me an idea of Grigor, but Sophia is the one I'm most interested in."

Daphne raised her eyebrows in a teasing query, and he laughed. "Not like that. Not as a woman. Mother of Mary, save me from women like her... No, no. I'm interested in her as an operator. Those breach of promise cases... The club... What sort of woman has she grown into? Where does she get that 'you-can't-stare -me-down' attitude? She'd be terrifying if you let her get to you. Where does that come from?"

Daphne shook her head. "It's always been there. Either she was born with it, or she adopted it as a very young child."

Jack nodded. "So, do you know anything about her business interests, apart from the club? I suspect that's not the only pie she's got a finger in."

Daphne hesitated. She shook her head. "Not really. Over the years, there have been rumors, but that's all. Nothing concrete."

"Rumors?" Jack sounded interested. "What rumors?"

Daphne hunched forward and lowered her voice to a rough whisper.

"The sort you shouldn't really even discuss in public." Her eyes narrowed, and she leaned in closer.

"Like various nefarious propositions. Stories she operates a string of brothels throughout the state. That she's not averse to taking on very young children to work around the places."

He felt a chill up his backbone.

"What? You mean like indentured servants? Orphan train gone wrong stuff?"

"Pretty well. Not illegal, but unsavory and unethical. Working them long hours with no pretense at providing even basic education. You know the stories you hear. Of people taking some of the so-called 'orphans' that are sent out here and selling them on as cheap labor. She doesn't appear to have any sensitivity about stuff like that. If it suits her, she does it. She seems truly immune to basic morals and what other people think."

"Is there any chance she's still involved in that sort of thing now?"

"Honestly? If it was profitable and she could get away with it, it wouldn't surprise me. Grigor moved in questionable circles, and she was always there at his side. She probably heard and saw things that were quite inappropriate for an impressionable young girl."

"Questionable circles? Any names?"

She shook her head. "No, sorry. But I tell you who might help there, and that's Pania Russell. She was married to her manager, Harvey Miller, in those days. Harvey was a lot older than Pania and didn't want to go out as much as her. She used to hang out with 'Sir' John and a guy called Eustace Mountford? Some rich-boy heir from back East. They were a tight threesome. They mixed in very wide circles because of Pania's concert career. She might remember something."

"Thanks," said Jack, his hopes deflating like a burst balloon.

He'd been hoping for some damning detail, a hard fact he could latch on to and run with.

All he'd got, really, was an hour of tasty gossip and airy-fairy suppositions.

"I'll see if Pania Russell knows anything. If she'll talk to me."

Thirty-eight

Sophia was hovering at the bar, watching head barkeeper Ned clean up for the night, when Hector approached. It was getting late. The theater crowd had drifted off home and the remaining patrons were at the billiards tables or getting quietly drunk in corners.

"Sophia. We need to talk." His voice was solemn, direct. He wasn't looking for small talk. That was plain. "Have you got a few minutes to join me somewhere private? It won't take long."

They locked eyes. Her stomach still churned from the row she'd had with Grigor, but she could see by the steady calm with which he regarded her that de

Vile had no inkling of what had taken place.

"Certainly, Senator. Ned, you're fine here to close up, aren't you? Call the last round in." Her eyes flicked to her diamond-encrusted wristwatch. "Say, in thirty minutes?"

She wasn't willing to keep staff on when the profits weren't there.

She led Hector out of the big public bar and into the secluded quiet room, which Pania and Graysie had vacated more than an hour ago. A faint lingering of female fragrance reminded her their season was coming to a close. Pity. They'd brought a crowd of new patrons into the place, chaps who may not normally frequent the Imperial. She was hoping for an influx of new memberships as a result.

"Make yourself comfortable," she said,

gesturing to an armchair. "Can I get you another brandy?"

"No thanks. I've had my nightcap. More than one." He gave her a quick, acknowledging smile.

"You run a good operation here, Sophia. I'm impressed."

She reached out a smooth white hand with its groomed red nails and stroked his sleeve.

"See. I knew you would be."

She sank into the tub chair opposite him, reluctantly relinquishing hold of his arm as she did.

He immediately pulled back, increasing the space between them.

"Yes, from what I've seen, you've got an excellent business here," he said, his voice sounding formal and awkward.

He shifted uncomfortably in his chair.

"But…" He paused and squared up to

her, his eyes meeting hers with a resolute steeliness. "That's as far as it goes. I want you to understand. Any arrangement we might come to starts and end with the business."

She felt her back teeth clench together in a reflective response. *Relax,* she told herself. *Tremors in your cheeks will betray you're clenching your jaw.*

Rejected. Twice in one night.

She couldn't afford to let this bird escape, not after the showdown with Grigor.

She eased her teeth apart and marshaled her steely will to soften her expression.

"You don't want to rush things. I understand that, Hector."

She re-settled herself in her chair, drawing her feet closer to the base, sitting forward with her hands clasped in her lap. What she thought of as her "Duchess Pose." Everything calm and controlled.

"I appreciate you understand what we've got here. It's an excellent proposition, and I have a lot of ideas for how to make it even better. This experiment with the Golden Queens singing here. This is just a start. I think we can raise the prestige of the place. Attract all the best people."

She gave a tinkling little laugh, when inside her heart felt like lead.

"Not that we don't do that already, of course. More of the best people, should I say?"

She stared into his eyes, and he flicked away from her.

I'm definitely losing my touch. Can't hook them like before.

"Let's delay no longer. You've done

your due diligence. I respect your position. Why don't I get my lawyer to draw up an agreement and we'll seal the deal before the end of the week? No more fuss about it?"

De Vile's jaw dropped, as if he couldn't believe his ears.

"Really? That's it?"

She nodded. "That's it."

"What about all the palaver? The threats? Your girl with the trinkets?"

"Trinkets?" She acted puzzled, her brow drawn into querying lines. "Oh. You mean Isla... the bracelet. Just put that down to me getting your attention. Nothing serious."

The senator's throat bobbed like he'd swallowed a goldfish.

He stared at her, disbelieving. He wanted to ask her more. Lots more. She could see that. But if he did, he'd be acknowledging he'd known all along what she was getting at. That he knew what she knew. Or thought he did.

But you don't. And you won't, until I decide I'm good and ready.

He cleared his throat.

"Err. The bracelet. Where did you get it?"

Her eyes roved over his face. He was still a handsome man for his age, with tanned, strong features, dark-flecked eyes and steely hair. A sweaty sheen glistened under the lock that fell over his right eye. She let the question hang in the silence between them.

She took in a deep breath. Drew her hands up to her throat and fingered her necklace. Her emerald and pearls tonight. She drew strength from them.

"I really can't remember," she lied. "I picked it up somewhere... I've had it for years now, just lying around in my jewelry box. Where did I get it? Was it from Grigor? Or Bertha?"

She flicked her attention away into the middle distance, as if trying to recall where she picked up the inconsequential object.

"I really can't recall. Why? Is it important?"

"Oh no," said de Vile with a sharp intake of breath.

"I was just curious."

#

Just one more before I go to sleep.

Hector de Vile perched his backside on the edge of his luxurious four-poster bed, his feet in woolly slippers thrust out to keep him steady, and swirled the amber liquid. It caught the light of the bedroom lamp and threw a golden reflection on the gilded wallpaper.

I told her I'd had enough for tonight, so why am I still drinking?

He stared into the clear depths and searched his soul for the answer.

Am I celebrating an escape? Or am I mourning a loss?

Bertha. She mentioned Bertha.

His throat closed over at the recall.

What about it, Hector? Are you winning or losing at this point?

He slipped his feet out of the woolly scuffs and pivoted against the mountain of pillows nestled at the head of his bed.

He lay back and began a conversation with himself. As he'd grown older, he'd done this more often, because there was no one else to talk to.

Strike one to you, because she now accepts you will not marry her.

He considered that for a moment,

staring down at the nautical-themed coverlet.

Accepts it for the meantime, he corrected.

So I still might have a chance with Elizabeth.

Strike two to her, because she's still got all that old history she's holding over you. So why has she eased the noose for now?

She's playing a long game. It will come back to haunt you. That she mentioned Bertha's name proves it.

I wonder what Grigor thinks about all of this? He's already warned you off once. Maybe I should find out.

I don't know what's wrong with me. I've gone soft in my old age. Once upon a time I'd think nothing of arranging that woman's demise.

He took a big swallow and savored the

burn as it ran down his gullet.

But no. No more killing.

I've got sons to think of now. And if it's not too late already, I want to die with them thinking well of me.

You can't just leave it there. What if she goes directly to Alex?

No. I can't leave it there. I have to tell Alex before she does.

He took the last swig of brandy and turned out the lamp. He rolled over with his knees clasped to his chest. But it was a very long time before he went to sleep.

Thirty-nine

Grigor strolled through the magnificent white marble columns that bordered William Chapman Ralston's Bank of California, the pillared pile on the corner of California and Sansome Streets, and a sense of deep security enveloped him.

There was something about the Italianate building's two floors of serried arched windows, built in stone quarried from nearby Angel Island, that anchored a man.

They'd trimmed each archway with smaller columns and piers, conferring a sense of permanence and wealthy grandeur on all who entered its doors. People referred to it as "Ralston's Bank" because he'd been the mastermind behind getting it up and running in 1864, and he'd certainly used it as a personal source of funds ever since.

Grigor pursed his lips in the closest resemblance he gave to a smile. He'd been in San Francisco longer than Ralston. He already owned a couple of important commercial buildings when Ralston was still a shareholder in a struggling steamship company. And although Billy wasn't a close friend, they went way back. He knew his secrets. And there was no way he'd refuse him the favor he was about to ask of him.

An immaculately tailored assistant stepped forward as soon as Grigor came out of the sunlight into the shaded interior. Billy was expecting him. He'd already made an appointment to discuss this matter, which had become so important to him. Probably one of the last important things he'd do on earth.

"Mr. Grigor," the associate said, peering at him over gold-rimmed spectacles. "The bank president is expecting you. Let me take you through."

After the heat outside, the inside of the building was gratifyingly cool. As the deputy manager turned in his navy blue jacket to take him through to the big man, Grigor wiped his sleeve across his forehead. He'd worked up a sweat just getting here, and he hadn't started telling Billy what he wanted from him yet. He chewed his lower lip.

Ralston lounged behind an enormous mahogany desk, the very picture of a man who controlled the city. His tireless advocacy for San Francisco, his commitment to funding the development of Nevada's Comstock silver mines by opening a branch of the bank in Virginia City, had seen the city boom over the last decade. All thanks to this man.

His face was boyish and debonair, his ruddy complexion and jovial expression set beneath a wide domed forehead and prematurely receding hairline.

He rose from behind the desk as Grigor entered and leaned over to offer him a warm handshake. "Grigor, my old friend. What can I do for you? Your note sounded urgent."

"To me it is."

Grigor sat, and they chatted amiably about stocks and shares and how Billy's work on the Palace Hotel was going until a secretary had served them coffee and cigars. As soon as the man had left, closing the door behind him, they got down to business.

"I've got a nice payment coming into our accounts in a few days," Grigor said. "I wanted to alert you."

Ralston was nodding, invested, and pleased. As Grigor was talking, the banker tore pieces of paper into fragments and let them drop as he listened.

"Always like to hear that our customers are doing well for themselves." He grinned. "The more money for them, the more for us."

He took a pull on his cigar and blew the smoke out with a chortling laugh. "What have you done this time?"

Grigor shrugged. "It was Sophia's idea, actually. I wasn't that keen at first. But she's persuaded old Hector de Vile to take a stake in the club. The place is going ahead in leaps and bounds. He certainly won't lose his money. But to me it felt like we were building a three-wheeled bicycle."

"So, how can we be of help?" Ralston's voice was quiet and patient.

Grigor reached into his pocket and drew out the paper he was carrying.

"I've got a requisition here, signed by my lawyer. When de Vile's payment comes through, these are instructions for it to be transferred to a trust account with Benedict and Arnold. It's important it's done immediately. I want no time lost."

Ralston took the paper and read through it in half a minute. "No problem there, Grigor. We'll send on the $30,000 as soon as it lands. And I'll make sure McElroy sends a confirmation as soon as we've got it."

"Thanks," said Grigor. "I appreciate it."

Ten minutes later, after more chitchat about the palace construction, he left the bank, humming an old Irish air Ashling liked to sing, a new lightness in his step.

Forty

"I've invited Elizabeth along to be my witness."

Hector ghosted his arm around his companion without actually touching her, shepherding her into the "Green Room" to watch the signing of the agreement of sale.

Sophia scrutinized her in sharp-eyed silence while Grigor dipped his head in acknowledgment of her presence.

Elizabeth suppressed a smile.

Neither of them is exactly delighted to have me along.

Hector had warned her, and the politics didn't concern her.

When he'd come asking if she would

join him for this occasion, she'd been surprised and initially resistant.

"Really Hector, it's got nothing to do with me," she'd protested.

"I value your judgment and your support," he'd said. "I don't want my dealings with this pair to come between us. Whatever happens, I want us to deal with it. For it not to spoil our friendship."

That had touched her, even though she sensed he was still not offering full disclosure. This was a step in the right direction toward mending the frayed edges.

She'd decided on one of Daphne Partington's most elegantly understated jacket dresses to mark the occasion, a simple white "Garibaldi" shirt over a smoky gray skirt, topped with the fashionable bright red Zouave military-style jacket, trimmed in a double row of black Russian braid from the collarless neckline to the slim cuffs.

A style statement at once eye-catching and discreet.

She forbore from acknowledging it was "the opposite of what Sophia represents" because they weren't in any sort of competition, were they?

But the look on Sophia's face when they arrived made her very glad about her choice of dress, and very clear on the competition—or lack of it. They were in a catfight to the end. She saw that as soon as she walked into the room.

Well, good then. Bring it on. See if I'm the milk and water doxy you think I am. You'll be surprised.

Grigor stepped into the silence that had fallen after the introductions.

"I want to give full credit to Sophia for today. With her remarkable foresight, she's drawn together a new alliance which will see the club go from strength to strength."

He put his hand around the back of her neck and patted her right shoulder.

"Well done, Sophia. Forgive an old man for being initially rather unenthusiastic. You've won me over."

Elizabeth could see his words pleased Sophia. Her complexion pinked up and her lips curled in a triumphant tilt.

"Oh Grigor, you're the one who got this place established. We'd never have done it without you. That's obvious. Thank you for being the most wonderful father substitute all these years."

Elizabeth flashed a quick smile at de Vile that said, *Do we really have to listen to this session of mutual admiration?*

He gave her the briefest of shrugs, which said "I don't have a clue what's going on here either."

Elizabeth felt her heart warm toward him. It had been a dispiriting few days, contemplating breaking off her relationship with Hector. Maybe even clearing off to Dolphie in London.

She confessed she enjoyed these secret little wordless exchanges. That deeper level of communication between them was still there, which was comforting.

De Vile's eyes swivelled back and forth between Grigor and Sophia. He was picking up on an underlying tension between them that contradicted their words.

Elizabeth studied her old friend, and saw the way fleeting expressions flashed across his face, too fast for anyone to read unless they knew him exceptionally well. Which she did.

He was asking himself questions such as , "Why does it feel as if they hate each other, despite their praise fest?", "Who's the praise fest meant for? Us or them?" And "What's the hidden game I'm missing here?"

She caught his eye and gave him an infinitesimal nod of affirmation.

Because there was no doubt something off key was going on here, and they both knew it.

#

Elizabeth and Hector were at the point of leaving the signing session, standing at the top of the Imperial Club stairs. Hector had stretched out his hand for Grigor's final handshake.

He hesitated. Beside Grigor, Sophia appeared resolute in a slim-skirted buttermilk-colored dress with a mandarin collar worn with a long jacquard gilet over the top. But when she spoke, her voice carried an edge of anxiety.

"So you'll arrange the funds to be transferred immediately?"

The words quivered in the empty, echoing space.

"I will instruct my bankers first thing tomorrow," Hector said, poised and staunch. "Don't worry. I'm a man of my word."

Sophia looked to Grigor, suddenly the junior looking for reassurance.

Then she pulled back her shoulders and laughed.

"Oh, I'm not worried. I just wanted to be sure we understood each other."

She took Grigor's arm purposefully and turned back into their lair.

Forty-one

Jack had left a note with Pania's housekeeper, asking if he could call that afternoon. He guessed that if Pania had to perform that evening, she'd want to rest earlier in the day, but she could possibly give him some time before she had to go to the club for the show.

And so it had turned out. He presented himself at her doorway at 4:30 p.m. and a pleasant Spanish-Mexican woman showed him into the Russells' San Francisco library, a small feminine room so different from the masculine version of the same room he usually saw, smelling of cigar smoke and whiskey fumes, all heavy brown furniture and leather-bound books.

There were a lot of books here too, but big double-hung windows offered a view of the garden and a cream paper dotted with spring primroses lined the walls. The shelves were painted a fresh apple green. Potted maiden-hair ferns on the windowsills added to the sense of lightness and the intrusion of the natural world.

Pania bustled in within minutes of him sitting down, and he could see she was already wearing the costume she would assume on stage tonight, a burnished gold sequined top with matching gold satin turban and satin skirt.

He jumped to his feet, and she dismissed the gesture with a wave of her hand. "Oh please. Sit. We haven't got a lot of time." She peered at a slender gold-banded bracelet watch on her wrist.

"I have quite a warming up process I like to go through every afternoon to prepare the voice, so let's get down to business."

He liked her focused attitude. No wonder she enjoyed the success she did.

"Lady Russell," he began, and her peal of laughter rose to the ceiling, and the soprano followed it, half rising from her chair. "No, no, Mr. Cabot. I am Pania. My husband, John inherited that dusty old title from his grandfather—a very unusual situation, but there were special circumstances to do with his predecessor's heroics during the First Opium War in China. We won't go into it now."

She sank into her chair again. "It's a pleasant reminder of family legacy, but that's all. He puts no weight on it and neither do I. So. Pania, please."

Jack grinned. "If you say so, Pania."

He launched into his explanation. About meeting Daphne at her concert a few days before. "I was blown away, I must say. It was a fantastic night, and not just because I met Daphne."

Pania laughed. "She's quite a trick, isn't she? I'm sorry she closed up shop—she ran a very good design studio, but she wearied of it."

"She was telling me about Grigor and Ashling and Sophia, and all the rivalries that arose."

He was purposely keeping it general. Not going into personal details.

"I had an ulterior motive for being interested, I must confess."

He felt the familiar tightening in his belly, the rising sense of panic he experienced whenever he allowed himself to think of Cordelia.

"I've never had a wife or children, but I did have a precious niece, Cordelia. My sister married a fellow of no substance, a pretty-boy card sharp who was good at catching women's eyes and then running out on them.

"He went as far as marrying my sister, but after she died, he wanted to go back to his old ways. He had no room in his life for a little girl."

Suddenly, he had no more air in his chest to continue. He couldn't breathe. He bent over in desperation, trying to free the tight band under his ribs to get himself flowing again.

Pania jumped up and was at his side in minutes with a glass of water in hand. She gently tapped his shoulder. "Here. Sip this slowly. And give yourself a few minutes to recover."

He sipped and coughed and went red

in the face.

"I'm sorry. I find this extremely painful to talk about."

"Don't rush it. And I quite understand. I've lost a sister. I can guess what you're feeling."

After several minutes, he resumed.

"Cordelia's father sold her to some New York merchant—a wealthy couple with no children. Like a reverse orphan train. I didn't realize what he was planning until it was too late to stop him. And my lawyer tells me he had the right as her father to dispose of her as he chose. I couldn't prove money had changed hands, and I had no grounds to intervene. I haven't seen her in seven years."

Pania got up and refilled his water glass.

"I understand that's an awful personal

situation. But what has it got to do with Daphne, or Grigor, or Sophia? I don't see the link."

Jack nodded, appreciating her level-headed rigor.

"Daphne hinted to me there were faint rumors that Sophia might have dealt in something similar. Goodness knows. She might even have been the one who gave Cordelia's father the introduction. I know that's pulling a long bow, but you see where I'm going with this?

He gazed at her over tense, linked fingers, wordlessly communicating his powerlessness.

"And the other part of this is just as painful. I was a good friend of Elizabeth Westerhoven's. She knew my sister and Cordelia, and she's concerned that Sophia might be attempting to blackmail Hector de Vile. She's heard a suggestion that it may be related to Alex, his adopted son."

He sensed Pania stiffen beneath the sequined gown.

"I know this is an enormous cauldron to stir. It might be baloney soup. But if there was ever any suggestion that Sophia or anyone else in that circle was involved in selling children for profit... well, I honestly don't know what I'd do. I want to satisfy myself as to the accuracy of it. And if there is any truth to it, I would try to stop it from ever happening again."

Pania's eyes went to her watch. "Jack, I'm running out of time. This a big issue, and there's a lot to say."

She rose to her feet, charged with a restless energy that hadn't been there earlier. Her dark eyes glinted with deep knowledge, but she gave a brief, denying dip of her head. She wasn't going to be drawn on anything more now.

She picked up his empty water glass and returned it to the silver tray on her desk.

"Even more importantly though, there's someone I think you need to meet. To talk to about this."

He lifted his head and stared in expectation.

"Oh really? Who?"

"Graysie Russell, née Castellanos. Alex's half-sister. I know she'll be transfixed by what you have to say. And she may contribute some vital clues. Why don't you come by the Green Room tonight after the performance and I'll introduce you?"

Forty-two

De Vile was finishing up his Wednesday clinic, his regular fortnightly session for meeting with voters, which he held whenever he was back from Washington, when a doorway commotion interrupted his concentration.

The pale-faced widow who'd been complaining she'd been deprived of her deceased husband's military pension was wringing her hands anxiously.

De Vile rose. "I'll walk you to the door, Mrs. Stuyvesant. And I'll set my assistant about looking into your husband's service record."

They walked to the door, and he paused, sheltering his visitor protectively.

The strident tones of a female voice penetrated down the hallway.

"I must see him. Now…"

He opened the door and saw his secretary Tom Bedford, a young, fair-haired man with little physical presence, being charged down by an angrily protesting woman.

De Vile stepped out and shepherded Mrs. Stuyvesant out of the way down the corridor.

Tom was attempting to impede Sophia Morrigan's progress to his door while simultaneously calming her, and he was having little success with either strategy.

De Vile braced himself for the onslaught.

"Tom, it's fine. You can leave this in my hands…"

He looked Sophia straight in the eye. Not a simple thing as she barreled forward, her head slightly lowered like a charging bull.

"Sophia." He spoke her name loud and sharp, and he got her instant attention. She stopped mid-stride and made a swatting gesture toward the unfortunate clerk, as if dismissing an irritating fly.

De Vile repeated his earlier instruction. "Tom, it's fine. I can handle it."

His electoral manager slowed, nodded at him, as if only now registering his presence, stepped around Sophia, and melted back down the hall.

Hands on hips, sapphire eyes flashing in fury, Sophia glared.

"A man of his word. That's what you said."

He took a deep breath.

"Sophia. Calm down. Come in, and tell

me what's wrong. No need for this display."

His steady, slow instructions had the desired effect.

He pointed to the chair placed in front of the desk at just the right positioning for importune voters to make their appeals.

She took two more steps and slid into it, never taking her eyes off his face.

"Now, tell me. Why are you upset?"

"I'm not upset. I'm justifiably angry."

He tried again. "And why are you angry, justifiably or not?"

"You said you'd pay out on our deal, and you lied. The money should have come in two days ago, and it's still not showing in the account. I checked with Billy Ralston on my way here."

De Vile felt a prickle of concern trickle down his backbone.

"It certainly should be in the account.

I deposited it myself yesterday morning, just like I said I would. I didn't want to take any chances of an error or delay."

She rolled her eyes in disbelief, her face flushed, her cheekbones shining points of red.

"Well, it's not there. I hardly need to remind you what will happen if it's not there by tomorrow."

His throat closed over, so that it took him half a minute to swallow and regain control of his voice.

Then he felt the slow pulse of anger start in the pit of his stomach and fire through him.

"I admit I am not entirely clear what you are referring to," he said in a menacing, clipped voice. "Perhaps you could enlighten me."

She seemed oblivious to the warning note in his voice.

She continued to glare at him, a self-righteous set to her jaw. De Vile flicked his eyes to the door, to ensure Tom Bedford had withdrawn to the outer office, and was pleased to confirm they were alone. He got up, went to the door, and firmly closed it.

"Well? Tell me, do." The words sounded more like a threat than a request, but still she did not adjust her stance.

She put her hand to her neck and flipped out a leather thong with something dangling from it.

The bone ring—bracelet, teething ring—whatever it was. The matching twin for the one he'd ripped out of the girl's hands in the spa two weeks ago.

She flashed him a contemptuous smile. She still thought she held a winning hand.

"I'm sure you wouldn't want your miraculous son, the one who so conveniently appeared just when you needed him, to find out about this."

She rattled it in her fingers.

"He might be upset to know you colluded in his disappearance. That you 'adopted' him, knowing full well that his father was alive and desperately seeking him."

De Vile felt the blood that seconds ago had heated, chill in his veins.

This was it. The first full declaration of what she believed she had over him. What she thought was so valuable to him that he'd do anything to keep it a secret. Even marry her.

And he saw in a flash what a fool he had been. He had paid her the money which she'd said would be payoff enough. What had happened to it, he did not know, though he could hazard an intelligent guess.

But in those few seconds, it was as clear as lightning in a thunderous sky that as long as Sophia Morrigan thought she had this noose around his neck, she'd keep drawing the knot tighter. He would never be free of her.

And he recognized the thing he'd dreaded most, all along.

He would have to get to Alex and tell him what really happened the night his mother died before Morrigan did.

Alex and Elizabeth.

His jaw clamped tight. He felt the color draining from his face and knew she'd take that as a sign of his capitulation.

When he spoke, he fought to make his voice as penetrating, as convincing, as Abe Lincoln giving his presidential acceptance speech.

"I do not know where my money has gone since it left my account, Sophia. I suggest you go back and ask Billy Ralston that question. And if you've already asked it him once, ask him again. Ask him if he's done any special favors for his old buddy Raizney Grigor in the last forty-eight hours. I don't care who you talk to, but find out why your own house is in disorder."

He rose slowly from his chair, his meaty hands fixed on the desk edge, and loomed over her, taking advantage of his size and breadth.

"And when you've done that, come back to me, as your newly appointed shareholder in the Imperial Club, and apologize. Then you can explain to me why I should ever take seriously anything you say, ever again."

His eyes were flashing daggers.

He raised his right arm and pointed to the door.

"Don't you ever threaten me again. And now get out, before I call security, and have you thrown out."

Forty-three

"I'm here to throw myself on your mercy, Elizabeth."

Hector gazed at the woman he'd grown to love, and his heart was a stone locked in his ribcage.

He brought his hand up to his chest and pressed it flat against his fluttering pulse, reassuring himself it was still pumping.

Her dark brown eyes opened in shock as she caught the desperate note in his voice, and her mouth fell open.

"Oh, Hector." She started forward. "Are you all right? Sit down. I'll get them to bring some water."

He grasped the back of a garden

bench and shook his head sadly.

"It will take a lot more than water to fix what I'm about to tell you," he rasped.

He stepped around the chair and sank into it with a grateful sigh.

He'd gone straight from his confrontation with Sophia up the hill to Elizabeth's house. He didn't know how much time he had before the club owner descended like a petulant goddess to wreak carnage on his life and reputation, but he was determined to get in first if he could. First with Elizabeth and then with Alex, anyway.

He'd found Elizabeth in her back garden, where she'd directed he be brought when he'd rung her door bell midmorning on a weekday. She hadn't been expecting any visitors, and wore a simple, pale cream day dress printed with a delicate deep gold and green botanical design.

It was the sort of dress she'd worn when she was twenty, and she seemed hardly any older than that now,as she stood, dewy-skinned, her eyes at first crinkled in amusement at his surprise visit.

A shallow crescent of a basket hung from the crook of her left arm, while her right hand held a wooden-handled pruning knife. He'd interrupted her cutting flowers for display in the house, and he could see from her relaxed, joyful expression as he'd entered she was enjoying her simple interlude.

A trail of rose petals showed her progress across the watered green lawn, for many of the roses in the surrounding beds were at their summer height, full-blown and fragrant, already dropping pink, yellow and deep red petals.

Mingled with them were white daisies with big yellow centers, purple sweet peas, blue cornflowers and black-hearted red poppies, lying in a profusion on the wicker, releasing a glorious fragrance. He took in a deep breath and inhaled the bouquet's fresh, woody green perfume with sweet high notes.

He paused, regretful he was about to destroy her idyllic mood. The stone masquerading as a heart restarted with a lurch as he realized when she'd heard his story, she may never look at him again with the same unfiltered shining eyes. Elizabeth's amused and affectionate "What's he done now?" look.

Elizabeth searched his face and understood he was facing disaster.

She dropped the basket to her feet

and stepped to where he still leaned against the seat for support.

"Something's happened." She searched his face, her eyes narrowed and calculating. "What is it? Has someone died?"

He gave a low, guttural laugh.

"Not quite, but they may as well have."

She stared another half a minute. "You need water. Do you want to stay out here or go back inside?"

He let go of the seat and pulled himself up to his full height.

"Out here's good. Quieter." He gestured to the gazebo further down the garden, a white octagonal retreat with a tiled conical roof and intricately carved balustrade, inside which sat two basket chairs and a small round table.

"Down there's perfect."

She ran her hand over her forehead. He could see that under the brim of her straw hat, her face had a healthy pink sheen.

"I could do with a glass of water, even if you don't need one."

She picked up the flower basket and turned for the house. "I need to get these into water, too."

As if by telepathy, the back door of the kitchen opened and Mrs. Roderiquez stepped out. She strode toward her mistress.

"Let me take those, Mrs. Westerhoven. And can I bring refreshments? Some lemon squash?"

"Perfect." From where he stood, Hector could hear the satisfaction in Elizabeth's voice. She hated not fulfilling her role as the generous hostess.

"Bring a jug and glasses and then

advise the rest of the staff we're not to be disturbed."

#

They wandered in silence to the gazebo, Elizabeth lost in a brief reverie, Hector swallowing to moisten his throat and steel himself for what was coming next.

"Lovely place you have here," he said. "I hadn't realized you've done such a lot of work in the garden."

She nodded appreciatively.

"It's one of my favorite places," she said. "I spend a lot of time out here."

She gestured to a novel that lay on the small table, a bookmark protruding halfway through.

De Vile picked it up and scanned the cover. "*Little Women*, by Louisa May Alcott," he read. "Any good?"

Elizabeth smiled. "I'm enjoying it."

There was an awkward silence, broken by Mrs. Roderiquez's arrival with the refreshments.

Elizabeth poured two tall glasses, and they both gulped down welcome icy mouthfuls.

Then Elizabeth settled her hands on her lap and turned to him.

"Now Hector. What's wrong? What have you got to tell me?"

He gazed at her composed face, memorizing every feature, wanting to remember her just as she was today. After today, he may not be welcome in her house.

"You've known something's been wrong these last few weeks, Elizabeth. You're too smart a woman to not know. And I've been fobbing you off, hoping to sort it all out so no one would be left upset or disturbed."

He gazed into her eyes, which were calm but questioning.

He flicked his thumbs nervously and sighed loudly.

"But I'm afraid the situation has got beyond me. I can't keep the lid on any longer. And I wanted to make sure you heard about it from me before anyone else."

He sighed again. He did not know this was going to be so hard.

Still, she stayed silent and waited. She took another measured sip of lemon squash.

Then, when he still didn't speak, she said in a quiet voice, almost a whisper: "It's to do with Sophia Morrigan, isn't it?"

Her eyes flicked to his, searching him out.

"I knew there was something going on there."

Hector nodded. "She's ruthless. She claims to hold damaging information about events that happened years ago. Things I regret, though I can't honestly say I wish they'd never happened. It's more complicated than that. But when she brings it all out in the light, which she is threatening to do, it will be damaging. Very damaging."

He stood abruptly, unable to stay still anymore. His blood was firing up, his legs were twitching. He strode to the gazebo's outer perimeter and leaned against one of the vertical uprights supporting the roof, his long legs crossed in a deceptively relaxed pose, and continued.

"I'm seriously considering resigning. I'll have to see how the scandal plays out." He spun around and gazed out over the garden, his back momentarily turned to her.

"That's not the worst of it." He spun back to face her and in a couple of quick strides resumed his seat facing her.

"The thing I fear the most is how much it will hurt you and Alex."

She nodded, her back rigid, still showing no sign of response.

There was a long, heavy silence.

"Well. Carry on." Her voice was terse, business-like, determined to face the music. She reminded him in that moment of the girl he'd first met, daughter of a missionary family, staunch Protestants who'd gone to Hawaii to bring salvation to the Paradise Islanders. There sat the righteous young woman who'd lied to him about the death of his children because she believed it best for everyone.

Elizabeth had always had a strong moral code. And in the early years, his behavior appalled her, he was certain, though she was too polite to say so.

"When I got Alex..." He cleared his stopped-up throat and started again. "When I was offered Alex for adoption twenty years ago, it wasn't a righteous arrangement. He wasn't a poor orphan child whose parents were both dead. His father was alive, and I knew it."

Her face drained of color. "You what?"

He shook his head, unable to suppress his rising tension.

"I knew his father was alive," he said more loudly. "And I ignored it. I did nothing about it."

"Oh, Hector," she said, tears springing to her eyes. "I don't know what to say."

She brought her hands up to her face and held them there for a long minute.

When she brought them down again, she asked in an icy voice, "And did you pay for him? Did you buy him from whoever was a purveyor of defenceless children?"

Her eyes were blazing.

The words stuck in his throat.

"Well. Did you?"

He nodded, robbed of words.

And then summoned the strength to face what he'd done. The whole calamity of it.

"Yes, I did. One hundred dollars, to be exact."

She covered her mouth and sat, saying nothing for a long time.

When she looked at him, her eyes were desolate.

"I feel sick," she said. "I don't think I can handle any more of this today."

"Please, Elizabeth," he begged. "I want to explain. I want to tell you how it happened."

"You bought a child, and his father died of a broken heart. What else is there to say?"

"I know. I know. It's reprehensible. But there were extenuating circumstances."

She rocked her head.

"I'm sorry, Hector. Please. Leave now. I can't discuss this any further right now."

He rose from his seat, his bones stiff, muscles sore, barely able to support his weight.

He felt like he'd suddenly aged to eighty years old.

Forty-four

Ask Billy Ralston. Ask him if he's done any favors for his old buddy Raizney Grigor...

A sense of righteous purpose carried Sophia straight out of Hector de Vile's office, headed for the Bank of California. She was on a wave of consuming energy, capable of conquering any enemy.

But when she got out onto bustling Montgomery Street and the early lunchtime rush enfolded around her, she slowed her feet, and her confidence deflated like a popped balloon.

Ask Bill Ralston again.

The old man sounded very sure of his facts, and however much of a ruthless rogue the senator had been in getting rich, they knew him to be straight up.

And Grigor was acting strange lately. She'd given up trying to understand him. What with this carry on over his son out of nowhere, and his objecting to the way she wanted to organize the share float?

Could Grigor have pulled a fast one on her?

She sauntered back up Montgomery Street to the club, enjoying the warmth of the midday sun on her face, turning everything over in her mind.

She could be married to a wealthy Irish earl's eldest son and living the high life as mistress of all she surveyed back in New York if she'd played her cards right. If she'd ditched Grigor and set sail on her own, instead of working in tandem as they'd always done. She'd faithfully followed all his instructions in entrapping James Willoughby into the breach of promise action that had given them their first pot of gold.

Willoughby's snobby family was gagging to pay for her to just melt away; they'd been easy marks. And she and Grigor repeated that trick with differing amounts of payout another two or three times, with Grigor doing the work of identifying the target and setting it up for her. She was the one who'd got them the nest egg which enabled them to open the Imperial Club. And now he was stealing it back from right under her nose?

For what? To pass it on to Ashling's son?

By the time she reached the cool marble entryway to the Imperial Club—looking remarkably like the entryway to the Vatican library—her pleasure at the heat of the midday sun was turning into an uncomfortably fiery rage at Grigor's audacity.

They'd always trusted each other. She'd told herself they never kept secrets. She paused halfway up the stairs to the Imperial Club bar. It was early, but there would already be members there enjoying a light lunch. She had to hold herself in check and not let the mask slip for a single moment.

She was the beautiful, the mysterious Sophia Morrigan. The gossip columnists were stoking rumors she was about to marry Hector de Vile, and she was confident she could still pull that off, no matter what he'd said a short time ago.

First, though, she had to knock her long-time guardian and business partner back into shape. He had to come to terms with just who was in charge now, and it wasn't him.

#

Grigor was with Ned at the long bar when he saw Sophia enter. She was wearing the slimline French dress with the patterned gilet—one of her business outfits, so he could easily guess why she was striding defiantly toward him, her cheeks flushed red.

She'd been to the bank and discovered the money wasn't there yet. He was tiring of the way she'd been acting lately, as if she was the mastermind of everything—enlisting de Vile, harassing him for immediate payment, like this business was all her doing.

Well, she was in for a few nasty shocks, including the discovery that Hector de Vile's deposit was missing. Is that what she'd concluded? Or had she already harassed de Vile about the cash?

He felt a rush of relief that he'd lined up Billy Ralston on his side. The Bank of California president owed him a few favors, so it wasn't hard to convince him to tell a couple of small porkies on his behalf to delay her realization of what had happened. What he'd pulled off. Keeping everything shipshape. That's how he liked to live.

His back to the open room, he grinned to himself as he wiped down the glittering bottles that lined the shelves like enticing jewels and waited for her approach.

"Grigor." Her voice sounded friendly, but carried a peevish undertone.

Yep. She knows the account's empty, and she's wondering if I've got anything to do with it.

He turned around slowly, his eyes focused behind her into the middle distance, as if she'd caught him daydreaming.

"Oh, Sophia. Hi. Having a nice day?"

She sized him up through narrowed eyes.

"Nice enough," she said, with a curt edge. "You?"

"Yes, I'm fine, thanks. What's happening?"

She leaned against the public side of the bar, resting on her elbows, and regarded him.

"That's what I wanted to ask you. Got a minute?"

She nodded to the library room, the current Green Room. The singers wouldn't be in for a few hours yet, but it was still closed to members, so it was all theirs.

"Sure." With languid ease, he dropped the damp cloth he'd been wielding, wiped his hands on a dry towel and called to Ned, who was cleaning further down the long stretch of wood: "I'm out for a while, Ned. She's all yours."

And he followed Sophia to the Green Room.

#

She pulled the door closed behind them and slouched into a chair, giving a convincing display of being at full ease in the sultry afternoon.

He matched her manner, settling on the other side of the table.

She eyed him for a long minute before opening her mouth to speak.

"I went by Bill Ralston's place this morning, and discovered de Vile hasn't put his money in yet, the son of a bitch.

Billy says he hasn't seen it."

Her face opened like a flower, a sight he'd seen so often over the years when she was a child appealing to him for special favor.

"What should we do, Grigor? You're the wise old one. Can you believe it? He'd risk us exposing his secrets by not paying up?"

Her voice rose in a frustrated crescendo.

"Doesn't he think we're capable of telling the world what he's done?"

She pushed her body back and up on her two elbows as she spoke, like a hungry cat stretching her frame before the kill.

"I asked Billy twice. He denied knowing anything about it. So I went to de Vile."

For the first time since they'd entered

the small hot room, Grigor's body stiffened, and he instantly knew that, like a cat stalking a bird, she'd noticed.

"Really? De Vile? Wasn't that premature? Maybe there's just been a delay with the transfer. It happens."

She didn't reply. She watched his face closely.

Reluctantly, he followed up with the next obvious question, the one he knew she waiting for him to ask.

"So what did de Vile say, anyway?"

"He threatened to throw me out of his office."

She laughed, as if enjoying a big joke.

And then, in an instant, her mood and her expression changed.

"Oh, and he told me to ask Billy if he's done any favors for you in the last forty-eight hours."

She turned on him, like a viper rearing

up in preparedness to strike.

"So has he, Grigor? Billy? Has he been telling lies for you? Just like you've been telling lies to me for a very long time."

Grigor's heart raced, and his poor, battered lungs worked overtime to maintain steady breathing.

"Lies?" His voice broke on the one short word. "What are you talking about?"

"Yes, Billy. Lies. About that boy of Ashling's. He's your son too, isn't he? You never told me about him."

"Nothing to tell," he said defiantly. "He's got nothing to do with us."

"Is he your son? Or just some spawn of Ashling's with some other chap?"

"None of your business," he said, his voice getting dangerous.

"And did you take de Vile's money? The $30,000 that was supposed to be for his share in the club?"

"What if I did?" he said, charged with defiance, tired of having her act like some Celtic demigoddess.

"I've put my life into this place and I will not be around for much longer to draw benefits. Call it interest on my investment."

"Your investment," she scoffed.

"I'm the one who paid the price to get us started. The one who's still paying the price. Without me, we'd be going nowhere. With de Vile, we're set for the major league."

Grigor shook his head. "How many times do I have to tell you? You're dreaming, Morrigan."

He stared at her, his tarnished Madonna, and felt a rush of sadness. She really did not understand. She'd always overestimated her power because men fell at her feet in the light of her beauty. But that was not the same as wielding true power. They'd made the best of it while they could.

"Face it, Morrigan. You've lost this round. But you've still got the club. You're still earning a pretty profit. And when I'm gone, you'll have a new partner. Not de Vile. Someone you'll need to nurture along in the same way I've nurtured you."

"Oh, yes? And who's that? Jack Cabot? He wouldn't be bad. Or that friend of Jack's who was here the other night? Phillip someone?"

Was she being deliberately obtuse?

"No, no, no. Lochie O'Riordan. My son. I've had a new will drawn up. He'll inherit all my shares in everything. The club, the properties... the lot."

Her mouth gaped open. She clasped

at her chest, as if she was about to collapse in shock.

Then she rose from her chair, a coiling, hissing force from beyond the reaches of this world.

"Like hell he will," she seethed through gritted teeth.

"I'll marry de Vile before that happens."

Forty-five

When Alex answered his front door and saw Hector standing on the front steps, he knew instantly something was wrong. His father seemed to have shrunk since the last time he'd seen him. He was unsteady on his feet, and his eyes darted around Alex's face as if he was unsure of his reception.

"Father," he cried. "What's wrong? You look dreadful."

He stepped forward to take Hector's arm to support him inside, but the old man growled.

"I'm not dead yet, boy," he grumbled. "I've just had a rough day."

Alex stood back respectfully. "Oh, I

see. Well. Come in and sit down. I'll get refreshments. What would you fancy?"

Hector appeared to stumble over the threshold as he entered, and Alex didn't feel reassured until he'd got him settled in one of the leather chairs in the sitting room.

"I don't need a drink," Hector said testily. "I've already been at Elizabeth's this morning and she filled me up with lemon squash."

Must be serious, Alex thought, if he's already called on Elizabeth.

"Alex, I'm here at this minute because I have something I want to talk to you about," Hector began.

Alex smiled. "That's good, Hex, because there's been something I wanted to talk to you about too. Who goes first?"

Hector raised one eyebrow.

"Something on your mind? Pray tell."

Alex felt a queasiness in his stomach, and his tongue fattened up and so filled his mouth he had difficulty in framing his first words.

He hesitated, hemming and hawing, coughing and clearing his throat.

Hector sat back in his chair.

"I've never known you to be tongue-tied, Alex. Is something wrong?"

"No, no. Well, I don't think so, Father, that's what I wanted to check on, really."

He took an almighty breath and rolled into it. "The other day I had a spat with Graysie. I got angry because she was making preposterous suggestions, and when I objected, she wouldn't back down. In fact, she got more obstreperous the more I objected. I admit I ended up walking out on her."

Hector frowned. "That's not like you two. It seems to me you've always got on remarkably well.'

Alex felt some of his tension melt away. "That's quite right, Papa. I knew you'd understand."

"So what was the disagreement about?"

"I suppose it all started because I mentioned a few things about our last conversation—you remember when you talked to me about Grigor? I asked her about the night our mother got killed and what she told me about some of it and, well, it just all went downhill from there."

"Downhill? In what way?"

"Graysie had this ridiculous idea that we should ask you if you knew anything about that night. She made it sound as if you might know more about it than you've admitted."

He gazed at his father, as if seeking reassurance. Giving him time to interrupt and deny everything there and then. But he didn't do that.

His eyes flicked away to the window.

"I told her it was absurd, insulting even, to suggest you had any involvement. I mean, when we discovered the identity of my father—when I discovered those photographs, you remember?" He paused and his eyes sought his father's, questioning him with his eyes...

Hector sat there, dumbstruck. He didn't respond in the reassuring way Alex was hoping... expecting...

"Well. You were as surprised about it as I was, weren't you? You said nothing then, and that would have been the obvious time if you'd known anything?"

Alex couldn't help himself. His voice

rose in tone as he progressed, so that by the end he was asking a question rather than making a statement. When he finished speaking, a long, awkward silence opened up.

When Hector's voice came through, it had turned thick and rasping. It was taking him more than the usual amount of strength to get the words out. Alex could hear it in his voice.

"You're right, son. It would have been the obvious time."

He hesitated, and his face when he gazed into Alex's eyes carried deep lines of grief his son hadn't noticed before. He was usually so buoyant, his vitality must have masked them. But not now. His face carried the full weight of his fifty years, and the losses he'd borne showed.

Hector had taken another long break, as if he found it too hard to continue. He took a huge breath. "And I very much regret that I did not take the opportunity then to admit to some events from our shared past."

If a thunderclap had rung out overhead right at that moment, Alex couldn't have been more stunned. In his head, it felt like a bolt from heaven.

What is he talking about? Hector was involved with my father somehow?

His head spun as he tried to make sense of his father's vague confirmation that he hadn't been upfront.

Graysie is right. He is hiding something.

He felt sick with dizziness.

"I don't understand," Alex said, his voice wavering and questioning. "What are you talking about?" The exasperation he was feeling leaked into every word.

"There's a lot you don't know, Alex. And that's why I am here. To tell you everything before someone else does."

Forty-six

Jack waited for Pania Russell in the private dining suite on the third floor of The Old Poodle Dog restaurant on the corner of Bush and Grant Street, nervously flicking his attention around the set table, making sure everything a special guest might expect was in place.

He needn't have been anxious. The Old Poodle Dog, situated right on the edge of Chinatown, was one of the great French restaurants of the city—some said the greatest—begun in the very year of the Gold Rush, 1849, and still going strong over twenty years later.

Chefs and staff were thoroughly practiced at meeting every need a guest might express, and his lunch today was modest compared with many they had hosted.

The Dog's multi-storied building offered family dining on the ground floor, lavish banquets on the second, and sumptuous private dining suites on the upper three levels, the latter reached by a side entrance and a private birdcage elevator.

As if on cue with his roaming thoughts, he heard the elevator rumble and then the metallic slide of the screen as it stopped on this floor and the outer door rasped open.

He stepped out into the hallway to greet his guests and found Pania and John Russell exiting the lift.

"As we'd hoped, John's back in town for a few nights," Pania said. "So, it's all worked out perfectly."

Pania wore a creamy satin day dress with lace-edged sleeves flaring to the wrists from bows tied at the elbows. A narrow mauve ribbon circled her waist, falling into a broad informal bustle at the back. A small matching mauve hat perched on the front of her head, completing the chic look. At her side, her husband measured up as a fitting escort, in a simple but elegant dark slim line bespoke suit.

Jack greeted her with a light peck on each cheek in the French manner and turned to Sir John, his hand thrust out in a confirming handshake. "Sir" John topped six feet—equal in height to Jack's own—and had the groomed assurance of a man who was used to getting his own way.

But his hands were stronger and more calloused than those of the average desk-sitting magnate. His grip was firmer, too. Not your average "Rogue Baron" barking orders and leaving all the work to his lackeys, then. Jack liked him more with every passing minute.

"Pania's filled me in on the background." He flashed an open grin at Jack. "I'm not at all sure I can tell you anything useful, but I'm happy to try. It was all a rum business and none of us came out of it looking good."

Russell drew his wife closer. "As Pania knows, I'm not proud of the part I played, and I want to be assured before we even start that what we discuss will be treated in confidence."

Jack gazed into his face, and a pair of piercing eagle-black eyes stared right back at him.

"I quite understand, Sir John," he said. "None of us reach the age we have without having made choices we regret in hindsight. I know for sure there are plenty of things in my life I'd handle differently the second time round."

"I'm reassured." Russell smiled as he took off his hat and gestured to Pania to precede him into the dining suite.

"If it's fine with you, I thought we might take the table d'hôte menu," said Jack. "That's five set courses of the day—and let the staff get on with what they do best while we talk. That way, we're not distracted by the food. Does that sound good to you?"

The Russells nodded in agreement. "What fun," said Pania. "It's always great to leave it to the chef to make the recommendations. Nothing better."

Within minutes of the Russells' arrival, The Old Poodle Dog's accommodating servers offered them drinks and explained the day's menu. They'd already set the table with five-piece settings—fish knives, dessert forks and the rest of it—and they each had something to drink from one of the three glasses, plus water, that sat at each placement.

Pania took off her gloves and relaxed back with a sherry.

"Now, let's not waste any more time about getting down to business. First, maybe just give John a quick rundown."

Jack had done as Pania had suggested at their previous meeting and called by the Green Room last night after the Golden Queen's performance. Graysie had been welcoming but said she really didn't feel she had anything to add to what he already knew about the night of her mother's death.

"I was only a child, as you well know,"

she said with a faint smile. "My memories of that night are a confusion of fact and fiction. I didn't know until many years later, for example, that Eustace had anything to do with it. That he'd caused the crash with his madcap scheme to intercept my mother and persuade her to run away with him. None of us knew anything about that until recently.

"Honestly, I don't think I have any additional information that would be useful. Nothing that Pania doesn't already know. But it's possible John knows something new, because he was there and he knew the key players."

She clasped her hands in front of her. "I think it's best if we wait until John's in town and get Jack to talk to him as well."

Jack gave John a quick introduction and then they switched to less contentious topics, such as how the show at the club was going now that the season as drawing to an end—extremely well—while the staff brought in the first courses: consommé or sorrel soup followed by self-serve cold meats and salads including French imported snails, and filet of Sole with tartare sauce.

Once they'd finished their soup and were free to graze amongst the meat and salads, Jack reintroduced the reason why they were there.

"I'd like to speak frankly, and I don't want to slander anyone, so as you've already suggested, can we treat everything we say as for our ears only? That gives us the chance for a frank and open discussion."

John raised a hawkish brow. "You're getting more intriguing by the minute, Jack. Please. Proceed."

Jack took him up on the invitation, explaining about his suspicion that Hector de Vile was being blackmailed by Sophia Morrigan, and that whatever she held over him could relate back to the wider Russell family—to Graysie, Russell's sister-in-law and her half-sister and half-brother Isabella and Alex.

"I've got no personal interest in the family. I mean, I have no intention of prying," Jack assured them.

"What I'm interested in is how all of that came about, the disappearance and re-settling of the twins, I mean. I'm affected by a similar situation—not exactly the same—but the same consequences. A child alienated from her bloodline for many years. It's something that is very close to my heart. And our situation remains unresolved, unlike yours."

As he'd been speaking, the joviality John Russell had displayed when he arrived—pumped up with the excitement of seeing his wife again, perhaps—had faded, replaced with a penetrating interest. He seemed to draw back into a deep well of silence, though his eyes still glittered with attention at Jack's every word.

Pania was the first to speak. "I'm sad, and I'm sure I speak for John too—deeply saddened—to hear you speak of your own family loss," she said. "We have some understanding of what that might involve. We've both, in different ways, lost people dear to us, and when they are unexpectedly restored, it's the most marvellous thing."

She turned to her husband.

"You know a lot more about this than I do, John, though whether we've got anything that could help Jack is maybe doubtful."

She hesitated. "It's an odd coincidence that I had a talk with Graysie about this same thing only a day or two ago. I find that disturbing."

Russell turned his gimlet eyes on his wife. "The same thing? What exactly?"

Pania paused as the waitstaff arrived to refill glasses, clear away plates and bring more dishes, and then resumed.

"Graysie says Hector made some vague remarks to Alex about Grigor. How he might somehow know something about Elanora's death and the subsequent events. Something that has never come out. That was the impression Alex got from de Vile, anyway."

Russell stiffened in his chair. "Really." The tone of the word was downward, and Jack caught the remnant of a blue blood

English accent, a leftover from his childhood as the son of a Scottish merchant and servant of Empire to the English queen, Victoria.

"That's not all. When we were talking it over, we remembered that odd incident in Grass Valley a couple of years ago, when Graysie was staying at Gold House and Minette went missing. Do you recall that, John?"

"Never forget it," said John with alacrity. "I've a secret fear of it happening again, with Robert, our own lad."

"What was that about?" Jack sensed there was a lot more to it than they were saying.

Pania ignored him and gave her husband a direct, burrowing stare. "You know, a repeat of that disaster is highly unlikely, John. For two reasons. Madame

Ring is no longer a player. And neither is de Vile."

Russell screwed up his mouth, as if preparing to dispute with his wife.

She stared at him, saying nothing, until he broke eye contact.

Pania's eyes darted to Jack, full of meaning.

"Nothing was ever proved, but it was all a bit too coincidental for our liking."

That word again. Jack didn't believe in coincidence.

"Tell me about the coincidence."

"Minette disappeared from John's house in the middle of the night. They probably subdued her beforehand. We concluded it was impossible for a four-year-old to have just wandered off under her own steam.

"Thanks to Nathan's connections with the Chinese hotel staff—the Russell boys all picked up some Cantonese when they lived in Hong Kong—he found her the next day, hidden in the cellars at the Exchange Hotel. The place was run by an old crony of de Vile's and she was blamed for the entire episode. She was gunned down a few days later, but Nathan's always believed she didn't act alone.

"He believed she was the scapegoat. Our suspicions fell on Hector. He was a majority owner at the hotel—Ring only had her job there by his favor. And he was intent on bullying Graysie into selling him a gold mine she'd inherited.

"Threatening the child seemed like a calculated way to frighten her. To force her to abandon the idea of working the mine and get out of Grass Valley. Most single woman facing a man like that would have dropped it all and run."

"And did she? Abandon the mine, I mean."

"On the contrary, her conviction that it was worth continuing to explore has paid off a thousand times over. The Ophir is bringing in excellent returns up till today."

Jack sat back and set down his fork as the Poodle Dog server returned. "Ready for dessert, sir?"

"Give us another ten minutes," said Jack. "Then we will be." He turned back to his guests.

"That's a horrible story. Let me get this straight. Hector de Vile was a party to kidnapping a child for leverage and extortion. Not to put too fine a point on it. And this was what—three years ago?"

Russell nodded, a dark cloud over his face.

"That's what it amounts to, yes. But

we had no proof. There were other undesirables in the mix—some fellow from Sydney with a grudge against Nathan. It could have been all his work. But probably unlikely. And totally unprovable."

"And what about the earlier episode involving the twins?

"That's even more nebulous," Russell said, glancing uncertainly as his wife.

"How so?" asked Jack.

"Well, we all know now that Elanora and Rafael's twins disappeared from the stagecoach accident site in the hours before the rescuers reached them. For years there was speculation wild animals had taken them.

"Elanora was friendly with Bertha, another playgirl, who'd help her out with the children and go out for coffee with her when Rafael was away on his work trips. And Bertha was friendly with de Vile—more than friendly. I think they were romantically involved for a while."

John Russell's dark gaze roamed from Jack to Pania. "If you're suggesting Sophia has got something over de Vile, and de Vile is hinting it relates to the children, then I'd be wondering if Bertha was involved somehow. She's the common factor.

"She knew them all, and within a few weeks of the crash Bertha's sister and de Vile are 'coincidentally'"—Russell made quotation marks with his index fingers—"both 'adopting' orphaned children of vague origin. I'd be asking myself if Bertha was on the stagecoach with Elanora and saw the opportunity to take the children and run. Hard to believe. But possible."

Russell, who Jack guessed was

normally a controlled man, threw up his hands in disbelief.

Pania chimed in. "To be honest, we have wondered privately in the middle of the night if de Vile knew where Alex came from. We found out twenty years later that he got him from Bertha—and you have to wonder how much she told him at the time they arranged it. We've never wanted to question it openly because of Graysie.

"We felt she should be able to enjoy her elation over finding her siblings again without us raising too many questions. And Bertha's long dead and gone. We can't ask her."

Jack nodded. "So the question is, did Hector know who Alex was when he adopted him?"

Pania nodded. "At the time the twins were 'found,' both de Vile and Bertha's sister Huldah, Isabella's stepmother, claimed Bertha told them the twin's parents were dead. They'd perished in a snowstorm or drowned or some such vague story. That's quite believable. Those kinds of things happened all the time in those years. People getting caught out in terrible weather.

"But did Hector know the truth? Did he pay Bertha for Alex? Did he know Alex's father was alive and pining for him? You just can't imagine it. But is that how it happened? I don't know the answers to those questions. Maybe the only person alive who knows is Hector himself."

Jack interceded. "Or Grigor. Do you think he could have had something to do with it?"

Jack made the question sound like a casual inquiry, but he'd lit up with a burning conviction, deep inside.

His sister was a party girl. Just the sort to drift into circles frequented by the Berthas of this world. That's how she'd got snared by gambling man Dan "Dandy" Durkan.

He'd just got one step closer to finding how Cordelia was stolen from him, he was sure of it.

And the buzz within was better than any opium high.

Forty-seven

Hector stared at his son's lovely, artless face and saw his usual open beauty clouded with dark suspicion.

"Before someone else does? What are you talking about? You mean you wouldn't be doing this except under duress?"

Alex jumped up from his chair and turned away, so Hector couldn't see his face.

The silence stretched between them, increasing the emotional distance the longer it hung there.

Finally Alex swung around, his face thunderous.

"So, Graysie was right all along?

You've been keeping secrets all this time? And I thought she was being unfair to you…"

He gave a bitter half laugh.

"Well, let's get it all out now, Hex." Using his pet name had a heavy, ironic edge. "Leave nothing under the carpet, please. What else do you want to tell me 'before someone else does'?"

"And who is the 'someone else' anyway? Can I guess? Grigor? Or Sophia, by any chance?"

His countenance crumpled in disbelief.

"I trusted you," he protested, and it sounded like an accusation.

De Vile's heart felt like he had been stabbed. He wished he had been, if he could spare Alex this pain.

"I wasn't on the coach. So no, I wasn't there when it crashed. I was not a witness. I saw nothing. I was miles away in Sacramento, waiting for its arrival, along with your father, but I didn't know him then.

"We were just two men, waiting for a coach that never came. He, of course, was waiting for his family. I was waiting for Bertha, a friend of your mother's and mine, who was traveling on the same coach, giving Elanora a hand with you children, something she did frequently in those years."

Alex glared at him, and then resignedly slid back into his seat, as if he was being forced to listen to a story he didn't want to hear.

"When you were overdue by several hours, we set up a search party and went out looking for you. It was hours later, in lashing rain—it was a horrible night—when we came upon the wreckage.

"It was immediately clear that Elanora was dead, and that Bertha and you children were missing. Your father was utterly vanquished. No other word for it. He was practically cataleptic with shock and grief. We sent him back to Sacramento with Elanora's body and Graysie while the rest of us set up a search party to look for you."

"And Bertha," Alex said in a hollow, bitter voice.

"Yes," de Vile said quietly. "And Bertha. As you now know, our search was fruitless. There was no sign of you. We rode far and wide until well into the next day. Then there was nothing else we could do but return to town empty-handed."

He paused, gazing at Alex, who was hunched forward, watching him closely, reading every line in his face. De Vile's throat was tight and dry. He regretted turning down the offer of a glass of water.

"So, what then?" said Alex, a resigned note in his voice, as if someone had forced him to take bitter medicine.

"I did what I could for Rafael, but he was past help. The woman who rented him his lodgings was looking after Graysie. The shock destroyed Rafael. He couldn't eat, couldn't work. I had to walk away, Alex."

Alex stared blankly, refusing to soften into understanding.

Hector sighed. He deserved this, and much worse.

"I completed my business and went back to San Francisco. When I got there, I found Bertha, living with her sister Huldah. And with her, she had you and Isabella. Huldah had already taken over

Isabella. And Bertha wanted me to take you."

Alex pitched over, holding his chest.

"So you knew all the time! You knew who I was. You knew my father!" His cry was like a knife in de Vile's side.

"How could you?"

"Alex, I know I should have said something sooner, and I'm sorry. But try to see it from my viewpoint. You were safe, well fed, and well cared for. I could give you a good life. And your father was overwhelmed looking after Graysie and grieving for his wife. It made plain good sense."

Alex looked at him belligerently.

"And I suppose the fact that it gave you an enormous advantage in claiming your family legacy had nothing to do with it," Alex spat out. "Tell me, did you pay Bertha for us? Did she ask for money in return?"

De Vile felt the blood drain from his face back to his madly pumping heart.

The question he found hardest of all to answer, to justify.

A weighted silence hung between them.

"I paid for you, Alex. Yes. Bertha always wanted coin."

He gazed at his son, his eyes wet with tears.

"And it was the best one hundred dollars I ever spent, son. I'd make it a thousand if I had the chance to do it all over again."

He stood shakily as Alex curled his hands into fists and pressed them into his eye sockets, as if he no longer wanted to see his father or the world he inhabited

"Sophia Morrigan is trying to blackmail me, Alex." De Vile's voice was hoarse with pleading.

"She is threatening to blacken my name by making it look like I colluded with Bertha to abduct you. I want to make it clear: Bertha acted alone. I had nothing to do with the original abduction. But I went along with providing you with a new home. And with not telling your father you were still alive. I understand now wrong that was. And how painful that would have been for him."

He leaned heavily on his walking stick.

"I hope we can get over this, Alex. You are the most precious thing in my life. Far beyond lands, or dollars or status. Raising you is the best thing I've ever done, even if it has proven to be a house built on sand."

Alex did not raise his head. Did not utter a word. So Hector de Vile walked out of his son's life, holding himself as erect as he could in his crumbling grief.

Forty-eight

Perhaps it was the loosening effect of the third glass of lunchtime wine, or the false sense of security that comes with eating good food, that sense that the world is a loving, nurturing place and nothing will ever go wrong again.

But somewhere after the Old Poodle Dog's staff had cleared away the dishes and leftovers of the third course—mains of braised chicken casserole, liver brochette and duck—and they were waiting out a slight hiatus while dessert arrived, Pania got to ask Jack a question that had been needling her since her first talk with him.

"Jack, do you mind me asking? This

personal family loss that you've mentioned. Could you tell us a little more about that? And what could we do to bring it to some conclusion?"

Jack shot her a one-sided smile. "You've been very understanding in allowing all your family business to be exposed to examination," he said. "I guess I can only expect to reciprocate."

He was trying gamely to make light of it, but his eyes lost their sparkle, even as he spoke.

"I had a sister, Tasmin—I called her Tammy—who sounds a lot like Bertha. She was a frivolous young thing, attracted to parties, crazy adventures and the wrong people."

He shook his head and gave another smile, a sad one this time.

"And listen to her big brother talk, seeing the way I've been living my life the last few years. As if I've been a shining example."

He glimpsed the servers bringing in dessert—a selection of fruit tarts and chocolate fancies served with coffee.

"Ah. Something to sweeten our talk. Much needed, I'm afraid," he joked.

"She got lured into eloping with Dan Dandy Durkan, a black sheep from our own circles back East, who, as you might guess from the nickname, always assumed the garb of a gentleman even if he didn't act like one.

"His family pushed him into a military career—he was a third son and the oldest one had inherited everything—so they sent him to West Point. But Dan fancied himself as a poker player, not a soldier. He convinced Tammy to run away to the West on their grand adventure."

He shook his head. "I feel some responsibility for that. I think she copied me by turning her back on the family fortunes—but as you will have already picked up, things didn't go so well..."

Pania nodded consolingly. "Surprising that. Don't worry. I've seen many a girl like Tammy who thinks life out West will be one of freedom and adventure, all excitement and good fun. They probably end up in much the same place as your sister."

"Yep. A delightful bubba at home and a husband who is out most of the night."

Jack grimaced.

"Tammy's Cordelia—her daughter—was the recompense for all this, of course. I saw a lot of her in those four years after her birth, dropping by to make sure they were fed and cared for. I fell in love with Cordelia, I have to admit.

She was a little treasure."

Jack sighed and stared down at his coffee.

"When Tammy died suddenly from a fever, I talked to 'Dandy' Durkan about letting me take over as her stepfather or guardian. Dandy had no interest in or talent for rearing a daughter, and my parents had withheld Tammy's dowry, so there was no money in it for him."

Jack's face was a mask of pain. "But no such luck. Through some unknown intermediary, he sold her to fancy schmanzy New Yorkers who had everything they wanted in life except a child. They shipped out on the next train, in a manner of speaking.

"We've not seen or heard from her in six years. The last time I saw her, she was crying for me on the railway platform seconds before a white-uniformed nanny headed for New York whisked away with her."

John Russell clenched his jaw, as if Jack's story required special strength to listen to. The table fell silent and then John commented in a quiet voice: "This is a quest. A passion for you, Jack, isn't it?" He spoke slowly, the words laced with understanding and sympathy.

"You want to find who is behind these awful transactions, where they treat children like merchandise. It won't be Bertha responsible this time, but whoever it is, you want to know and stop them."

Jack picked up a tray of tarts and offered them to Russell in response. "You understand it perfectly, John. My aim is to identify, and if I can do it, stop them.

"They must be a tight little circle of conspirators, don't you think? I mean, I know children barely have any rights under our law as it stands, but surely the milk of human kindness still operates? If they were exposed, maybe they'd stop doing it."

"'They?'" Pania said, with emphasis. "Have you got any suspicions who 'they' might be?"

"I honestly don't, although a friend with very good networks into the underworld suggests Sophia Morrigan might be one who'd wouldn't mind getting her hands dirty if there's money involved. And I wondered if by any chance Sophia knew, or learned, a thing or two from Bertha all those years ago."

John Russell gazed at him.

"You could be onto something there, Jack. As I might have mentioned earlier, Grigor and Sophia arrived in San Francisco around the time Elanora died. Grigor was one of Bertha's friends. In fact, they lived in the same lodging house at one time—the three of them—Bertha, Sophia and Morrigan. It was only a temporary thing, as I recall. Bertha moved on. She never stayed in one place for very long. But they certainly knew each another."

Jack's eyes sparked for the first time since he'd launched into his story.

"I *thought* we might be onto something…"

"Sophia is blackmailing Hector over something that happened a long time ago… something possibly involved with Elanora's death. What if that something was that he colluded in abducting the twins, knowing their father was still alive? I mean, even that is probably not against California law, but what would the voters think if it ever got out? And would his son ever talk to him again?"

Forty-nine

Here Grigor was, back at the Cobweb Palace, but this time he was waiting for Jack Cabot, not Hector de Vile.

De Vile.

The man's very name stuck in his craw.

As he tapped the table impatiently in between taking pulls of his draught beer, Grigor argued in his head about the situation he faced.

Sophia was already swanning around as if she was a society hostess in Washington.

I suppose if she's back East, she won't be messing with Lochie.

Don't worry. That won't stop her. Not

if she's got a big name like Hector de Vile at her side. She'll run roughshod over everyone.

He cast a glance around the palace, which was pleasantly empty before the lunchtime rush which would come soon. Out on the sidewalk, tourists ogled the cages of bears and rainbow-colored parrots and macaws with foot-long tails.

But still no sign of Cabot. Grigor was here in response to a mysterious note from Jack hand delivered to the club, for his eyes only.

If he hasn't turned up by the time I've finished this pint, I'm leaving.

And as if on cue, Jack Cabot sauntered in with one of the palace's tame monkeys on his shoulder. When he spotted Grigor, he made straight for him, paused before the table and set his arm out at right angles. The beast scampered down it and alighted beside Grigor's beer as if to say, "Well? Are you going to offer me some?"

Grigor was leaning his elbows on a chest-high table.

"Very well-behaved animals he's got here," said Jack with appreciation. "Better than most of the children I see."

Grigor laughed.

"Spoken like a true bachelor," he said. "Can I get you a pint?"

Jack shook his head.

"Iced water will do nicely, thanks."

Grigor raised his hand for a carafe and a serving maid appeared like magic and poured them both a glass of water.

"So what gives?" said Grigor, with no buildup. "What's so urgent you wanted to meet here?"

Jack took a long glug of iced water and slapped the glass back down on the table.

He wiped his lips with the back of his hand.

"My, that's good. I was so dry." He searched Grigor's impassive face.

"Sorry," he said. "Let's get down to business."

"Good idea," Grigor said. "Get on with it."

Jack searched his features for a long minute, as if trying to read his deeper thoughts.

"I get the powerful feeling you can't stand Hector de Vile's guts," Jack began, reading his eyes as he spoke. "But I'm not entirely certain why that is."

He gazed over the room and then came back to him.

"He's an arch rogue in my book, too. I wondered if we might work together on getting rid of him."

"'Getting rid' in what way?" asked Grigor.

"Not as in beating the living daylights
out of him, so he no longer draws
breath," said Jack.

"Just as in 'make life so damned
uncomfortable, he's got no option but to
withdraw from public life and
disappear.'"

Grigor scowled. "Chance would be a
fine thing," he said.

Jack pounced. "But that's just it. From
what I understand, you already have
something on him. You can create your
chance."

Grigor's scowl deepened.

"What gives you that idea?"

"A lot of things. The way Sophia is
hanging off his arm for starters. He's got
designs on the Countess, as far as I
understand it. He wouldn't be putting up
with your piece of fluff for another
second, pardon the expression, unless

she had something over him."

He stared long and hard into Grigor's eyes. "Despite the gossip columns puffing it out as the love story of the month, it will not happen."

Grigor felt a wave of disquiet rattle through him.

"My piece of fluff?" He glared, knowing that his eyes were more glacial than ever.

"I thank you to speak of Sophia with more respect."

Jack waved him away with a calm hand.

"Grigor, let's not doodle around here. If Hector can have Elizabeth Westerhoven, why is he wasting his time on Sophia Morrigan? It makes little sense unless she's blackmailing him. So I'm asking you. What have you got on him?"

"What's it to you?" Grigor asked.

"Why are you so keen to take him down?"

Jack gave him a long, calculating look.

"I want to nose out if there's any truth in the rumor that he's involved in buying and selling children. And if he is, by God, I'll get him for it."

"Ahhh," said Grigor, his innards warming with satisfaction. "Why didn't you say so at the beginning? You've come to exactly the right place then."

Fifty

The years since Tammy's death had been cruel to Dan "Dandy" Durkan. That much was clear to Elizabeth as she eyed the droopy-lipped, balding man sitting opposite her on a mosaic-topped table in Kate Buchanan's parlor.

Around them, visiting gentlemen and Kate's "ladies" murmured stilted conversations against a backdrop of clinking glasses and the gracious sounds of a string quartet anchored in the center of the room under potted palms. Kate's establishment was nothing if not refined, Elizabeth thought with an inner smile.

Durkan had once fully deserved his handsome sobriquet "Dandy." But no longer. It wasn't just his thinning hair, the lifeless parchment complexion, the bulging belly that hung over shapeless trousers.

His pale gray eyes, once dancing and lively, now sat hollow and dead in their sockets. The once finely sculpted mouth was slack and expressionless, the skin on his lips dry and flaky. He exuded an aura of unkempt hopelessness.

And no wonder. Elizabeth had it on good authority from Kate's house manager Jake Bernstein that Dan was up to his eyeballs in debt to a notorious poker boss. Unless he paid up in twenty-four hours, Dan Dandy Durkan was likely to be found dead in one of the city's Barbary Coast back allies, a slug in his skull and no one, especially not the cops, curious about how it got there.

Elizabeth hooked a finger to summon

the bartender. "Another whiskey for my friend," she said. "He's especially thirsty tonight."

Dan gave her a death skull smile that had no humor in it.

"Funny lady," he said. "I bet you're enjoying this."

She exhaled a long, tired breath.

"Dan, I don't take pleasure in seeing others fall into trouble. But if anyone deserves it, you do."

His dead fish eyes flicked up in half a heartbeat. Not so demoralized as to be blind to his situation, she thought.

"We needn't pretend we're friends, do we, Dan? We never were and never will be friends. So let's cut to the chase. I'm here because you're in desperate need of money if you're to keep breathing for longer than the next twenty-four hours. And I'm willing to pay you for information. Good information."

She eyeballed him, her mouth set in a hard line.

"If you tell me lies, sling the hatchet, talk twaddle, or gild the pill, then I'll find out and I'll make sure your poker boss man hears about it, don't you doubt it. You know the score."

She'd worked enough years in these shady communities to have earned respect from the most unlikely fellows, and Durkan knew it. His already pasty face turned a shade paler.

"Who did you sell Cordelia to? And who managed the transaction? That's all. Two names and you can go back to driving yourself into an early grave."

She paused and stared at him. "Just make very sure they're the right ones, or we'll find out and come after you."

Dan Durkan made a choking noise in

his throat and his head swivelled around nervously.

"No one is listening." Elizabeth said. "The men here have other things on their minds. Spit it out, Dan. I'm not waiting all night."

She hesitated and drew her reticule from where it rested on the foot of her chair. She opened it up and drew out a notebook and pencil.

"Better still, write the names for me. Then I won't forget them."

She pushed the notepad across the table to him.

He hesitated, reaching for his glass. He brought it to his lips and swallowed noisily.

Then he picked up the pencil and began writing.

Fifty-one

Jack eased his back against one of the spouts in the Imperial Spa's tiled tub and groaned with pleasure as the hot flow massaged around his neck and over his shoulders.

Lounging an hour away in a private pool with Grigor certainly had its compensations,

His eyes ranged over the domed ceiling and around the walls, lit with candles in bricked niches. The lovely dim light was soothing on his eyes. The fragrance of lavender and eucalyptus that rose from the water was at once invigorating and relaxing. It would have been an all-around sublime experience, if it wasn't for the contentious issues being tossed back and forth between them.

This was their third session of talking and they were coming close to either hammering out an agreement or walking away from it altogether. Which was why they were lolling around in a private pool going over the same old ground.

"I want the dirt on Sophia and her activities with children," said Jack, fighting to keep the hint of impatience out of his voice. "Is she selling them to the highest bidder? Sending them into positions of lifelong servitude? That's what I want to know.

"And you? You want to scotch the idea of Hector and Sophia as a couple, and to see your son Lochie protected from the Warrior Queen if anything happens to you. Have I got that in a nutshell?"

"If anything happens?" said Grigor

acerbically. "I keep telling you, my end is not far off. So get ready."

Grigor was looking haggard, Jack had to admit. He watched as the Irishman ran one of the pleasantly abrasive scoria stones provided down his arm, from shoulder to wrist, while the hot water dripped through his fingers.

Since their "meeting of minds" session at the Cobweb Palace a few days ago, Jack realized he didn't really care about de Vile, apart from anything pertaining to the mistreatment of children. And Grigor seemed to care about de Vile the most, mainly because he feared if Sophia and Hector joined forces, Lochie's interests would be at serious risk.

"I keep telling you, I've made it my business not to know Sophia's business," Grigor said, sounding tetchy. "Slavery of any kind is repugnant to me. You can't stand on the ramparts for workers' rights as I did in my youth and support slavery of any kind. Sophia's father died on those ramparts. Whether or not that matters to her, it matters to me."

Jack sank his shoulders under the velvety water and asked himself once again if he was wasting his time. From what he could see so far, it was all rather one-sided.

Grigor was desperate to provide for and protect Lochie. Despite his brave-faced insistence of his imminent death, he'd left estate planning too much till the last minute.

By his own admission, Lochie was an artist like his mother, not a businessman. Grigor had not only omitted giving him any estate management training, he'd also kept his very existence secret from the woman who would be his business partner, Sophia Morrigan.

"Tell you what, Grigor. I'll step up as a guardian for Lochie's business interests if you set aside a share of the estate for me to use in pursuing child traffickers. How about that? Does that sound fair?"

Grigor's eyes glimmered with humor. "You're a cheeky cove, I'll grant you that," he said with a grin. "But you know, that's not a bad idea."

Grigor rolled onto his back and gazed up at the ceiling, as if in a trance. "There's one other thing I could do to make looking after Lochie worth your while, and that's give you the bracelet Bertha took from Elanora's son before she sold him to de Vile."

Jack rose like the biblical sea monster Leviathan, water streaming off his body.

"You what?" He was in shock. He'd

been banging on about child labor for days, and this was the first time Grigor had mentioned anything about de Vile and the exchange of coin.

Grigor grinned across in delight, and Jack saw the flash of his odd, pointed gold tooth as it caught the light. Like a cunning old shark, he thought. Hold on to the best until just before the point of fracture.

"Explain that to me, Grigor. Why have I been wasting my time? What bracelet? What sale?"

Grigor laughed uproariously, perfectly aware he'd saved the best till last.

Before he could explain, the heavy oak door into their cubical pushed open, and a shadowy figure stepped into the intimate space.

A chiming, like a sweetly sonorous alert, sounded inside Jack's head. He'd seen that girl before, at the club. She'd caught his attention for all the wrong reasons. Too young. Too vulnerable. And too sophisticated.

Hair as pale as ash, nearly as white as Grigor's. A fine, solemn face, with sharp cheekbones and elegantly arched brows. She wore a simple white tunic and clasped her hands in front of her body, as if to anchor her nervousness.

Grigor responded sharply. "What is it, Isla?"

She stared into the darkness, her relief at not having to progress any further into their private space, clearly discernible on her features.

"Madame Sophia says she needs to talk to you urgently," the girl said.

She stood rigid, as if uncertain what to do or say next.

"Thank you. That will be all," said

Grigor, and turned back to Jack.

There was a long moment of silence between them.

Then Jack said, "Who was that?"

"Oh, just one of Sophia's helpers," Grigor said with a shrug.

"One of her helpers? Helpers to do what?"

She wasn't a cleaner or a kitchen hand. The marrow in his bones told him so.

Grigor shrugged. "I don't really know, to be honest. I keep out of it."

Not any longer, you don't. Not if you want me to be your young Lochie's champion and defender.

Jack sunk beneath the water and let out a succession of satisfied bubbles.

When he surfaced, he grinned like a cheeky monkey.

"You'd better see what the Angel of

Death wants," he said. "Can't keep the Warrior Queen waiting."

He laughed at Grigor's answering scowl.

"I think we're making some progress at last," he said. His arms, his legs, felt newly invigorated, despite the deep relaxation of the soak they'd just enjoyed.

"Next step, you'd better introduce me to Lochie."

Fifty-two

**A Telegraph to the Rev. Teddy
Kalama: Kalama Legal Chambers, 52.
West Street, New York City.**

URGENT

**Request regarding health and
wellbeing of Cordelia Susannah
Cabot, granddaughter of Ebezener
and Alcesta Cabot. STOP**

Mr. Dear Teddy,

**Cordelia went missing six years ago
after sudden death of her mother
Tasmin Sanderson Cabot. Believe**

child then aged four years old sold to an unknown family of an unknown location, possibly somewhere in New York. STOP

New information shows she resides with Thomas and Sylvia Carterton, at 99A Fifth Avenue, New York City. STOP

Can you please investigate whether Cordelia is still at this address with her "adoptive" parents, and advise of her general health and wellbeing? Her uncle, Jacob Mortimer Cabot of San Francisco (known to our family), urgently requests details. Your loving cousin, Elizabeth. Matthew 25:40 STOP.

Teddy's reply came back immediately:

The King will reply, "Truly I tell you,
whatever you did for one of the least
of these brothers and sisters of
mine, you did for me."

Fifty-three

"So, where exactly are we?"

Jack gazed around him in wonder. They'd taken a short train ride south of downtown and the Mission District, but he felt as if he was in a different country. Behind him rose a rugged hillside dotted with golden California poppies. Eagles and hawks circled in the air high above their heads, riding hot thermal draughts.

Below him lay a rural landscape of unsealed roads, a few fine houses but mostly modest cottages, cows grazing on the tough native grass, and vegetable lots of squash and sweet peppers.

"Bernal," said Grigor with a hint of pride. "I bought a five-acre lot here in

1862. Nearly ten years ago. It was part of one of the original Spanish grants owned by José Bernal.

"Lots of us Irish Micks bought here. I suppose that's why the Catholics built St. Mary's College out here three years ago."

His arm pointed to the horizon. "Military engineers laid it out during the Civil War, so they named lots of the streets after generals."

He stood sideways and made a sweeping gesture. "Welcome to Bernal Heights."

They were standing in front of a simple two-story cottage with a sharply sloped V-shaped roof and a balustraded upstairs balcony.

Grigor knocked on the door and the copper-headed youth Jack had glimpsed at the Golden Queens concert stood in the opened doorway.

"Grigor." Lochie's face lit up with a delighted grin. "What are you doing here? Come in." He peered over Grigor's shoulder and noticed Jack standing in the shadows. Delight turned to confusion. Grigor grabbed Jack's arm and raised it.

"Lochie, this is Jack Cabot. It's important that you two get to know each other. I'll explain when we sit down."

Jack stepped forward and proffered his hand. "Nice to meet you, Lochie." He hesitated. "As Grigor says, he'll explain everything."

They passed into a spacious main room. Brilliant light from generous-sized windows lit a dazzling display of paintings—watercolors of delicate artistry and gemlike colors sang from the walls like a harmonious choir. They framed a multitude of flowers and fruit, still life studies that vibrated with the joy of creation.

Jack stopped in his tracks and stared. A lump formed in his throat, a choking recognition that while he'd buried himself in self-pity in scabrous dives, someone was creating works which shone with unquestioning joy at life's inevitable ebb and flow.

He saw a kaleidoscope of flowers, some in fresh bud, others dropping their last petals in the final stage of senescence. On one wall, a stunning night picture, an owl on a branch under a glittering sky, held pride of place. Everywhere the eye turned, there was something new to see. He could spend a day looking at the work around him and not tire of it.

His eyes were wet. How many years had he wasted while this artist was watching creation blossom in its every hour?

Grigor's usually austere face was soft and proud. "Ashling never lived here. She died before I had the chance to buy this place. But this is the sum total of her life's work, with some of Lochie's slowly being added to it."

Their moment of quiet reverence was broken by the bustling arrival of a rotund matron from an adjoining room Jack took to be the kitchen.

This must be the woman Daphne mentioned, who kept things going after Ashling died. What was her name?

"Ahh, Mr. Grigor! You didn't say you were coming or I could have made something special for lunch!"

"Nan Waters, meet my friend Jack Cabot. And don't worry. We're here to see Lochie. We don't need feeding."

"Of course yah need feeding," she exclaimed with an Irish lilt. "Whoever heard of not feeding men?"

Her face was as brown, round and wrinkled as a walnut, and she had an explosive merry laugh. Tanned and muscular forearms protruded from a white pinafore apron. He knew immediately she would keep and milk a cow and dig potatoes with equal relish.

She was all bustle as she insisted they sit and allow her to bring in coffee and bread and cheese. "Made it myself this morning," she said with a wide smile, and Jack wasn't sure if she was referring to the bread, the cheese or both.

By the time Lochie had taken them on a quick guided tour of the garden, which contained exactly the sort of overflowing vegetable plot Jack would have expected from Nan Waters, coffee and a

Ploughman's lunch with pickled gherkins and onion jam was awaiting them.

They'd dulled the edge of their appetite before Grigor paused with a sense of ceremony and spoke.

"I know you'll be wondering why I brought Jack here today, my boy. When I look back over time, I haven't been here often enough, and for that I offer my regrets."

Lochie shrugged. "I know you've got business in town, Grigor. Don't apologize. We get on pretty happily here. Nan's a wonder."

"I know, I know, boy. But I've got things we need to discuss. Things that are going to affect your life soon."

He rubbed his face wearily and Jack saw the day was taking its toll on his friend. There were dark circles under his eyes Jack couldn't remember seeing earlier.

"Jack is a man I trust. He's got experience that you lack, in the world and in business. I've never brought you alongside and given you a business education, and you're going to need it. Jack will be the one I want you to use as a close confidante in all things to do with money, in particular."

Lochie's brow furrowed, and his eyes narrowed in concern.

"Why the big speech, Old Man?" He grinned with affection. "You're the money magician. I don't need anyone else for that."

A long pause followed, interrupted only by the subdued clink of the knife on the plate as Jack cut another piece of cheese.

"Thing is, Lochie, I won't be here forever. Not even for much longer."

Lochie's Adam's apple jerked in his throat.

"What are you saying, Old Man?"

"Lochie, I'm ill. Very ill. I'm sad to say I won't be around much longer to guide you. And I've left it all a bit too late to make the plans I should have made."

Lochie's face lit with up alarm.

"What do you mean? You're as tough as old boots, Grigs. You always have been."

"Not for much longer, son. I haven't been the father I wish I'd been, and I'm running out of time to become a better one."

He spread his fingers wide on the table edge, making a play at cracking hearty.

"What do they say? 'All good things come to an end.'"

Lochie half rose from his seat. "No! I don't want to hear this." He brought his hands over his ears protectively.

Grigor gazed at him with a sad smile of understanding. "Sit down, my dear boy. This is the day you become a man. I'm leaving you in the best possible situation, and in the safest pair of hands."

Lochie hesitated, and then reluctantly sank back down into his chair.

"We're going to go over things with you. I'm proud to say I will leave you well provided for, but that will disappear in a puff of smoke if not managed wisely. That's where Jack comes in.

"I want you to be reassured. Everything is taken care of. You'll be able to continue with your work as an artist undisturbed. I believe you will be just as brilliant as your mother someday. You'll hardly notice I'm gone."

Lochie's head dropped to his chest. He clutched his throat and silently sobbed.

Fifty-four

Grigor returned from Bernal Heights worn out but warmed by an inner sense of quiet elation. At last, he was doing what he should have done months ago. He was ensuring his personal legacy as he wanted it. When he drew his last breath, he could do it with a sense of completion.

He'd filled up on Nan's fresh-baked bread and cheese and had only wanted a cup of hot milky tea when he entered the dining room in Sophia's private apartment that they shared for most meals.

Best to put in an appearance and reassure her he was following his usual routine, he surmised. He'd pushed the buzzer to summon Scottie O'Callaghan when Sophia sauntered in dressed for dinner in what he laughingly described as her Tsarina dress—a heavily brocaded dusky ice-blue evening gown with gray pearl buttons down the front and a bright Ming blue sash across the shoulder, anchored at the waist with a big diamond brooch.

"Goodness, special occasion, is it?" Grigor asked.

"I'm out for dinner," Sophia said, a haughty distance in her voice. "You weren't around to ask."

"You don't have to ask me," said Grigor with a breathy laugh. "I've had a busy day, so I thought I might get an early night."

"Oh. So what's kept you so busy?"

"I had property issues to sort out," Grigor said vaguely.

"Property issues? What property?"

"Stuff you don't need to know about," said Grigor bluntly

She tapped the table with her fan. "Oh, it's like that, is it? More secrets."

"We've never lived in each other's pockets, Sophia. There are plenty of things you do I know nothing about, I'm sure."

"Like what?" She eyed him coldly, continuing her impatient tapping.

"Well, now you mention it. Where you found Isla, for example? And why do we need a girl like her, anyway? She should be in school."

"My, my, we are on our high horse tonight. Just for the record, education in not compulsory in California. And anyway, she's learning more useful life lessons with me."

Avoiding answering the question, he

saw. He tried another tack.

"It's unnecessary to send a young girl like her into a private spa where men are bathing. What was so urgent, anyway? I was going to take that up with you yesterday, but when I got back here, you were nowhere to be found."

"I've got my private business to attend to just as much as you do," she said, her jaw locking tight.

"Right. So that's what Isla is? Private business?"

"Keep your nose out of it, Grigor. You've never been interested before."

She picked up the bead-covered reticule she'd dropped on the table when she walked in, turned her back, and stalked out.

She's right, thought Grigor. *There's been a ribbon of girls like Isla who've passed through our portals, and I haven't bothered to ask about any of them before.*

#

Grigor stood in the middle of Sophia's bedroom and allowed his eyes to swivel from one wall to the other. Where would she keep the bone bracelet Bertha had given her? Or that she more than likely stole from Bertha?

Start with the most obvious, and work from there, he thought. *If you're wrong, you've still got plenty of time. Goodness knows what she's off doing, but she's taken a lot of trouble getting dressed for it. She's expecting she'll be out for the night.*

His gaze fell on her dressing table, and his eye caught the carved rosewood jewelry box he'd given her as an eighteenth birthday present, along with drop pearl earrings to put in it. He wondered if she still had those earrings.

He crossed the room in two strides and gently opened the decorative brass latch.

Gingerly, he fingered through its contents, memorizing them as he went so that he could put them back in the right order. The traditionally styled box had several drawers and hinged layers that opened up to reveal more underneath.

It was a journey down memory lane to see her armor laid out on the dressing tabletop like this. The first string of pearls she'd ever owned, gifted to her by the earl's son. The matching bracelet, from her next "romance." Grigor rolled his eyes at the memory.

She'd acquired a lot more loot since those days. When he saw just how much of it, he confirmed something he'd always known but hadn't wanted to acknowledge. She had substantial income from sources he knew nothing about, to afford all this. Because he calculated that even Sophia Morrigan, with her elegance and beauty, hadn't had enough beaux to account for all of it. She had to be buying—or stealing—a good portion of it herself.

His keen ears picked up a far-off noise—someone running up the club stairs at a fast clip, a woman's shoes ringing on the treads as she came. He still hadn't found the child's token. He reached into the very bottom receptacle, overflowing with layers of blue tissue paper, and his fingers touched something soft. A suede pouch with a drawstring closure nestled amid the paper. He drew it out and tipped the contents onto his open palm.

The amulet! He'd found it! The noise of feet and raised voices was coming closer. He thrust the empty bag and bone emblem into his jacket pocket and hurriedly replaced Sophia's treasures back into the box, hopefully close enough to the order in which he'd removed them,

He'd barely closed it up and slipped out the door into the main corridor before he heard Sophia's voice.

"There you are," Sophia said, standing at the other end, eying him suspiciously. "You've got a visitor."

Her chest rose and fell. She was out of breath from running.

"What's going on?" he said. "Why aren't you still out enjoying your big night?"

"Something came up," she said, abruptly cutting him off.

She stared at him through narrowed eyes, as if trying to read his inner thoughts.

"Jack Cabot is waiting for you in the library. He ruined my night."

Fifty-five

When Grigor strode into the library, he found Jack relaxed back into one of the capacious sofas, arms flung along leather backrest, with a satisfied smile of a cat that had just got the cream.

"Sophia seems unusually shaken up by whatever's happened tonight," Grigor said. "You look like you're celebrating a victory. What's going on?"

Jack grinned. "Finally, my stars are in alignment. Maybe the Good Lord in Heaven has seen I've done my penance and now I'm getting my reward."

Grigor sat down some distance away with an irritable *harrumph.* "Stop talking drivel and tell me why she's back early. I nearly got caught red-handed."

Jack's smug look vanished, and his eyes on Grigor sharpened.

"Oh? What happened?"

"No. You first."

Grigor stood and walked to the decanter that sat on a silver tray at a small bar. He picked up a glass and waved it invitingly. Jack shook his head. "Not for me."

Grigor filled one for himself and turned to his guest expectantly.

"Well? Get on with it."

"Total coincidence. I ran into Sophia dining at The Old Poodle Dog with a couple of fellows I used to know really well. They're swindlers and worse—both of them. So I was curious about what business she had with them. My friend was happily distracted chatting up a lady at another table, so I invited myself to join Sophia and asked some pointed questions about her companion's activities."

"Who were they?" asked Grigor.

"Dan Dandy Durkan and Flash Fingers Jo Diamond. One the owner of notorious poker dens. I'm sure you recognize the name. The other likely to be up to his ears in debt to said dens. Do you know either of them?"

"I've come across Jo Diamond from time to time. A nasty piece of work. 'Dandy' Durkan? Only heard of him by reputation."

Jack scowled. "Dandy Durkan lies as fast as a dog can trot, and Jo Diamond is even worse."

"So why was Sophia upset?"

"I got onto a line of questioning with Dandy that Jo didn't like. Related to some unfinished business I had with

Durkan. It put the wind up Jo. I got the impression he wanted rid of Dandy anyway, so it gave him an excuse to scarper."

"What did your previous business with him relate to?"

Jack's face glowed in triumph.

"Funnily enough, selling kids. I wasn't doing the selling, I hasten to add. Dandy was."

He waggled his brows at Grigor.

Jack's enjoying himself rather too much.

Grigor felt a gush of acid in his gut.

"If I was a betting man, Grigor, I'd say Sophia was planning to talk to Jo about expanding her prostitution racket into his poker dens."

He nodded his head, as if confirming his mock surprise. "And yes, Grigor, she keeps bawdy houses. All over the state.

Did you know? I suspect that's where she puts the Islas of this world to work."

Grigor's face flushed a reluctant pink, but he remained silent.

"My guess is that Flash Fingers is keen as mustard to get in on the 'painted lady' escort service Sophia's talking up to him. But the thought that she might be mixed up with Dandy Durkan in indenturing kids into jobs that are really lifelong slavery? He's a bog-trotting Catholic with six children. At the mention of child slavery, he couldn't run away fast enough."

Grigor stared into the last inch of liquor in his glass and then downed it in one gulp.

He pulled something out of his inside coat pocket and passed it to Jack.

"That kiddie's bracelet Sophia got from Bertha? Don't know if she was given it or stole it. I didn't know she had it until ten days ago. It's all yours. Depriving her of it makes it that much harder for her to blackmail de Vile into marriage, and that's all I'm interested in.

"Do with it what you like. Just don't mention my name."

Fifty-six

Grigor had quietly seen Jack out—the
club was full and still roaring along on a
busy Saturday night—and was returning
to his private quarters when Sophia
descended upon him like a whirlwind,
one hand clutching her jewelry box.

"Where is it?" she demanded, holding
the little rosewood trunk with one hand
and pointing at it with the other.

Grigor instantly schooled his face to
blank innocence.

"Where's what?"

"You know damn well what, Raizney
Grigor. What stupid game are you
playing? 'Thwart Sophia at every turn,' is
that it?"

The "Tsarist" brocade she still wore gave her the presence of an avenging queen, her face lit by rampaging indignation.

Grigor stood on the thick carpet, his shoes in one hand, caught out attempting to pad-foot it to bed to avoid this very confrontation.

They stared at one another in silence, and then Sophia stepped right up to him and stretched out her hands to run them up and down his jacket.

He took an indignant half step backward.

"What are you doing?"

"I'm patting you down, looking for the bracelet. I know you took it. I suspected something was off when Jack brought me back."

He felt assaulted by her arrogance, but he stood his ground quietly.

She approached again and ran her hands roughly up and down his sides and then undid his jacket and rifled through his inner pockets. When she came up empty-handed, she stepped back with an angry, heaving breath.

"You think you're so smart," she said. Her cheeks flushed red with frustration.

"I could accuse you of similar hubris," Grigor said stoutly. "What right have you to keep it? Or to have the cheek to search me like you've just done. It was never yours to keep. Bertha stripped it from a defenseless child. To my mind, taking it was as tasteless as stripping the dead."

Sophia's mouth dropped open, and bright red spots highlighted her cheeks.

"Anyway, you of all people should know I'm not into women's jewelry. Maybe one of the staff took it. What about Isla? Now, wouldn't that be poetic justice? You steal it from Bertha and Isla steals it from you. Is that what you mean by learning from life?"

Sophia scowled. "Isla wouldn't steal from me," she said. "She knows her life's not worth it."

"So tell me. I'm curious. What was your business with Flash Fingers Jo and Dandy Durkan? If it was to do with the club operation, then why didn't you ask me along?"

Her already redder-than-normal complexion darkened further.

However, when she spoke, her voice was ice cold.

"Grigor, you won't be around for much longer, and you wouldn't want to know."

Fifty-seven

Hector de Vile draped the antique piece across his big palm and fingered it delicately with his other hand. Jack himself had cleaned the initialed tiny silver shield, so it shone against the mellow cream of the aged bone.

"What sort of bone do you think it is?"

"It's probably ivory," said Jack. "Though I'm no expert. Someone obviously commissioned it as a special piece."

Hector glanced up, his eyes misty.

They were sitting in de Vile's Russian Hill breakfast room, with sunlight streaming in from the wide windows onto the garden, hot coffee and Boudin's croissants on the table before them. The room smelled of strawberry jam and a sharp resinous marigold fragrance from flowers that shone gold and fresh in a vase beside the coffee jug.

Jack felt enveloped in wealth and well-being that had once been familiar, but which he hadn't known for many years.

He'd carried the heirloom home last night, using soap and water to polish and dry the intricately carved silver shield before wrapping the whole in a soft cloth soaked in glycerine overnight.

He'd wasted not a minute in taking the stiff early morning walk up the hill to Hector's doorstep, arriving unannounced. He figured the cargo he was carrying would open doors, and the welcome couldn't have been warmer.

De Vile had been surprised, and then—when he understood the full import of Jack's delivery—overwhelmed.

"A. R. C.," Jack said, gazing across the table. "You know who or what those initials stand for?"

De Vile locked eyes with Jack.

"It's obvious it's Alejandro Rafael Castellanos. Elanora or Rafael had it specially made for their son."

His face tensed and a fleeting embarrassment flickered in his eyes.

"I know my part in this business is reprehensible, Jack. But I didn't know about the bracelets. And I want to ensure that this one finally goes to the person they intended it for, my adopted son, Alex."

From Jack's point of view, another piece of the bigger puzzle was falling into place. His sheer good luck in bumping into Dan "Dandy" Durkan last night had reignited his determination to understand what was going on with abuses in child labor on the coast.

He took a special pleasure in seeing that although he might not be in the best of shape himself after his last few years of despair and self-punishment, Dandy was in far worse condition.

And he deserved to be, he told himself, devoid of mercy. He'd gleaned enough from his relentless questioning last night to be convinced that Dan had sold Cordelia to Sophia, and she'd then arranged the child's transfer to the new parents.

He could read it in Durkan's guilty yellow-faced denials, and by the shifty way he kept looking to Sophia to rescue him. She had not given an inch in acknowledging her part, but he could read the non-verbal signs between them.

Durkan might even have regrets, but

if he was, Jack suspected it was for purely selfish reasons. Perhaps he calculated that if he'd kept Cordelia in his life, he might have enjoyed some flow-on benefits from her family connections.

The only thing that left him bamboozled was Dandy's reaction when he'd first appeared at the table. The fellow had reared back as if he'd seen a ghost, and accused him of persecuting him, when it was the first time he'd laid eyes on him in six years.

Jack shrugged at the memory. Maybe his alcoholism was so far advanced he was seeing or imagining things.

Whatever his state, Jack knew he was getting closer every day to putting all the pieces together and avenging Cordelia's fate.

He realized Hector had addressed a question to him.

"What was that, Hector?"

"What do you want from me, Jack? I appreciate it's a big thing you've done for me here. What do you want in return?"

"Glad you asked, Hector. I'm on a mission to rid this state of abuses in child labor, and I'm asking for your help with that. I'm happy to negotiate a price. However much you feel it's worth for you to return it to Alex. And however much that is, I promise I'll devote it to rooting out the evil, however long it takes."

De Vile suggested a very generous sum, and Jack went away glowing with a surety that the magnate was aware of the mess he'd go into, and was doing his utmost to gain Alex's forgiveness.

Fifty-eight

Isla's eyes widened in wonder as she stepped down from Elizabeth's Rockaway carriage and gazed up at the front of the Nob Hill house, with its turreted tower and pitched shingled roofs.

A long-haired smoky blue cat lounged across the front doorstep, as if awaiting the party's return. The girl's eyes alighted on the cat and momentarily her face shone. Then, as if remembering she shouldn't reveal her feelings, she closed down again.

"That's Artemisia," said Elizabeth, guiding Isla gently up the path to the front door. "She loves to be stroked. Let's go inside and you can feel how silky her fur is."

Luminous blue eyes reflected a fleeting anxiety that the child successfully hid in the rest of her face. Like many of the women Elizabeth had known in the Tenderloin, she'd schooled herself to believe no one and trust no one.

As they progressed to the front door, Jack hung back, happy to let Elizabeth take the lead. Isla seemed comfortable with her, and he didn't want to do anything to interrupt the chances of a rapport being established between them.

Grigor had organized for Isla to escape her duties at the club while Elizabeth was out all the afternoon with a session at the dressmaker's. Jack had reluctantly enlisted Elizabeth's help because he knew the girl would feel much more comfortable with a woman present, and Elizabeth had the experience to deal with her sensitively.

"I basically want to just get as much information as we can on Isla's history," he told Elizabeth. "Where is her family and why isn't she with them? How did she end up with Sophia? If we knew that, we'd be much better placed to judge whether there's anything wrong here."

They paused on the front steps and Elizabeth bent down and scooped the cat into her arms. Turning to Isla, she offered up the purring cat's supine form. "There you are… Stroke her back. She won't scratch you."

Isla gingerly put out her hand to stroke along Artemisia's sprawled form. After a couple of long strokes, she bounced on her toes in delight and whispered, "Oh, her fur's all warm from the sun! And so silky!"

The door opened and the smell of

home baking followed the motherly figure of Mrs. Roderiquez, Elizabeth's housekeeper, onto the porch.

"Oh my, Mrs. W., you're just in time. The apple tart is cooling on the rack right now. Come on in and our guest can give Artemisia a saucer of milk."

Isla scanned Antonia Roderiquez's friendly face and giggled. Her hand went up to her mouth instantly, as if to cover her reaction. She hesitated.

"Can I really? I've never seen such a beautiful cat."

Roderiquez had set the parlor table for afternoon tea, but Elizabeth quickly decided she'd rather they sat in the gazebo in the back garden. "Isla will be more comfortable there… with more space to play with the cat if she wants to," she said by explanation, and it was all quickly rearranged.

As they wandered outside and Isla danced off on the lawn, trailing a long lure of ribbon the cat jumped after, Jack came alongside.

"A perfect setup, Elizabeth. No spies to report back to Sophia. I can't thank you enough for being willing to help."

Elizabeth shrugged. "It's the least I can do," she whispered.

#

After Isla and Artemis had exhausted each other—Elizabeth wasn't sure who had been the first to give in—and they'd gorged on egg and lettuce sandwiches, apple tart, and chocolate cake, Elizabeth shot Jack a meaningful look.

If they were going to get down to questioning the child, now was the time. She was satiated on food and as relaxed as she was ever going to be with newcomers like them.

Over the course of the meal, Elizabeth realized what a boon the random appearance of the cat had been, because it had sparked a spontaneous delight in the child that she suspected she showed nowhere else.

She'd eaten with a mechanical blankness, showing little pleasure in her food, even though Elizabeth was confident the spread laid before her was almost certainly better than anything she'd eaten in at least the last six months, if not longer.

When she wasn't playing with Artemis, Isla sat unusually still, as if she'd absorbed the ancient rule that children should be "seen and not heard" into her bones.

She maintained a rigorous sense of apartness, which wasn't at all the same as restfulness or placidity.

"Have you had enough to eat, Isla?" Elizabeth asked.

Isla nodded contentedly, but didn't speak.

"You know, Jack and I brought you here because we wanted to ask you more about yourself. We will not tell anyone else. It's our secret. Not Sophia, Not Ned, not Grigor. No one else will know anything about it."

Isla's eyes flickered in momentary surprise, and then the light went out again.

Jack spoke up quietly. "Do you enjoy your work with Sophia, Isla?"

She turned and regarded him thoughtfully.

She had a finely featured pale face, with a strong patrician nose and knife-edge cheekbones that smudged out any reminder of babyhood softness and gave her a look of wisdom beyond her years.

"I enjoy it better than the place I was in before," she said, after careful consideration.

They let the answer lie there for a long minute

"And where was that place?" Elizabeth asked softly, and sensed rather than saw the shudder that went through her.

"A horrible place. They told me if I went there, my sister would be safe."

"Your sister?" said Elizabeth. "You have a sister?"

Isla's glance was shot through with panic.

After another long silence, she said, "Yes. She's my baby sister. Her name's Cassie. She was only four."

"And Cassie stayed with your mother?"

Isla shook her head. "No. My mother's dead."

"Oh, I'm sorry. So who was Cassie staying with?"

"She was in the orphanage with me. We were both there." She gazed steadily at Elizabeth and her eyes filled with tears. "But when I turned ten, they told me I couldn't stay there any longer. First, they said I had to go out to work to pay for our food."

She dropped her eyes to the table. "But then in a little while they said I couldn't live at the orphanage anymore either. And I couldn't see Cassie anymore."

She suppressed a dry sob. Her fingers threaded through the fabric of her skirt, squeezing it into tight balls.

Elizabeth cleared her throat. She felt like bursting into tears herself at the girl's tightly held anguish.

"And who were the people who told you this, Isla?"

"My stepfather Finney. He said we had to go to the orphanage when Mother died. He didn't want us. He didn't have enough money to feed us. He sent us to the Dragon's Den in Portsmouth Square."

"The Dragon's Den?"

"That's what we called it. I had to do lots of work and we didn't get enough to eat, but at least I could look after Cassie."

"And then? When did you go to Sophia?"

Her brow furrowed as she considered her answer.

"I think Sophia bought me when I was ten, but I didn't live at the club then. I got moved to a place in Stockton." She blushed. "A flash house. Lots of molls and men coming through all the time. Some girls weren't much older than me. I washed sheets with Molly and hid as much as I could. Then Sophia brought me here."

"How long were you at the flash house?"

"Two years. I'm twelve now." She gazed out over the garden with a faraway stare, as if remembering.

"That means Cassie is six now…" She paused, and added: "If she's still alive."

Her eyes chopped back to Elizabeth.

"When I got back here, I sneaked out one night to Portsmouth Square to see if I could find her." The corners of her eyes narrowed in misery.

"Looks like the place burned down. There was a black hole where it used to be."

Her eyes flicked back to the garden, as if the view was the only thing that gave her relief from her worst fears.

"Even without a fire, a lot of the kids died in that place. I hope Cassie isn't one of them."

Fifty-nine

Telegraph from the Rev. Teddy Kalama, Kalama Legal Chambers, 52 West Street New York City. To Elizabeth Westerhoven, 18 Pine Street, Nob Hill, California.

URGENT

Sylvia Carterton died two months ago. Daughter Cordelia in poor health—suspected TB—and in mourning. Thomas largely absent from home. She remembers Uncle Jack with great fondness.

Psalm 34: 17-18 STOP

And Elizabeth Westerhoven's reply:

Warmest thanks, Teddy. Please await further instructions.

Psalm 34:17-18: "The righteous cry, and the LORD heareth, And delivereth them out of all their troubles. The LORD is nigh unto them that are of a broken heart; And saveth such as be of a contrite spirit."

Sixty

Grigor stepped into the Imperial Club's rooftop garden and, despite himself, caught his breath. Laid out under a silky San Francisco night, with a dome of glittering stars hanging overhead and a soft sea mist rolling in at ground level, the expansive rooftop garden felt like a place of secret rendezvous, mysteriously set apart from mundane life.

Already, a colorful crowd gathered in anticipation of the memorable party to celebrate the Golden Queen's closing night.

He paused at the entryway and, as he gazed around, he had to concede the place had never been more enchanting.

From the points of his leather-nosed shoes to the white-columned outside walls stretched an expanse of watermark-patterned pale pink Italian marble. Half a dozen bulky bronze whale oil pots dotted the floor, set with fires that sent sparks like fireflies up into the night sky.

At strategic points around the generous open-air area, bundles of six-foot-high flaming brands stood upright in cylindrical urns, like knots of giant sunflowers, lit by the relatively odorless sperm whale oil that was readily available in a town which had resurrected its whaling industry in the last decade.

And looped around the outside of the rooftop garden were flowering archways of vibrant red and mauve bougainvillea, their rampant growth springing from pottery urns at ground level.

To finish it all off, a rotunda decked in red velvet curtains stood in the center of the space, occupied by a string quartet playing lively popular pieces as silver-tray-carrying waiters in black evening suits circulated, offering drinks of choice.

Never one to hide her light under a bushel, Sophia was making a statement about the desirability of the venue as she marked the occasion on the San Francisco social calendar.

Good, Grigor thought.

Two can play that game.

He surveyed the room. It was just after eight p.m., and none of the key players had yet arrived. The "Queens" show had begun at five, and had just ended. Pania and Graysie and their husbands were enjoying a brief break in the Green Room before making a grand entrance.

Their audience were traipsing up from the theater on the lower levels, taking up their second or third drinks of the night and looking around them in quiet wonder. Any minute now Hector de Vile, Jack and Lochie would arrive and the fun would begin.

#

Sophia cruised in a few minutes later, looking supremely confident in the blue brocade "Tsarina" gown she'd worn to her failed meeting with Joe Diamond a few nights back. Grigor swallowed a smile. The dark blue sash she wore across her breast tonight, anchored by the diamond pin at her waist, announced her supreme authority over the occasion.

She spotted him immediately and sidled up, getting close.

"Everything meets your approval?"

she asked. She was smiling, but she couldn't keep a sour note out of her voice.

He turned to face her. "You've done extraordinarily well, Sophia. Congratulations. The place is captivating."

A flash of surprise crossed her face, and Grigor felt a pang of guilt. Her contribution to getting the club to the level it was couldn't be denied, and he didn't begrudge her the recognition. The way they were falling out right at the end of it all was regrettable, but unavoidable.

And a misplaced feeling of gratitude toward you will not divert me from my one last act.

\#

Two hours later, and Grigor judged it was time to make his move. He knew

Sophia was about to summon in the waiters to serve supper. The string quartet was ready to take a break, replaced by a fiddler, banjo and harmonica. It was time for Grigor to make his stand.

As Sophia assumed the stage to announce supper was about to be served, Grigor stepped up beside her and clapped his hands for attention.

"Ladies and gentlemen," he said. "I know Madame Morrigan is about to announce supper, but before she does, I have an announcement to make."

Jack and Lochie were standing off to one side with Elizabeth and Daphne Partington. He beckoned to the men to come and stand with him.

As they stepped up, an awareness seemed to permeate the crowded floor. Something of import was happening. It was rare—indeed unheard of—for Raizney Grigor to occupy such a prominent position. No one could recall it ever happening before.

An eerie silence fell over the gathering, and Grigor felt his throat close up with a sudden attack of stage fright. For a moment, his vocal cords locked. He swallowed hard, put his arm lightly around Lochie's shoulder, and began.

"Ladies and gentlemen, I'm here tonight to thank our wonderful performers, Pania and Graysie Russell, for an outstanding season of entertainment which will long be remembered in this city, and to thank my co-owner in this enterprise, Sophia Morrigan, for having the foresight to organize both that show and this wonderful party."

He scanned the crowd, gauging

response. Sophia was standing to one side, looking stunned. The rest of his audience was enthralled, on tenterhooks for whatever was to come next.

"I realize it's generally known that Senator Hector de Vile has also joined the ownership of the club, and I'm sure in years to come, he will prove to be an excellent asset. But what won't be so well known is the announcement I have to make here tonight."

He drew Lochie more closely into his side. He could feel his son's tense breath. This was all totally new for him as well.

"I have long planned to retire from the Imperial when I reached a certain personal milestone, and that time has come tonight. I am passing my share in this enterprise to my son, Lochie O'Riordan." He was running out of breath. He stopped speaking and heard a multitude of indrawn breaths from the gathered onlookers.

People were staring at Lochie as if he had just appeared out of a birthday cake.

"Yes, everyone," he said in a louder, firmer voice. "This is my son, Lochie O'Riordan, a brilliant artist like his mother Ashling. And he will be my sole heir."

He smiled at Jack.

"Lochie will take up this new opportunity under the careful and wise guidance of Jack Cabot, who is known to many of you. For a small percentage in the Imperial operation, Jack will stand alongside Lochie and tutor him while he learns the ropes of our business."

His eyes moved to where Sophia stood, hovering like a dark, avenging angel. Her face was roiling in thunderous fury, her hands clenched at her sides.

He stepped aside, an enormous sense of lightness filling his chest. He felt as if he might float out of the rooftop garden and ascend to the glittering stars. He grasped at Lochie's shoulder even tighter, and Sophia stepped up.

"How noble of you, Grigor," she said through clenched teeth. "And Jack, Lochie, welcome aboard the merry ship."

She turned to the floor. "Supper is now served, everyone. Please do enjoy."

Then she turned and stormed out.

Sixty-one

Unbelievable.

It was the only word she could summon to describe her reaction to the words that had tumbled from Grigor's mouth.

May the first drop of water to quench your thirst—may it boil in your bowels.

A fury boiled up from inside, so hot and raw she could barely stand up under it, and the old Celtic curse didn't reduce her feverish rage.

May your limbs wither and the stench of your rotten carcass be too horrible for hungry dogs.

May you fade into nothing, like snow in summer.

An image of Lochlan—she refused to call him Lochie—standing beside Grigor with his father's arm around his shoulders, looking so like Ashling, rose in front of her eyes.

May these curses of the Ancients rest on your children. This, I pray.

She strode out of the rooftop garden like an empress, but once she reached the privacy of her own quarters, she collapsed into a chair and panted like a hunted stag.

What had just happened? Grigor had humiliated her in front of the most important people in the city. She would never recover her prestige.

She poured herself a glass of water and sipped it as her mind raced.

Only one thing for it. She'd put the screws on Hector. At the very least she'd attach herself to him for the rest of the evening. Renew the impression something was going on between them. That idea was still being floated in the local gossip columns. It hadn't entirely died. She could stoke it up again.

She doused herself in fresh perfume, downed another glass of water and sallied out.

And in the meantime, she would kill Grigor. If his body didn't give up on him before she got to him.

A black hole opened up inside her.

Her old soul mate.

He must sense the end was near for him to take this radical step of a public announcement. A sense of impending doom loomed, and she wasn't at all certain whether it was hers or Grigor's.

She bared her teeth at an invisible enemy. The man who had guarded her like precious treasure her whole life was about to discover his deathbed truth.

Hell hath no fury like Sophia scorned.

Sixty-two

Sophia cornered Hector at the supper table, where he was loading his plate with cold meat and salads, ready to carry it away and eat it in a quiet corner.

"Hector," she said with enforced gaiety. "Just the man I wanted to see. Mind if I join you?"

He peered up from his plate in mild surprise and then nodded with casual indifference. "If you want."

She picked at a savory snack from a passing waiter's tray and trailed behind Hector as he sought two chairs under a flowered arch butted right up against the exterior colonnade. A light evening breeze lifted the blooming sprays.

"You've put on a marvelous show tonight, Sophia," Hector said gallantly. "Congratulations."

"Thank you, Hector. I like to think if it's worth doing, it's worth doing well."

He gave her a clipped smile and turned his attention to his plate.

"You must have been a little surprised by Grigor's announcement?" he inquired, concentrating on his food. "Did you know it was coming?"

"Did you?" she countered. "You're a shareholder too."

He peered up from his plate, his fork loaded with potato and mayonnaise.

"Not anymore," he said. "Hasn't Grigor told you? He bought me out."

"He what?" said Sophia.

"Oh yes. He bought me out. I think that means he—or rather, his estate— owns a little over fifty percent. That shouldn't cause any problems, though, should it?"

"Hector, you must be mistaken," she said. "You need my agreement to make a change like that."

"I don't think so, Sophia. Grigor had all the legal documents already drawn up. All I needed to do was sign them."

"But what about Alex? What about the whole town knowing about what you did to Castellanos?"

Hector stopped eating and put his fork down on his plate.

"Oh Sophia. Stop this nonsense, do. It's gone on quite long enough."

"It's not nonsense. You know that as well as I do. What about the bracelet?"

As soon as the words were out of her mouth, her throat closed up.

The bracelet. She didn't have it anymore. Grigor had stolen it.

"The bracelet?" Hector set his plate on the floor at his feet and pulled something out from his inside jacket. He dangled it in front of her.

"Oh. This trinket, you mean? The one that Jack sold me. For a considerable sum, I might add. But I didn't mind. The money is all going to a good cause."

He got to his feet. "Yes. Jack has got some bee in his bonnet about starting an organization to put an end to children's indentured labor. Or any abuse, really. All seems rather ahead of its time, to me, but good luck to him."

Sixty-three

Sophia leapt up and grabbed at Hector's swinging arm to create the impression they were still—what was the word—dallying?

That was it. Sophia Morrigan and Senator Hector de Vile were dallying. She felt his instinct to pull away, but he didn't disengage. Nor did he slacken his steps. She matched him stride for stride as they made their way back across the rooftop, with her babbling a stream of numbskull small talk to create the impression they were still "together."

While underneath the flow of nonsense, her mind moved sluggishly, like a deep and stagnant river, eddying around her jabbering tongue, trying to compute what had just happened.

The men in her life—all of them—had sold her out. And she was now in real danger of losing everything.

What was it Hector had said?

The money's all going to a good cause….

Jack's got a bee in his bonnet about child labor…

How blind could she be? She'd been so taken up with her own importance, so ready to count her chickens before they hatched. And now the fox had got into the coop and stolen the whole clutch.

She thought back to her aborted meeting with Joe Diamond a few days ago. The one Jack had gate crashed and blown up.

Only a few minutes before Jack turned up, Dan Dandy Durkan deposited himself at their table, uninvited as well. He was eager to get back in Joe's good books and flush with money. In one swoop, his debts were all paid up, and he was asking Joe for more credit.

And Dandy was the guy on whose behalf she'd sold that kid years ago now—the one who went to New York. It came now, a vague memory, that Jack was related to the kid's mother somehow? But so what? She was dead, anyway, wasn't she?

Her veins turned to ice as the jigsaw pieces dropped into place. By the time they reached the other side of the big room, she understood just how much ordure she had on her shoes. She was ankle deep in the stuff. Make that knee deep, she thought as she stopped in her tracks, gazing ahead.

There before her, in a cozy little

group, chatting like they were best friends, were Jack and Grigor, Lochie and Elizabeth. And Isla. What the hell was Isla doing here with them? She let go of Hector's arm. A high-pitched buzzing drowned out any other thoughts in her head.

In a blind fury, she grabbed up one of the flaming torches from a nearby urn. Her efficient staff were constantly renewing the torches, and so it was good and ready. Then she lunged at the man who'd been her savior, and her destruction.

Sixty-four

Grigor was closest to her, physically speaking, and he was also the one who had brought down her house of cards by refusing to go along with her plans, and then turning all paternal on her and introducing this son she'd known nothing about to the entire world.

Ashling's son. In her world.

She ran at the old man, and the flaming torch struck him at the base of his neck. His hair flared and fire ran up over the top of his head so fast she could hardly believe her eyes.

The man who'd once been the Arctic Fox was a fireball as he fell backwards, tripping over his long legs as he dropped into an open chest that stood near him. A chest that contained fireworks she'd planned to light at midnight as a brilliant party finale.

Grigor raised his arm and ran it over his head, desperate to smother the flames. An agonising, high-pitched wailing, like an out-of-tune Irish flute, pierced the air. Then, for a few long seconds, there was just the hiss of the flames as the fire took hold of Grigor's clothing.

His right sleeve smouldered, and he collapsed into the chest with a thump. Long before anyone else understood the danger, Sophia saw what would happen next.

A chest crammed with fireworks—Sky Rockets and Catherine Wheels, Enchanted Rain and Pegasus Fountains, the very best of Chinatown merchandise—was about to explode around them. And amidst the 150 guests from the cream of San Francisco society trapped with them.

She gazed in silent horror at the man who had been everything to her, flopped back like a babe at rest, flames licking up around him.

It already seemed as if he'd passed to another realm. He didn't scream or struggle. He simply lay back in surrender.

Then there was a howl on her right, the sound of a tormented animal, and she turned to see Lochie, flame-haired boy that he was, being restrained by Jack, as he struggled to reach for his father.

"No, Lochie. No! I'll get Grigor. You make sure the women are safe."

He gazed beseechingly at Elizabeth,

who grabbed the boy from the other side and dragged him away, scooping up Isla with her other hand as she turned.

Sophia's paralysis vanished, and a fresh surge of energy galvanized her. Like father, like son. She wasn't letting the cause of it all escape. He was inheriting the business she'd sweated her whole life to create, and he'd done nothing for it. Nothing!

She grabbed up a second brand and turned on him, ready to pursue him to the gates of Hell. She raised the torch to strike him from behind. And then Hector de Vile was in front of her, blocking her attack.

"No more, Sophia. You'd done enough harm."

He raised his hands in defence as she rushed him, forcing him back, back, retreating, fingering the flaming torch with his bare hands.

He hit the edge of the rotunda and fell backwards, just as Grigor had done minutes before. Someone grabbed Sophia from behind, and she felt tough arms like a chain around her waist, hauling her off de Vile. She hurled the torch with as much venom as she could muster and saw another burst of flame as the velvet curtains flared to life.

She fought to get away, but her captor had iron control. Within seconds, he had her arms behind her, her wrists manacled.

A roaring fizz whizzed overhead, narrowly missing them, hitting an elderly woman who fell, screaming. The first of the fireworks had ignited.

Grigor's redheaded son was howling like a wolf. One of the Russell men rushed to Elizabeth's side—Graysie's husband Nathan, Sophia thought—and took control. Isla trailed behind them like a shadowy wraith.

She struggled to see what had happened to Grigor. Jack Cabot was holding a thick blanket and was attempting to smother fireworks that were erupting around him like popcorn in a tin.

There was no chance, she could see, of him ever being able to extract Grigor—her precious, inscrutable, valiant Grigor—from his funeral pyre.

Sixty-five

Hector de Vile lay back on his pillows in the airy, light-filled room and smiled fondly at his visitors. His thickly bandaged hands rested on the top of the sheet. A second heavy bandage covered the flesh from his right ear to the top of his head and wound round under his chin, obscuring part of his speckled gray and white beard. Any skin not concealed by the bandage was a blotchy red.

Graysie felt a surprise rush of affection mixed with guilt for the old goat. He was humble, subdued. He'd lost his hubris, and she much preferred him this way.

She glanced across at Alex. They sat,

one either side of Hector's massive four-poster, separated by an expansive finely worked quilt patterned with sailing ships and quadrants. The tinkling sound of children's laughter drifted in from opened windows. George and Mimi were playing chase around the rose beds under the watchful eye of Nanny Blanchet.

Right now, though, she wasn't watching her children. She knew they were safe, and she and Alex had more urgent business here at Hector's bedside.

"I'm so pleased you could come," Hector said in a soft, hesitant voice. "It means a lot to me."

Alex bent over him solicitously. "Hex," he said in an exasperated tone. "You couldn't keep me away. The only thing I want right now is for those burns to heal and you back to your old self."

He spontaneously reached out, as if to pat the back of his father's hand, and then sharply pulled back. Hector's hands weren't ready to have anyone pat them yet.

Hector gave another wan grin and turned to Graysie. "And Graysie. I know you're a busy mother. I appreciate you making the time to see me."

She patted the bedcover in front of her instead of his hand and smiled. "It's a pleasure, Hector. In one way or another, our lives are entangled. Have been for a long time now."

He nodded appreciatively. "They have indeed, and that's exactly why I invited you here today. I wanted to sort a few things out. Ancient history it is, but it's important to me."

He hesitated, as if momentarily

uncertain of how to continue.

"You mean you want to talk about our mother's accident?" Graysie's voice was hesitant. He nodded.

"Really? I never thought I'd see the day…" And she laughed, a tinkling sound that was remarkably similar to the music coming from the garden.

They all relaxed back for a long minute, letting the beauty and serenity of the morning settle around them.

"Grigor was there that night, you know? Not when the crash occurred, but for the aftermath."

Suddenly the genial peacefulness evaporated, and she was on high alert. Alex pulled himself bolt upright in his chair. He felt it too.

"He was there?" he echoed. "Tell us about it."

"We were both at the Sacramento

Wells Fargo station, waiting for friends to arrive. I was waiting for Bertha. He was waiting for a friend on another coach entirely, from Marysville, I think. But when word went out that a vehicle was overdue, it was all hands on deck. The weather was dreadful. A full storm raging. We both went out with the rescue team to see if we could help."

Graysie's hands were chilled, as if even talking about that night brought back the memory of the icy cold temperatures, the black despair she'd felt.

"It took us hours to get there, and when we arrived, a dreadful scene awaited us. Wreckage strewn all over the place. It looked as if they'd veered off the road and hit several trees, peeling back part of the siding, before rolling down a bank."

De Vile's eyes rested on her, and Graysie could see a nervous pulsing under the right one. He dabbed at it with his bandaged hand and masked a wince.

"It's a miracle anyone survived, let alone tiny children."

He hesitated and cleared his throat nervously.

"I'm sorry to say it, Graysie, but it was quickly clear your mother was beyond help. Her body was unmarked, but I suspect her spine snapped on impact. She'd been thrown out and was lying under trees. She could have fallen asleep with you tucked in under her arm."

Tears sprang to Graysie's eyes, and Hector faltered.

"I... I'm sorry," he whispered. "Am I saying too much?"

"No!" Graysie's exclamation was

sharp and instant. She took a deep breath. "Sorry. Didn't mean to sound alarmed. I want to hear this. No one has ever talked to me about it. No one who was there. It was a forbidden topic at home."

She gazed into Hector's eyes and saw the tears falling.

He squeezed them shut and then gazed at Alex. "Are you OK, son?"

"Yes Hex, fine. Thank you for this. I know it's costing you."

"We knew Elanora had three children with her. I was expecting to find Bertha, who was travelling with you. So you can imagine, I expected the worst when we could find no trace of you—Bertha or you children.

"It seemed the logical thing to fear wild animals had taken you. It had been hours between when the crash happened and when we got there. We scoured the area for the rest of the night and all the next day, trying to find you. To understand what happened to you. All to no avail. In the end, we had to pack it in and give up."

Alex interrupted. "Graysie seemed to remember Rafael came with you. Do you recall if that's right?"

Hector seemed to sink into himself, his chin dipping further into his bandage, before nodding. "Yes, Alex. Graysie's right. Rafael was at the Sacramento station as well, waiting for you all to arrive. When the coach was late, he was beside himself. And when we arrived at the scene and found Elanora dead and you missing, he went wild with grief. He was hardly conscious of where he was. We lost him to it.

"The coach driver and an elderly

couple were injured and unconscious, and first up we had to get them out. The Wells Fargo chap running the rescue sent Rafael, Graysie and Elanora back with them. It was too hard for everyone having him there with us. He was so distraught."

Graysie nodded, remembering her father's desperate kisses.

"You mentioned the fears about wild animals, Hector. There was a white wolf in a cave that night. I'm sure of it. I think I left Mother for a time and went looking for the twins. I couldn't understand where they'd gone. And then this majestic wolf appeared out of nowhere. It was like he was warning me of danger."

"How very odd that you'd remember that," Hector said, staring at her. "But you're quite right. There was a wolf there. Grigor took a shot at it, but it disappeared into the forest. I don't think he hit it. We never found a carcass."

Graysie felt a strange, enveloping warmth spread through her, supplanting the iciness she'd experienced minutes before.

"I'm glad," she whispered. "I'm sure he was my friend."

She heard a soft snoring. Hector had dropped into an exhausted sleep, his cheek still wet with tears.

#

They had to leave him then. They wandered back to the kitchen for morning coffee.

"Do you think he's going to be OK?" said Alex with an anxious frown. "He seems... different."

"I hope so," said Graysie, and to her

amazement, realized she meant it. "I'm still curious about the other part. The bit where we hear about Bertha."

Sixty-six

It was the next day before Hector was up to seeing them again, propped up against fresh-starched linen. His face was still drawn, but his eyes brightened as they tiptoed to his bedside.

"No need to creep around," he said with a twinkle. "I'm not dead yet."

"Oh Hex, don't even joke about it," said Alex, leaning over to kiss him on the forehead. "We want you here for many more years to come."

Hector smiled indulgently. "Has Mrs. Crisp already filled you up with coffee?"

"She has indeed," said Graysie with an answering smile. "And lemon meringue pie. The children are still finishing theirs with her in the kitchen."

"Then we'd better get on with it. Now where were we?"

The fleeting pain that crossed his face told Graysie he remembered very well where they had got to, and that the next chapter was going to be far more difficult for Hector than the last one.

She felt a surge of gratitude to him for being willing to open up like this for them. He could play the "forgetful old man" game and pretend he didn't remember.

Alex seemed to appreciate the point, too. He stroked his father's forehead and murmured, "I know this is going to be difficult for you, Hex. I'm eternally grateful you have the courage to do this. It means a lot to both of us." Graysie tilted her head in agreement.

"I've got something for you, Alex, but

with these darned hands…" He held up his bandaged hands, like a bear's paws… "you'll have to come and get it for yourself… in my robe pocket."

He was lying on top of his quilt today, and the maroon silk jacquard robe flowed around him. He gestured to a side pocket and Alex reached in and drew out a small leather pouch.

"What's this?" he asked, frowning.

"Open it," said Hector, "and all will become plain."

Alex widened the drawstring neck and tipped the contents out onto his palm.

A delicate bone bracelet caught a beam of sunlight from the windows as it fell.

"Ohhh," said Alex, transfixed. "This is the other bracelet."

"However did you get hold of it? She obviously wouldn't have given it up willingly."

De Vile grunted his assent.

"No, she didn't. We have Grigor and Jack to thank for this. Grigor got hold of it—I suspect he stole it—from Sophia and passed it on to Jack with his blessing. And Jack passed it on to me in return for a small donation to his latest cause, rescuing enslaved children."

His face shuddered in sorrow, but he forced a brightness into his words.

"I thought it the most appropriate way to start our conversation today."

Alex fingered the bracelet lovingly. "It's far too small for me to wear it," he said with a merry laugh, "But maybe, just possibly, one day I'll have a son—or a daughter—who will wear it for me."

He peered at the silver medallion. "A R.C. If it's a girl, it will have to be Alexandra Rachel Castellanos de Vile, won't it? Quite a mouthful."

He glanced up and saw tears were streaming down Hector's face.

"Oh Father, what's wrong? Have I said the wrong thing?"

Hector shook his head wordlessly and gasped for breath.

Graysie broke in as he regained his composure, her face wet as well.

"I think you said exactly the right thing, Alex. You'll see." Her voice was husky with emotion.

There was a long pause, as Hector regathered himself, and then Alex said brightly; "Now, tell me. How did Sophia get her hands on this treasure in the first place?"

So Hector told them.

Sixty-seven

When Graysie thought about that last meeting with Hector in the coming days, she always felt the most touching moment had been when Hector had given Alex his christening bracelet, and Alex had burbled on about the naming of his daughter—if he ever had one.

Alex was so invested in keeping his father alive that he hadn't allowed himself to see what was staring them both in the face. Hector's condition was deteriorating, not improving.

The hectic color in the glimpses of his face that the bandages weren't covering told her he fought a virulent infection, despite the physician's efforts to treat

him with the latest burns treatment—
Carron oil—discovered in Scotland,
involving frequent bandage changes
soaking the wound in a linseed oil and
lime-water liniment.

His brave decision to protect Lochie
from Sophia's rage had resulted in
severe burns to his hands, arms and
face, and the best of medical attention
had not prevailed.

It seemed fitting then that they were
sitting in San Francisco's Episcopalian
Cathedral with two caskets lined up side
by side in front of the altar.

Senator Hector de Vile on one side.
And the wily old Arctic Fox, Raizney
Grigor, alongside him.

As the first hymn opened, and the
bishop and choir processed as the
formalities began, Graysie couldn't
suppress a wry smile. They were both

old rogues in their own way. And they'd both died proving that underneath the tough exterior, they were ready to give their lives up for the ones they loved.

Sixty-eight

"I've got something to tell you."

Elizabeth winced at Jack's gloved hands and once again gave thanks to the heavenlies that he'd been spared the worst of the Imperial Club fire, coming out with only superficial burns and temporary breathlessness from toxic fumes.

"What is it?" Jack lifted his eyes from his coffee with a mischievous grin. He put down his cup and wiggled his fingers in the kid leather gloves he was wearing to protect against infection.

He's still like some children's magician, Elizabeth thought, but at least he has grown up a lot, and about time.

No one could dispute that.

He had been at the heart of the vain effort to save Grigor's life, but he'd had some protection from the thick blanket he'd been holding to smother the onslaught of fireworks.

Then the City Fire Brigade had made a quick entry and taken over and the building, apart from some water damage, had been saved. Some guests suffered minor burns or breathlessness, but the city had been spared a major disaster.

With Sophia in gaol facing two charges of murder, and Grigor and Hector both dead, Jack and Lochie were running the Imperial Club and Spa in the meantime. And while the spa was still operational, Jack was managing fire damage repairs to the rest of the building.

Elizabeth had heard rumors the new

design would incorporate O'Riordan artworks from both mother and son, something she was certain would have delighted Grigor no end.

"I've got news of Cordelia."

The cheeky grin Jack had plastered on his face a few seconds before vanished.

He stared, his tanned complexion draining of color.

"Not more bad news, I hope. Please Lord," he said.

"Relax," she said. "Not exactly bad news. She's alive."

"Tell me," he said with urgency. "Tell me everything."

They spent a long time talking about what to do next, and how to approach it.

"She can't have tuberculosis," Jack said. "She just can't. All she needs is some California sunshine."

He toyed nervously with his cup,

desperation in his eyes, pleading for her reassurance.

"You're right, Jack," she said. "People are far too ready to blame TB when young women get ill. And she's had a terrible time with her mother dying. It sounds like her father is away often. She's effectively got no family to support her."

"Well, she has now," said Jack. "And this time I won't let her down."

He stood and gingerly put his hands on the table in front of him.

"Oh, and Countess. A big thank you for putting the squeeze on Dan Dandy Durkan. That was a brainwave. Wish I'd thought of it."

He turned to leave and hesitated at the door.

"Makes me want to say all is forgiven."

"Really?" said Elizabeth, her heart bouncing with anticipation.

He grinned. "Almost. Maybe. But then again. Not quite."

She picked up one of Mrs Roderiquez's freshly baked currant buns from the plate in front of her and hurled it at him. He ducked, and it hit the top of his head.

"Now who's plain juvenile?" he said with a chuckle. And turned and walked out.

THE END

ACKNOWLEDGMENTS

Thanks are due to so many people for fielding my queries on weird and wonderful minutiae, and I thank you all, too many to mention individually. However, I can't overlook once again the sterling assistance I received from the New Zealand Library Service interloan facility, which enabled me to access hard-to-obtain books from specialist libraries across Australasia. In this regard, I'm especially indebted to the services of CJ Simmons, Interloan & Information Supply Librarian–Research, Heritage & Central Library, Libraries and Information - Ngā Whare Mātauranga o Tāmaki Makaurau.

Formatting of this volume in the series
was once again provided with alacrity
and wonderful attention to detail by
Jason and Marina at Polgarus Studios in
Tasmania. You are my author
champions!

Publishing books is such a team
activity, and I honestly could not have
got any further than producing a raw MS
without the assistance I've received.
Warmest thanks go to Stephanie Parent
for copy editing and Robyn Welsh for
proof reading. I'm so grateful to have
you both looking out for all of my errors.
I can't thank you all enough.

I wanted to also pay tribute to the
late Stephen Stratford, who worked on
most of the earlier books in the Of Gold
& Blood series as a developmental and
copy editor. Despite his status as one
of the finest editors of literary books in

the country, he didn't disdain working on a beginner's attempt at popular fiction, and gave me much appreciated encouragement and valuable advice when I was starting out. His sudden death has left a giant void in the New Zealand publishing scene and my condolences go to his family, wife Sarah and daughters, Madeleine and Sophia.

Dangerous Desires brings to an end the Of Gold & Blood series, but some characters who have appeared in these pages are getting their own stories in a new trilogy I am embarked on–Home At Last, with the first book, Sadie's Vow, due out mid-2022.

I am planning this as a kind of "Brothers At Arms–Three Musketeers" series, with Dolphie, Jack and Alex all taking lead roles in their own books.

I hope you, my loyal readers, will
continue to follow them and me in my
story telling.

WHAT'S NEXT?

If you liked Dangerous Desires, you will undoubtedly enjoy my next book, Sadie's Vow, Book #1 in a new trilogy Home At Last.

FREE PREVIEW - HOME AT LAST – SADIE'S VOW

One

The steamy summer night her sister Phoebe caught the eye of the Cobra, Sadie McGillicuddy lost the battle.

She just wasn't ready to admit it yet.

"You've got to protect her Daa," she murmured in Shamrock bar owner Bryan McGillicuddy's ear as she swung by his nonchalant form, leaning against the bar's end, her tray laden with tankards destined for the far corner table.

"She's only 19." He regarded her with twinkling blue eyes that shone from a ruddy, smugly satisfied face.

"What are ye worrying about, lass? She's more of a lure than you are, and that can't be bad for business."

Her stepfather cast his eyes approvingly over the heaving mass of drinkers, elbowing their way toward him for refills. His wide forehead shone with sweat beads under a tumble of sandy corkscrewed curls. It was one of the hottest nights of the 1872 summer, and her mother had been dead for exactly one year.

How could he look so pleased with himself? Didn't he even remember her anniversary?

She glanced down at the serviceable khaki pantaloons she wore below a long-sleeved white shirt buttoned right up to the collar and acknowledged that she was barely discernible as a woman. And that was the way she liked it.

She gazed into Bryan McGillicuddy's gratified face and told herself he had a business to run. A family of young uns, her three younger sisters, to feed. He didn't have the time to spare in mooning about, and neither did she.

As if to remind her of the fact, McGillicuddy said, "You'd better be moving that beer before it goes flat. We don't want the Cobra complaining." Her head swivelled involuntarily to the corner table expecting her delivery.

King Cobra was the boss man of the mobster syndicate that ruled the streets around The Shamrock, and the very last thing they needed was for him to take offense at the service.

"On my way," she said. "But I mean what I said. She's too young to be hanging out with the likes of them."

If she had a talent for being invisible, her half-sister Phoebe could not be missed. Her radiance lit up a room, even the dark little corner where she perched at a table with the Cobra, the New York chapter's second in command, Patrick Blackheart, and two flighty dolly mops, on a ditzy blond, the other a scowling red head, who regularly worked the floor for custom. Phoebe had hair the color of warm toffee curling over eyes that lit up like emeralds whenever anyone said anything she found half way funny.

Just sitting next to her at the table made your heart sing. As Sadie twisted her way through a forest of men's broad shoulders to reach her destination, the condensation from the icy brew on the pewter tray numbed her fingers, but her spirits sparked warmth at the sight of Phoebe.

She was the very picture of their mother, although by the time Sadie had made the deathbed promise, her mother's enchanting light had long since faded. That was probably why her stepfather was so indulgent with the girl, she thought, as she did the final pivot around a big waterfront guy to reach her waiting customers.

Someone - Cobra, probably from the way Phoebe was regarding him - had said something that amused her, and her exquisite face shone with delight, the pearly white teeth showing through the finely curved red lips as she laughed with a contagious merriment.

As if sensing her approach, Patrick Blackheart quietly rose and stepped slightly aside to allow space for her to reach in and place the tray on the table. She gave him a quick, grateful smile, which he acknowledged with a brief flick of one black brow. He was a big, olive-skinned fellow, with a darkly intense masculinity that set her nerves on edge.

Cobra's eyes were fixed on her sister. He was shorter than Patrick, but more burly and considerably older. She guessed Patrick was close to her age - late 20s or early 30s. Cobra was forty at least, the once black hair on the backs of his hands as he held the mug flecked with salty white.

"Thank you, Sadie," said Blackheart with a smirk. "For doing Phoebe's job."

Phoebe gave her elegant shoulders a feminine shrug as if to say 'More fool her,' and continued on as if she wasn't there.

Yes. Phoebe and her mother looked alike, but that's where any resemblance stopped. Her mother would never have behaved like Phoebe. She'd always been a demure Catholic girl, obedient to her husbands, undemanding of their attention.

For a moment, the roar of men's voices echoing off the heavy overhead beams, the energy-sapping heat, the smell of sawdust and hops and sweat - all of that faded away.

Sadie was back at her mother's sanctified bedside, her pale, lined face soft with her own holy peace, her breath coming in uncertain gasps.

"Promise me. Promise me, my darling Sadie. Look after Phoebe. Don't let her come to harm. She's too lovely for her own good."

Sadie squeezed the hand she held lightly and leaned over her mother's wasted, laboring form. "I promise Mother. If I die doing it, I promise. And now, you get some blessed rest."

Her mother's eyes fixed on her beseechingly. Her lips curled at the corners in the briefest of smiles.

"Swear it on the Bible." She had a well-worn Holy Book by her pillow. Please... do it now."

She released Sadie's hand and guided it to the black book's face; the title engraved in gold. Sadie mumbled the words, barely comprehending. "I promise by the Holy Mother Mary to keep Phoebe safe from harm."

Her mother's green eyes, so like her sister's, swam with gleaming gratitude.

Then the dark lashes, still long and curly, closed over her papery cheeks and her grip on Sadie's hand slackened.

A hard grip on her forearm called her back, and she came to with a jolt. "Sadie. Are you still there?"

Patrick Blackheart's ignite eyes showed concern. Cobra was watching too his yellow-brown orbs so like those of the serpent whose name he'd taken.

"Oh, sorry. Of course." She gathered her wits into a semblance of order, picking up the empty tray and drawing it to her chest. The drinkers had helped themselves while she'd been daydreaming of Maa.

"Can I get you anything else?" Directing the question to Cobra.

But he was already gazing at Phoebe, his tongue dipping in and out of wet lips. It wasn't forked, she thought with a crazy absurdity. But it might as well have been.

She whisked into a quick turn and headed back to the bar.

Oh mother, you see what's happening?

She exhaled her despair into the muggy, smoky air.

However am I going to keep my sacred vow?

Sadie's Vow will be published mid-year.

If you'd like to get updates by becoming a friend of Jenny's books and getting the latest news of releases and free book offers join us at:

www.jennywheeler.biz/free-poisoned-legacy-tangled-destiny-ebook/

Enjoy this book? You Can Make a Difference

Reviews are the most powerful tools in my kit for getting my books noticed. Much as I'd love it, I don't have the budget of a big publisher to buy bill board ads and other national advertising. But I have the promise of something more powerful–something publishers envy. And that's a committed and loyal bunch of readers. Honest reviews of my books help them gain the attention of others who might appreciate them, too.

Post Your Dangerous Desires Reviews Here:

For Amazon:

www.amazon.com.au/dp/B09RHTGY3H

For Goodreads:

www.goodreads.com/book/show/604972

83-dangerous-desires

For Apple, Barnes & Noble:

books2read.com/u/4jPOKD

ABOUT THE AUTHOR

Jenny Wheeler is the author of the Of Gold & Blood Old California mystery series:

Poisoned Legacy #1.
Brother Betrayed #2.
Double Jeopardy #3.
Tangled Destiny (Christmas novella and Prequel.) #4.
Unbridled Vengeance #5.
Hope Redeemed, A Spanish Novella, #6.
Boxed Set/Book Bundle Of Gold & Blood, Books 1–3.
Boxed Set Book Bundle #2 Poisoned Legacy and Tangled Destiny
Tainted Fortune #7.

Book Bundle /Boxed Set #3 Book #5 Unbridled Vengeance and #6 Hope Redeemed.

Book Bundle/Boxed Set #4 Book #7 Tainted Fortune and #8 Captive Heart.

Captive Heart #8.

Three Holiday Novellas–Book Bundle/ Boxed set Books #3, #6, and #8.

Ancient Deception #9.

Dangerous Desires #10.

Jenny's online home is at
jennywheeler.biz or email
Jenny@jennywheeler.biz

You can connect with Jenny on:
Facebook: @JennyWheeler.Biz
Twitter: @Jenny_Biz
Instagram: @jennysbingereading
Pinterest
www.pinterest.nz/Jennywheelerbooks
Goodreads:
goodreads.com/author/show/11371547.J
enny_Wheeler
Bookbub:
www.bookbub.com/profile/jenny-wheeler